THE SHADOW MASTER

"What do you see when you look out upon these wretches below?"

The guardsman shrugged. "I am a guard. They are the enemy trying to get into our city."

Sergeant Cristoforo thought upon that a moment. Wondered if thinking of them as the enemy made the task of standing here on the wall more bearable. "So would you attack them and drive them away?"

"I would."

"Would you put a case to the City Council that to defend our walls we must kill them?"

"No," said the guardsman, and spat over the ramparts. "No point in killing them. They are dying already. We just need to stand here and wait."

It was an interesting logic, thought the Sergeant. Then he asked, "But what happens when the number of plague people outside our walls is greater than the number of people inside the Walled City?"

"But that has already happened," said the guardsman. "That's when I gave up counting them."

ALSO BY CRAIG CORMICK

FICTION
Shackleton's Drift
Of One Blood: The Last Histories of Van Diemen's Land
The Boy's Own Guide to Wedding Planning
Kormak's Saga (novella)
Dig: The Unwritten History of Burke and Wells (novella)

FOR CHILDREN
Time Vandals
The Monster Under the Bed
Pimplemania

COLLECTIONS
The Prince of Frogs
The Princess of Cups
The Queen of Aegea
The King of Patagonia
Futures Trading
A Funny Thing Happened at 27,000 Feet
Unwritten Histories
When Angels Call (with Hal Judge and Steve Harrison)
A Meeting of Muses (Editor)

POETRY
The Condensed Kalevala

NON FICTION
Kurikka's Dreaming
Cruising with Captain Cook Amongst Cannibals
Shipwrecks of the Southern Seas
In Bed with Douglas Mawson
The Last Supper
Words of Grace

CRAIG CORMICK

The Shadow Master

ANGRY
ROBOT

ANGRY ROBOT
A member of the Osprey Group

Lace Market House
54-56 High Pavement
Nottingham
NG1 1HW
UK

Angry Robot/Osprey Publishing
PO Box 3985
New York
NY 10185-3985
USA

www.angryrobotbooks.com
A rose by any other name

An Angry Robot paperback original 2014

Cover art by Steve Stone @ Artist Partners
Set in Meridien by Argh! Oxford.

Distributed in the United States by Random House, Inc., New York.

ISBN 978 0 85766 515 7
Ebook ISBN 978 0 85766 516 4

Printed in the United States of America

9 8 7 6 5 4 3 2 1

To Sharon and Caèlan for creating the magic.

Special Thanks to Tessa Kum for her eagle-eyed reading of the early draft.

"A plague a' both your houses!"
     Mercutio, in *Romeo and Juliet*, II ii

I

"The city should be there before us, Capitano,"
the first mate said. But there was no city there. A
malevolent mist had descended around the ship,
reeking of piss and fear – though perhaps it was just
the stench of the crew at the oars as they approached
the maelstrom.

"Tar my bung hole and use me for a keg!" Capitano
Manzoni cursed. He was a tall man with a well-kept
dark beard and moustache, as most men of his House
wore, and he paced the deck of his galleon nervously.
He had followed the star-painted night skies across
the seas to guide him safely home only to find his
journey's end obscured. They had lost the sun and all
sense of direction and distance. If the fog did not lift
he could not see the Walled City. And if he could not
see the Walled City he might as well resort to the folly
of the sailor's incantation: blowing on his thumbs and
turning around three times in a counter direction to
the maelstrom. That had as much chance of guiding a
man safely through the whirlpool as he had of flying
his ship over it, he thought.

"Any sign of that Lorraine vessel?" he called to his first mate, but he knew the answer would be that they could no more see the rival ship behind them somewhere than they could see the Walled City ahead of them.

"No sign," the mate called back from the rigging above.

"Shorten the sails," the Captain ordered, and he heard the whirl and click of brass gears as the crew wound the *Windseeker*'s sails in a little. He could have as easily ordered the masts to be wound lower into the ship's hold, but he needed the crow's nest at maximum height.

There should be no fog, this time of year, Capitano Manzoni thought. Lesser men would believe it a bad omen. But he had been taught that was no such thing as ill-fortune or good fortune. Only good planning. And Galileo's secrets. The small tent had already been set up on the foredeck, to hide the instruments from the crew. You could never tell who might be a Lorraine spy, and galley slaves would trade any of the family's secrets for just the promise of a few copper coins. Though they'd more likely get their throats slit instead. Doing business with the Lorraines was as dangerous as doing business with a scorpion. Except that scorpions didn't actually do business, did they? He sighed. He had never been strong at the art of metaphors that conversation in the Walled City was ruled by.

He looked down into the belly of his ship where over a hundred men sat by their oars, sweating heavily despite the chill in the air about them. They were scared, he knew. For every two ships that negotiated the maelstrom only one survived. Each journey was a roll of the dice. A game of chance the Medici family was playing, with their lives, or deaths, as the stakes. That was a better metaphor, he thought. That would serve him well some time.

The crew foolishly believed that the forces of fate controlled their lives and the only intercession was through talismans and chants. They even felt their prayers had been granted when they were taken on as galley slaves. Yet who wouldn't want to be in service to one of the families of the Walled City? The only place in the entire civilised world free from the scourge of the great plague that had ravaged cities and countryside alike for six long years now. The Walled City had closed its gates and tried to block the mountain passes to the east, turning to the treacherous sea for trade. Galley slaves preferred to risk their lives to the fickle forces of chance that they believed ruled the seas, rather than the certain death from the plague. But in truth, the only forces that controlled their lives were those of the Medici family. And they controlled Galileo who controlled the forces of nature.

Well, except the fog, Capitano Manzoni thought. Though he would talk to the old man about that and perhaps he would invent some device that could dissipate it more quickly. A giant bellows mounted on the front of a ship perhaps. And such a device might also be used to blow a ship along in calm weather. He wondered why nobody had thought of that already. He would seek an audience with Galileo on the morrow to discuss it.

He paced back across the deck of the *Windseeker* and stared into the fog again. He was tempted to reach down into his pocket and rub the small gold charm his wife, Alaria, had given him upon his departure. "To bring you home safely," she had said, pressing her lips to his. He wondered if she would get word of his return and greet him on the docks. Just the thought of seeing her, so close now, filled him with a deep longing worse than any that had filled him while hundreds of leagues away.

Patience, he told himself. Almost home. He had been gone three months, sailing right out of the inner sea to the open oceans and down towards the heathen lands in search of spices and grain. For some captains, leaving the inner sea filled them with the most worries, but for him it was always the return home. He well remembered the apprehension he had felt on previous journeys approaching the swirling waters that filled the outer harbour of the Walled City. Eight times he'd made it through already. That made him a veteran. After ten successful journeys, a ship's captain could retire with a very handsome pension. It was both an incentive for the men and also a recognition that no man could tempt fate for too long.

That would all change now, though, he thought. Everything had changed. Although anything that raised the suspicion of the Lorraine spies had to be avoided. So perhaps he too would be allowed to retire after one more voyage, and he could then spend his days making love to Alaria. While most men he knew kept at least one mistress, he was still very much in love with his wife and had no inclination to chase other women. She was still beautiful after having borne him two children, and they could still raise a few more. As long as the spice trade continued they could all expect to live, safe from the plague. He would be docking in her harbour, as they liked to call it, when together that evening. That was one of Alaria's metaphors though, not his own.

"Stand ready!" he called out, to reassure the crew and galley slaves that he was in control of everything. And then, as if upon his order, the fog started to lift. He could already see the swirling edge of the maelstrom ahead, filling the outer harbour of the Walled City. Manzoni smiled. "Bring the ship around," he called and the slave master had the men on the port side of the ship stroke their oars once, then again, until they were facing directly towards where the red brick towers of the Walled City were now starting to appear ahead of them, seeming to dance as the fog broke up around them.

But it was the maelstrom that his deck crew were watching. They had to wait for one of the lulls in the waters as and then attempt a dash through. Hoping it would happen before the Lorraine vessel on their tail appeared, ready to fight them for their precious cargo.

But Capitano Manzoni knew it would be different today. He strode to the small tent at the front of the ship and stepped inside. The front of the small structure was open giving him a clear view of the city ahead. He waited until the fog had nearly entirely lifted and he could see that there had been changes in the many weeks since his departure. Several Lorraine towers had been pulled down, and there were two new Medici towers standing there. He smiled. That meant at least two more Medici ships had successfully delivered their precious spice cargo to make the spice wine that warded off the plague, and none of the Lorraine ships had gotten through. Cosimo the Great would be very pleased.

And now that he could see the city, he knew that another Lorraine tower would be pulled down, and another Medici tower built. He took out a small key and unlocked the wooden case at his feet and carefully lifted out the secret implements that had been entrusted to him. The first was a set of dials and cogs that he had to assemble. It was a difficult task, but he had practiced it many times. If they had been captured by the Lorraines they would not know what they had found if they could not assemble them.

He soon had the chronometer together and then took out two glass discs. He stood them at either end of the thick ornate cloth they had had been wrapped in and then rolled it around them and tied it tight with the ribbons on the end. So simple to construct but so difficult to know what it was if one had never seen a magnifier.

"Sir!" a voice outside the tent called urgently.

"What is it?" Manzoni asked crossly.

"That Lorraine ship."

"How far off?" he called back.

"About three leagues."

Too far to catch them, but close enough to witness him complete his ninth successful voyage. He searched for a metaphor. None came. He sighed. It would take some getting used to, being back in the Walled City.

"Rowers at the ready." He heard his order relayed to the nervous men. It was time. He wound the brass key in the back of the chronometer and the small gears and wheels began turning, each linked to another, a world of turning dials and cogs. It took a moment to feel its effect. He looked out the front of the tent and saw the swirling waters of the maelstrom were slowing. His heart, by comparison, was beating faster. He was filled with a feeling far beyond the excitement of captaining a ship far out beyond the inner sea. He was controlling time itself – that slipperiest of thieves, that most inescapable of prisons, that most irreversible of paths. Galileo had warned him of the intoxication of it – as well as the physical toll – but not the absolute sense of wonder that it gave him.

He wondered if he would break his vow and share this feeling with his wife. Wondered what playing the majestic butterfly with her would be like if he slowed time around them in their bed chamber. But also wondered what the toll on their bodies for that would be? Would she agree to that, or should he tell her afterwards?

Then he lifted the magnifier to his eye. It took him a moment to get the focus right, then he scanned across the blurred and magnified towers of the city until he found the one he was after. That is where the old man would be. He felt his heart beating rapidly with excitement. Patience, he told himself. There was a flash of light upon glass and he aligned his magnifier with the one on shore that was pointing at him.

And then distance was changed. Everything was changed. His vessel was halfway across the maelstrom before he even called out the order to row. The men in the belly of the ship had no way of knowing what was happening and the men on deck had no way of understanding it. Galileo's machines controlled time and distance, and he controlled the machines. He felt a tingling in his fingers as they shook a little and he grasped the instruments tighter to hold them steady.

The waters of the maelstrom now presented little difficulty to the rowers, sucking at the ship with no more force than that of an outgoing tide. Capitano Manzoni waited until they had reached the far side of the whirlpool before stopping the chronometer, as per his strict orders. He heard the roar of the waters fill his ears and the cry of the first mate, "Safely through!" The slaves at the oars let out a loud cheer and kissed their talismans.

The Capitano disassembled the chronometer, unrolled the magnifier and locked all the instruments in the case. He felt his fingers cramp a little and opened and closed them slowly, turning them over and looking for any signs of the change in them he had been warned of. The magic of science did not come without a price. There were no signs of the grey blotching on his skin and his fingers were just a little stiff. Surely that was nothing. He shook them a little and stepped out of the tent. He wanted to see what the Lorraine vessel behind them would do. Undoubtedly their Capitano was standing on the foredeck with his mouth agape like a triple-inbred Umbrian peasant. Which he probably was. Oh, that was a good one, he thought. He'd better remember it. But before he could even set eyes on the rival ship he felt the deck shake under him. It felt like they had struck something. But that was impossible. There were no rocks on this side of the maelstrom.

"Capitano!" his mate called out, still up in the rigging. "It's… whales!"

"What?" he asked, as if not comprehending. He strode to the ship's rail and looked over into the waters below. It had to be a Lorraine trick. But it was whales. At least three of them. He looked at their dark rough-skinned backs, looking like some leather-clad machines of Leonardo's, under the water there. But these were alive. Each as long as the ship's width, and they were attacking the *Windseeker*, nudging it backwards towards the maelstrom. "No!" he said. It was as impossible as… He searched futilely for the metaphor that might make it too incredible to be really happening. But the whales rammed the ship again, knocking him off his feet. A cry of panic ran up from the men at the oars as some took up their talismans in both hands while others tried to follow the order to row, so that the oars quickly became tangled with each other. They had lost forward movement and the ship started drifting backwards.

Capitano Manzoni started ranting in panic, not unlike a triple-inbred Umbrian peasant might, and he called to the first mate to try to regain order with the slaves as he tried to rush back to the tent with his instrument case. But his fingers were so stiff and clumsy and he knew he knew he would have no time. No time! The crew at the back of the ship were already pointing at the waters behind them in alarm. The whales were now pushing them back steadily and he felt the stern of the ship start to spin as the swirling waters fastened their grip on it.

Like a submerged beast devouring its prey, he thought. A good metaphor he'd never be able to share. They were dead. They were all dead. He would never retire after ten voyages and would not raise any more children with his darling Alaria. And Capitano Manzoni found all his teachings deserting him as he clasped the gold charm his wife had given him and cursed both the Medici and Lorraine Houses for killing him, and then blew on his thumbs and turned around three times in the opposite direction of the maelstrom as it sucked his vessel down into its embrace.

II

The assassination attempt was a bloody and clumsy thing. But that may have been a part of the careful planning of it, to distance any suspicion from those stealthy murderers employed by the Lorraine family. If they had used poison or employed a night-creeper to enter the Medici bedrooms while they slept, suspicion would have immediately been cast upon the Lorraines. But to attempt to stab Cosimo Medici and his brother Giuliano when they were attending a service inside the Grand Cathedral of the Walled City – surely only a madman or fanatic would attempt that?

If it had succeeded and the assassins had escaped into the crowds, the city would have been thrown into utter turmoil. Undoubtedly the Lorraines would have quickly produced unknown corpses to accuse of being the assailants. Foreign spies could have been blamed. The city guard would order everybody off the streets and the Lorraine family would offer to bolster the guards with their own much larger militia. The High Priests would have to support them for the sake of order and once granted military power over the city, the Lorraines would never relinquish it.

But that was not quite the way things had turned out. Only one of the Medici brothers lay dead and one of the assassins had been captured. And the city's bells rang out to let all citizens know to that chaos had descended upon them all.

Cosimo and Giuliano had been near the front of the crowd in the Great Cathedral during the service, as was their habit. Unlike many of those around them they had shown neither signs of fervour nor boredom during the long and near-hysterical tirade of the High Priest, as was also their habit. They'd appeared to be listening patiently to his rantings, but if they had actually been pondering the supply of spice, or the improbable attack of the whales upon their ship and what it might really have been, they had shown no sign of what they thought of the High Priest. Every now and then one of the brothers had turned his eyes to the heavens, but it might have been that he was studying the beautiful and ornate frescos high up on the huge domed ceiling of the cathedral, or counting the penises on the many cherubs, as most bored children did. The frescos showed layered scenes of how the world was viewed by the ancients, with the angels and saints sitting in heaven at the top of the huge domed arch above them, and the lower levels representing the lower celestial realms, with the Earthly realms at the edge of the dome, and finally the underworld of demons and punishment creeping down the pillars and walls closest to the congregation. Perhaps the Medici brothers pondered that they belonged to the higher orders on the dome. Not, perhaps, with the gods, but certainly above the common human masses.

They were starkly different for brothers. Giuliano was tall and thin, with a face dominated by his chin and nose, while Cosimo was shorter and more solidly built, with a flat and brutish face. Their nicknames amongst the populace were the Horse and the Bull, though of the two only Giuliano's nickname was said with any affection. They made a formidable duo – Cosimo with his brutal simplicity, and Giuliano with his skills at diplomacy – and together they increasingly outwitted, out-manoeuvred and out-imported the Lorraines. Until the appearance of the whales in the harbour.

The High Priest looked down at both Houses, proclaiming, as he did during nearly every service, that it was the sins of mortal men that had brought the plague to devastate the Earth, and it was only the hand of the Almighty that kept it from the Walled City. But the Almighty could remove his protective hand from any that were deemed to have sinned, he warned. Any that were driven by avarice. Any that engaged in the heretical practices of science. Any that put themselves above the Almighty in any way.

The service lasted a full half candle, though it seemed longer, for those not carried away by the High Priest's sermon, and when the good citizens were extolled to return to the light of the outside city under the guiding, yet watchful, eye of the Almighty, Cosimo and Giuliano began pushing their way to the rear of the cathedral with the others. In any other building, that might have been a cause for concern for the two men, or the family body guards, but inside the cathedral they did not even consider the possibility of danger. Not one of them would put a hand to a dagger's hilt, even involuntarily, or look around warily, until they had stepped outside onto the flagstones at the bottom of the cathedral's steps.

As ever the crowd was very slow to emerge from the vast building. The doorways were small and, with several thousand citizens either pushing forward or stepping back to perhaps allow a women to pass before them, it was a very tight throng at the doors to the building and the Medici brothers hung back a little, letting their guards push forward to clear a path for them. And that's when the assassins struck. There were three men, dressed in monk's robes with hoods over their faces, who suddenly drew daggers and leapt at them. The first that Giuliano knew he was being attacked was the sharp stab of steel in his back. Then again and again, pushing him to the ground.

But Cosimo, who had been half turned, saying something to his brother, saw the look of murder on the face of the man coming towards him. He knew he was in danger before he ever saw the flash of the dagger's steel. The assassin lunged forward, but had to push his way past a man in a dark cloak who suddenly stepped in front of him. It gave Cosimo time to throw up his hands and step back a little. The dagger found a mark, but only a glancing blow on his neck. It drew blood, but Cosimo acted as if he didn't feel it. He took a step back and met the assassin's eyes and the other man paused a moment, perhaps seeing the sudden rage and power in Cosimo. Perhaps seeing his own

death. And in that brief moment the future of the
Walled City hung.

The assassin stepped forward again for a second
thrust. Already Giuliano was falling to the ground
under the combined frenzy of the two men assaulting
him, hissing like tormented wild cats as they continued
stabbing into his back and head. One of the men
stabbed so hard that his blade became stuck fast in
Giuliano's head, and he was wrenching and twisting it
to try and free it. If they had been a little more careful
they might have prevented him from screaming,
"Murder!" as he crumpled to the cold stone floor, the
single word echoing around the high frescoed ceilings
and booming back to the crowd like a voice from the
Almighty above, as all turned to witness the attack.

They saw Cosimo face his attacker head on, his
only defence a fearless glare. Then he stepped into
the man's thrust. While the dagger struck him again
in the neck, it did less damage than the first blow.
Cosimo was a thick-set strong man who had killed
many enemies on the battlefields and when the
assassin raised his arm for a third blow, he found
the strong fingers of the leader of the Medici family
suddenly around his throat, the thumbs digging at his
windpipe. He changed the direction of his blow and
stabbed down at Cosimo's arms, hoping to dislodge
them. But although the blade again struck home the
grip on his throat did not lessen. He looked into the
dark eyes boring into his own, as if they too had the
strength to strangle him and he dropped the dagger as
he realised that the death he had been preparing for
all through the service was going to be his own.

He tried to mumble something. Perhaps a call for help or a curse upon Cosimo Medici, but his tongue would not obey him and lolled out his mouth insensible. The assassin's knees then began to bend, but Cosimo did not let him fall. He held him up, and shook him like one might shake a mangy dog one wanted to be rid of, and the man gurgled just before his windpipe collapsed. Just before his eyes rolled back in his head.

Cosimo was still holding him when his bodyguards reached him, to protect him, and he cast the corpse into their arms. By then the crowd were joining in the echoing call of murder and pushing even harder to get out of the cathedral doors. One of the two men who had assailed his brother had succeeded in throwing off his robes and joining in with the panicked crowd, but the other had been bludgeoned to the floor by the bodyguards while still trying to extract his dagger from Giuliano's skull. They had a blade to his throat now and were searching him for any poison or concealed weapon he might use to try and take his own life.

Cosimo walked across to him, dripping blood from his wounds, and stood on the man's neck. It took Cosimo a few moments to clear his head and understand that his brother was dead, lying there at his feet, in a puddle of darkening blood. It filled him with a black rage that strangling a dozen men would not diminish. Giuliano had been stabbed over forty times and Cosimo had already decided that a man would die for each stab wound. As he had already decided that the Lorraines were behind this attack. It would only take the required amount of torture on this surviving assassin to prove it.

His men were trying to press ornate cloths to the wounds on his neck and arms, but he shook them off and said, "I want all the bells of the city to be rung like the pealing from the heavens at the end of days. I want it to be known that my dear brother is slain and the two Houses are at war. And every citizen must declare himself. For whoever is not for us, is against us."

And then he spat on the assassin and said, "And keep this one alive. He'll have a tale to tell us, even if I have to cut it out of him."

III

"Show me again how the hands work," Lucia whispered to Lorenzo. He took up her hand again and spread the fingers with his own. "Inside your hand are three bones for each finger," he said. "And each bone is joined with a hinge, like on a door. And each joint has small wires that are attached to muscles that are like cogs or pulleys, that pull this way or that way, making it move." He closed his fingers around hers and she closed her fingers around his in turn.

"It is the same in the arms then?" she asked.

"Of course," he said, releasing her hand and tracing his index finger along her bare arm. "There are longer bones here, but they are also hinged, here and here." He touched her wrist and elbow. "And inside the arm are the same wires and cogs that move them."

Lucia felt goose bumps rise across her body as his finger touched the inside of her elbow. But it wasn't an altogether unpleasant sensation. She had been waiting for Lorenzo all evening. No, to her mind she'd been waiting for him for years. Waiting for him to climb up the outer wall of her tower with the use of those ingenious metal claws on his hands and feet, and enter her very bed chamber.

They had been aware of each other for years, since they first saw each other on the streets and each had given the other a smile. As if they had already met. And as they grew, their friendly smiles grew into something more knowing. Even when her mother took her away from the Walled City when she was twelve, to visit her relatives to the north, she had looked for his face amongst the boys around her. And when they had come hurrying back to the city, pursued by the plague, it was his face in the crowds she had looked for. His smile to reassure her that everything would be alright.

She chose to spend most of her time in her tower chamber, now, working on a large mural across one wall. It was the view of the city outside her window. But not just the city she could see. The city she wanted it to be. She wished that Leonardo were able to tutor her in painting more often, but he was always busy these days working on strange devices for her father, the Duke. She had once loved this city, but now saw it as a prison, keeping all of them captive. So she painted it anew, demolishing buildings that displeased her. Ridding the streets of the militia of the two Houses. Tearing down their stranglehold over the city. Taking away the large wall around them and adding flat green lands and rivers. Every time she fought with her father or mother she would come back to her chamber and paint away some of their power. Remove more towers and ships. And then she would paint small houses here and there, which she imagined she and Lorenzo would live in. Sometimes in the city overlooking a plaza, or sometimes in the countryside nearby.

They were both eighteen now, and this was the first time they had really talked together. Really touched. Though she had played this out in her own mind, many, many times. She had known it would happen one day. Known how they would sit and what they would say. There was so much she wanted to ask him about himself. She knew he was a ward of the Medicis and had no parents. Knew he worked as an apprentice to Galileo. Knew there was something that had always drawn them together.

If her father ever found out he'd have the poor boy skinned and turned out of the city, though. Or at least that's what he threatened to do to any of the men who he caught staring at her. But Lorenzo never stared. Not in that way.

"Lust is in men's hearts," he often advised her. "You will understand that when you are older." But nobody had ever warned her about the lust in her own heart. And now he was here, she didn't care to ask him those things she had wanted to know about him. It seemed much more urgent to talk about the workings of each of their bodies. Because she didn't just want Lorenzo to be there on the couch beside her. She wanted him to touch her.

But he was so shy.

"So is it the same for the feet and legs then?" she asked mischievously, kicking off her slippers and raising her gown a little so that her bare feet and slim lower legs were exposed. She watched his face redden a little and felt the same goose bumps rise across her body again. He was so much a boy still, with neither the beard of the Medici household nor the large moustache of the Lorraines, and that proved him something of neither.

When he had sat down on the couch beside her he had reached out a hand to brush back her hair. She'd grabbed his hand tightly to stop him, but he had said, "No. Let me look." And she had consented. Let him lift back her long, dark auburn hair and see the ugly plague scars along her neck, running down from her ear.

"The follies of the apothecaries," she had said. They had promised to mend the ravages of the ugly red welts that had burst forth on her skin in the north, but had left behind a mass of scars that looked even worse to her mind, like she had been patched up with spare skin from some animal, which had been burned into place.

She looked into Lorenzo's soft grey eyes and saw neither pity nor revulsion. And when he touched her skin there, so gently, that's when she knew. Now, looking at her feet and legs she saw a similar look on his face. Then, realising he was staring, he was filled with a moment of delicate shyness, and he turned his head away a little from her, not wishing to look at her, but then brought it back again, unable to not look at her.

"Yes," he said. "Though the bones in your toes are much smaller."

"Show me," she said.

He chewed his lip and then moved to take one of her feet in his hands. He ran his fingers over it as if it was a delicate object and traced out each toe, running his finger up the length of her foot, showing where each wire was that moved the parts inside. "You tell your foot how to move," he said, "and the engine that drives them all is here." He placed one hand above his heart. "All your limbs are tightly harnessed to it."

She put a hand atop her own heart, as if it was there he had touched. "My limbs are bound here," she said. "And bound to my will to move them where I wish."

"Well, sometimes your will does not control your limbs," he said.

"When don't I have control of my own foot?" she asked. And with something of a mischievous look of his own, he ran one finger along the bottom of her foot and it curled up at the sensation, completely unbidden. Again raising goose bumps.

"And what of more complex parts of the body?" she asked. "Like the lips." And she put out one finger and touched his soft red lips, letting her finger linger there. He looked into her eyes and, as if being able to read her desire, kissed her finger gently. Then he raised his own finger to her lips and she kissed it in return.

"We will be married," she declared to him then, telling him what she knew.

"Yes," he said, as if he'd never doubted it. As if it was the thing that he had climbed her tower to hear, strapping on metal devices that transformed his hands and feet into claws. No more staring at each other secretly in church. No more lying in bed at nights dreaming of the next time they might glimpse each other, or the next time they might risk just brushing against each other.

She had feigned illness today while the rest of the family had gone to church, in order that he might visit her. She had lain awake since before dawn, excited at the prospect of it. Unsure how he was going to manage it, slipping in and out of sleep, dreaming him there beside her.

This felt like a dream right now to Lorenzo. He was a lowly apprentice, but he was here, inside the tower of Lucia Lorraine, holding her and kissing her fingers. Something he'd imagined over and over until it seemed as much his imaginings as it was real. They'd planned this through small finger signs that they'd developed slowly over the years. Something they knew nobody else could understand. So they'd talked many times without ever exchanging a word. Until now.

"So how do the lips work?" she asked him. "There are no bones in them."

"It's very complicated," he told her.

"You don't know," she teased.

He shrugged. "I have not yet studied lips."

"Then we must work on that," she said, and moved back a little on the couch to give him room to lie beside her. He approached slowly without taking his eyes off her. His fingers were trembling a little. As were hers. Their first kiss. She wanted to close her eyes and wanted to keep them open and wanted soft music to be playing and wanted utter silence and wanted it darker and wanted to be in sunshine and when his lips touched hers she wanted to press herself against him so tight that he'd feel every bone and cog and wire in her body wrapping around him.

She felt her body was responding like her foot had when he stroked the bottom of it and could not say if it were voluntary or involuntary, the way she arched her back and pressed against him now.

Then his hands were around her and she felt his fingers touching her shoulders, moving up to her long dark auburn hair, sliding down to her neck. She could feel her heart beating rapidly in her chest and could feel his against her. Could feel his body moving against her, slowly at first, and then more rapidly, both pressing tightly against the other, all the cogs and wires moving the bones of their hands and arms and legs intertwining.

The shy boy had been replaced by her husband-to-be who had a right to touch her where ever he wanted, as she had a right to touch him wherever she wanted, and when his hand finally brushed against her breast she seized it and pressed it to her harder. She felt his legs quivering as he cupped his hand around her mountains of the goddess. Felt the pinnacles standing erect against his fingers. Felt a burning urgency start to fill her. She slid a leg over his and let him press his hips in closer to hers. Her pinnacles were not the only thing that was erect that she could feel.

He was feeling giddy. More so than when one of his claws had slipped out of the gap between the bricks as he was close to her balcony. He had looked down, certain he was going to fall, and clung to the wall tightly until the feeling had passed. He was falling now though. His head was spinning wildly as he pressed himself into her. Felt the pounding of blood inside him. Felt he had to cling to her more tightly than he had to the tower wall. Knew he would only be safe once he was inside. Knew it was wrong. Felt it was right. Knew if he did not he would fall into some darkness and keep falling. He reached down one hand and felt her own hand join his. Felt her fingers wrap around him. Felt the hands merge into one, the wires and hinges joining. Felt himself being anchored by her.

His lips were pressed against hers and she felt the taste of something warm rising up in her, flowing into him, and something sweet and warm flowed into her own mouth, as if their breath and blood was now a part of the one body. She moved a leg and felt his leg move with her. Closed her eyes and saw herself through his eyes. Opened them again and was looking at him through her own eyes again. She wrapped her arms around him tighter, feeling her hands reaching right inside him, their two bodies drawing closer together and she closed her eyes again, to see herself once more though his eyes, and was slowly filled with a revelation. By joining with her lover they were becoming something entirely new. By really joining with him they could change the very world. They could become a unified being while still being two, one that would have the power to somehow bring all the fractured and conflicting elements of their world together into a peaceful union.

He wondered if she felt it too. How his body was merging fully into hers. How he could feel the movement of her limbs and the breath she took. And that they were somehow changing the world about them into a new harmony. He looked into her eyes and saw her nodding her head. Urging him. He felt her skin against his skin, wrapping about his skin, inside his skin. His whole body trembled from the ecstasy of it.

She watched in amazement as her chest seemed to melt open and a large pink butterfly emerged, flapping gently as it rose from her and joined with a larger red butterfly that was emerging from Lorenzo's chest. He was just as astonished. The two creatures merged together in front of them, their colours becoming a swirl of patterns. Then she could feel them floating. Flying. Transforming. Rising above the bedchamber, the tower and the city. Could feel his marvelling at it. Could feel him pressing closer into her as she drew him in. The butterfly, not an engine, beating where their hearts had joined. He could feel her hearing the distant peal of bells ringing. Could feel his touch upon her skin. Inside her body. Could feel her hearing the cries of people in the streets below. Could see himself through her eyes. Saw what she saw as her head turned as the door to the room slammed open. Heard the scream of Lucia's handmaiden as she burst in on them and screamed, "*O Dio mio!*" Felt themselves falling suddenly apart. Felt themselves falling. Felt themselves hit the cold hard flagstones of the brutal city below.

IV

"Quickly, quickly, quickly," the handmaiden said as she bustled Lorenzo down the tower and out onto the street. She had him don an apron and carry a slops bucket in each hand so nobody would question him. The door to the building was guarded to stop people going in, but nobody was stopping people from going out. Though that might happen sooner or later.

"What is it?" Lucia had asked, over and over, "What has happened? Why are all the bells tolling?"

"It is trouble," was all the handmaiden said, over and over in reply. "Such trouble. The household is all astir. The whole city is astir. And this! This!" She pointed at Lorenzo, trying to refasten his clothes with his back turned to her. "*O Dio mio*! Your father will kill him as surely as night kills day and send you to a nunnery with your head shaven!"

"You must help us," Lucia implored of the handmaiden, grasping her shoulders. "I love him and you must help us." The handmaiden looked as if she were going to collapse under the sudden burden of this, but then she said, "Hurry!" She reached out and took Lorenzo by the hand. Lucia took his other hand, as if to hold him there a moment longer, but the handmaiden tugged mightily and dragged him to the door. "When will I see you again?" Lucia called.

"He will come back when he is a rich lord," the handmaiden said, "Though heaven help him if he has any connection with the Medicis." She slammed the door behind her and dragged Lorenzo down the corridor. "And heaven help you if you're found in the household today," she said. And so he was bustled down the stairs, carrying two slops buckets of turds, and pushed roughly out onto the streets.

"Thank you," Lorenzo wanted to call back to her, but she had already turned her back on him and gone back inside the household. He stood there for some moments, feeling that he had left a part of himself behind, but having no further desire to attract the attention of the guards, he made his way quickly up the paved street. There were people hurrying along the walkways all around him, muttering or crying as the bells continued to toll. It was the signal that the city was under attack, but how could that be? Who could attack them? An army of plague victims? Or had they assembled around the city in such numbers that they were battering down the gates to get in?

He tried to stop people on the streets and ask them what was happening, but each had a different story. "The ceiling of the cathedral has collapsed." / "Cosimo Medici has been slain." / "Hundreds are dead." / "An invading army is inside the city." He must see Galileo, he thought. If anyone knows what is happening, it will be him.

The old man would ask him where he had been, but he doubted he could ever tell him. He had broken the old man's trust and would be ashamed to tell him what he had done. But who else could explain to him what he had experienced? Galileo had taken him on as his apprentice when he was very young. An orphaned boy who had become a ward in the Medici household, in a manner nobody seemed to rightly remember. One more of many wards. But one whom the old man, Galileo, declared was possessed of a useful brain. That had led him to a different life than any of the other young boys of the household. No duties in the stables or kitchen or yards. No need to rise before daybreak in winter and cart water. No need to muck out horse dung from the stables. Instead he had grown up under Galileo's kind but firm hand. He had taught him to read. To write and do mathematics. And to think for himself.

Which he had found had become a two-edged sword. For as he grew he came to the belief that the old man was not letting him fully experience the wonders of their work. He was diligent and was industrious and loyal, but the old man forbade him from undertaking any science experiments of his own. It was not fair, he thought. He was the apprentice. He should be the one to trial the chronometer and magnifier, not those old sea captains. Had witnessed him perfecting other instruments. He had helped build them. He knew each device's workings and perils. He had even designed many science objects himself. Galileo had told him they were promising. But still Galileo forbade him to use any of the devices they built. He had told him it was dangerous in the hands of a young person. Told him that there were consequences for its use that Lorenzo should be spared from.

Galileo had been kind to him, but to deny him this was not right. He had a burning need to improve his position within the household. He was not one of the boys who lived on the lower floors of the palace, and was excluded from their games and comradeship. And he was not welcome on the upper floors. He was a boy in-between, with nobody to call a friend.

But he had Lucia, who he would glimpse once a week at church, or at a city festival. His special friendship with her had sustained him through his adolescent years. Allowed him to play out in his head the long conversations they would have about life and how the world worked, and everything he had learned. But he would need to have a higher station for that to ever happen. He would need to be more than just an in-between-floors apprentice.

And though Galileo might not appreciate that he used independent thinking to come to the decision, he had decided to steal the metal gloves and try them out. Use them to rise above his station. Use them to rise above the very city and climb Lucia's tower. Science would help him understand what it was that drew him to Lucia so. It was something he needed to understand, though even after having been with her now, he could never hope to explain it to another. Even Galileo. Now they had met. They had talked. They had touched. Something wonderful had happened between them. It was so powerful that he felt that he had emerged into a changed version of his city. As he felt changed himself.

He could still feel where Lucia's skin had touched his. Could still feel the fluttering inside his chest where something had transformed. He was both frightened and awed by it. And an invasion of the city, or a battle, seemed minor by comparison. He placed one finger to his chest, where he had felt the flesh open. It was more amazing than watching the metal gloves and all their cogs and wires melding with his hands and feet when he put them on.

He suddenly stopped walking. The gloves! He had left them in Lucia's tower. He felt a sudden sense of dread. Heard the bells tolling disaster loudly. His feet felt very heavy as he made his way quickly back to Palazzo di Medici, walking past the streets where statues of the ancients stood on pillars, looking down sternly. It was as if they knew that he had been arrogant and stupid. He had betrayed all his years of teaching. There was a story he recalled about one of the ancients who stole fire from the gods to give to mankind so that they could develop civilisation and industry, and he was punished by being chained to a rock where a large eagle would come and feast on his liver, only to have it grow back each day for the eagle to rip open his flesh and eat again.

He knew it was really a metaphor, but it suddenly seemed to be no more unreal that having one's hands turn to metal claws. When he finally reached the Medici palace he found it ringed by soldiers. It took him some time to find one who recognised him and let him through. Inside the building there were more soldiers everywhere, arming themselves and searching through rooms as if looking for hidden enemies.

He found Galileo in his chambers, calmly making sketches of some new invention. He appeared a little older to Lorenzo's eyes than he had the day before. He was dressed in black, with a white collar, as usual, his aged figure sitting squatly on his wooden chair. His skin seemed a little greyer. His fingers and limbs moved a little slower. Even his nose seemed a little more swollen, to Lorenzo, and his beard a little greyer, also, and his hair had surely receded a little more. Or was it just that he had been up all night once again, working on some fabulous device? All around him were cogs and wheels and lenses that he could assemble the most amazing things out of, and then disassemble again so that no one else could ever copy them. Only Cosimo the Great himself had copies of the final machines, and he guarded them closely.

Galileo's latest interest was in reflecting light and images. He was convinced he could capture images in some way. Freeze time into a single moment. It was incredible, but so many of his ideas were incredible. As his apprentice, Lorenzo had learned more than he could ever have learned in fifty years at school. And the master used his young and steady hands, and good eyes, to manufacture and assemble many of his experiments. The old man's eyes were failing, as was his steady grip, which was as closely a guarded secret as his inventions themselves.

"Ah, there you are," the old man said, glancing up at Lorenzo, which was his usual greeting to the boy.

Lorenzo could not say anything for some time and waited for the old man to ask about the missing metal gloves. But he did not. And he did not ask him where he had been. He was glad for being saved the need to lie. "What is happening?" Lorenzo asked Galileo. "The city is in an uproar! Have we been invaded?"

"Only by hysteria," the old man said. "Which will prove a much harder foe to fight than any army."

"Why?" Lorenzo asked. "What has happened?"

The old man put down his quill pen and looked at the young man. "There was an assassination attempt made upon Cosimo Medici in the cathedral this morning. His brother Giuliano is slain. Cosimo has been wounded, but not severely."

Lorenzo's face showed his shock. Galileo watched his apprentice and then said, "So, what can we assume from this using logic?" Lorenzo stammered for a moment. "Well there will be vengeance on the assailants."

"Of course," said Galileo.

"And who is responsible?" asked Lorenzo.

"The Lorraines are being accused of the attacks," said Galileo.

Again the shock showed on Lorenzo's face. "But... but... that means..."

"It means civil war. It means an end to the peace accords within the city walls." Lorenzo nodded his head, but he was thinking of Lucia. He was feeling a hole slowly growing in his heart where the butterfly had been. She would now be separated by rows of armed soldiers that would proclaim him a mortal enemy. He could not expect to see her at service again and could not expect to be able to climb up her tower wall unseen again. He felt sick in his stomach. Perhaps she would be taken to a nunnery where he would never see her again.

"And where was the attack?" Galileo asked him.

"You said in the Grand Cathedral," he replied.

"Which means?"

"I don't know. What?"

"Inside the sanctity of the Grand Cathedral," Galileo said.

Lorenzo nodded his head, as if he knew what that meant, but Galileo could see that he didn't. "And that means the rules of order have been broken," he told him. "*Daemonicus ex machine*. We are entering a time when we will be ruled by demons."

V

"Break another finger," Cosimo Medici said, staring fixedly at the man tied to the seat before him.

"They are all broken already," the torturer said nervously. But still the man refused to speak. Or even scream. It was unnatural, he thought. The man was either drugged or insane. They were the only people in his experience who could tolerate the pain. But they all talked in the end.

Cosimo Medici took two steps towards the stairs up to the half-demolished tower above them, then turned and came back. He wanted to leave the man there, dead or half-dead, for the Lorraine men to find when they came back to resume their demolition of the Medici tower. The cost of losing a ship was the loss of a tower that the Lorraines would use the stones from to build their own tower somewhere in their own part of the city. It was like moving pieces around a chessboard, this continual tearing down and building of towers in the Walled City.

A servant fussed over Cosimo's bandage, insisting that it be changed, but Cosimo kept waving the man away. He wanted to be present when the assassin gave up the names of his employers. He wanted to hear him say the name, "Lorraine".

The machine that they had him strapped to was a primitive thing, not like the wonderful torture cabinets made of metal cogs and sharp spikes that were in the basement of the Medici Palace, but this one would suffice. It was basically a wooden rack that had been roughly constructed to tie the man to. The art was going to be in the instruments used on him. Torture was a fine art, Cosimo the Great had long ago decided, and needed an experienced artisan to practice it. As one would only employ the best sculptors to extract the best sculpture from a block of marble, so one should only employ the best torturers to extract the best confession from a man. He had admired the Medici torturer's work for many years, watching the way he could extract a confession from a man without even touching him, just the thought of the pain that his instruments were going to bring could cause a strong man's will to desert him. But this assassin was something else.

He didn't curse them nor rant nor spit at the torturer. He kept his eyes shut and mumbled to himself over and over, like he was reciting a prayer. He had put himself into something like a trance, and they could not shake him out of it. When they touched the red hot poker to his arm pits and the smell of burning flesh filled the basement chamber, he had faltered in his mumbling and started shaking, but soon resumed it again as if nothing had happened.

"It's not natural," the torturer said again, for about the dozenth time. Cosimo had heard that there were some diseases, like leprosy, that caused a man to lose sensation in his limbs, but this man did not appear to have any disease. He did not even have plague pustules, so he must have been an inhabitant of the Walled City, yet nobody knew him. He was a mystery in so many ways that on another day it might have warranted deeper investigation. But today Cosimo only needed to hear one word from him.

But still he refused to speak. Cosimo had already had the man stripped naked and his body searched for any tattoos or symbols that might give away his allegiance, but there was nothing on him of any note, bar some scars on his back, as if he had been flogged at some time in his life. That told them he was likely low born. And yet his hands were not the deeply calloused hands of a worker. They were soft, with well-shaped nails. Another mystery.

"Use the lover's finger," Cosimo instructed. The torturer turned to his instruments and took up one, a long thin metal spike with a wooden handle. He looked across to Cosimo and made a questioning motion. Cosimo, waving the servant away from his bandaged wounds yet again, nodded his head in assent. The torturer in turn nodded to his two assistants. They knew what instrument he was holding and what effect it had on a man, and braced themselves either side of the assassin.

The torturer placed the long, thin end of the instrument into the coals of the brazier at his feet and let it sit there a moment to heat up. He looked up once

more at Cosimo Medici to make sure he wasn't about
to change his mind, but his face was set. The torturer
sighed and took the instrument out of the coals. There
were some tools that even he was reluctant to use.

"Hold him," he said to his assistants. One man
thrust a piece of leather into the mumbling man's
mouth and the other took hold of his serpent of sin
and held it up for the torturer. He stepped forward
and deftly slid the hot metal spike a small way into
the tip of it, hearing the sizzling of flesh. And this
time the man did scream. He looked down as if
suddenly aware of his surroundings and what was
happening to him and screamed an ear-splitting
shriek that filled the chamber.

The torturer withdrew the spike and the man
stopped shrieking. His head lolled forward and he
slumped against his bonds.

"Throw some water on him and see if he is willing
to speak now," Cosimo instructed.

The assistants threw cold water on the man until
he revived and he started shaking against his bonds
and crying. He was broken, Cosimo decided. Now
he would talk.

He stepped away from the stairs and came towards
the man. "Who sent you?" he demanded of him, as
the torturer had been demanding all evening. But
the man let his eyes roll back in his head and started
mumbling again. "It's not..." began the torturer, but
Cosimo cut him off. "I know it's not natural. But he's
a man isn't he? He'll talk if you do your job properly."

The torturer bowed his head and looked agitated,
promising that he was doing the best he knew how,

but this was beyond his substantial experience. Cosimo looked down at the man's bleeding, burned penis and turned away. He no longer wanted to know what the torturer did to the man. He could flay him bodily and make him eat his own skin if he wished, but he needed to hear him say the name.

"Get him ready again," the torturer said to his two assistants and one took the leather bit that he had spat out when he screamed and tried to stuff it back into his mouth. "Open up, damn you," he said and squeezed his fingers into the sides of his jaw, forcing the man's mouth open. Then the assistant turned to the torturer and said, "Master!" He twisted the man's head towards him. The torturer looked and shook his head. "No!" he said.

"What is it?" Cosimo demanded.

"He carries the wounds of a blasphemer," the torturer said. "The man has no tongue and cannot speak."

The assassin mumbled again and this time it sounded to Cosimo like mockery. Like he was telling him something the whole time that he could not understand. Telling him what a fool he was. The thought enraged Cosimo. Made the blood pump in his neck wound painfully. He was sure he'd opened it again and the servant would be in a panic about it. "Then make him write," Cosimo demanded. "If he can't speak the name of his employers he can write it."

"We have broken his hands," the torturer said forlornly.

Cosimo could feel blood running down the inside of his shirt and he pulled his dagger and walked across to the man, pressing the sharp blade's edge against his neck, pressing it in deeply. "Nod your head if it was the Lorraines you did this for!" he demanded. "Nod your head."

The man broke off his mumbling and focussed his eyes on Cosimo there in front of him. And Cosimo could have sworn that he saw mirth in them as the man violently shook his head, slicing his throat open on the blade.

VI

"Stand aside," the Captain of the Medici guard called once more as he led his band of well-bearded Medici down the winding thin streets of the Walled City boldly, flouting the public ruling that forbade more than half a dozen armed men to congregate together at a time, their heavy boots echoing loudly off the cobblestones. Some citizens looked out their windows from the tall buildings that shadowed the streets below and shook their heads, knowing there would be trouble. If the city guard, who were notably absent, dared challenge them they would undoubtedly be the worse for it. But the men were not charged with causing any trouble today. They were on the streets largely as a show of force, to let any Lorraine supporters know that the Medicis were a gathering of lions to be reckoned with.

But twice now they had come across bands of citizens who were setting upon each other and were unsure whether to assist or leave them be. Breaking them up was the charge of the city guard, and assisting them might be considered an act of aggression, but how were they to stand by watching while common citizens took up the Medici cause against Lorraine supporters? For there were few people in the city who did not support one or other of the Houses. Generally it was due to patronage, and so it was seen as mutual support, and that clearly argued for the Medici men to come to the aid of those civilians defending the Medici name. But sometimes family members were in conflict with each other over which house to support and sometimes people had switched allegiances as patronage offers grew or waned, and were one year Medici supporters and the next were in favour of the Lorraines, and they would side with whoever came out in front in this current war of the Houses.

Others may simply have been incensed at the brutality of the murder of Giuliano Medici, who was well-loved, and even if they were Lorraine men at heart, they were willing to stand up against the Lorraine supporters over it. It made deciding what action to take difficult for the Medici militia. Cosimo Medici would not thank them for escalating civic unrest, but he would surely understand if they were defending the lives of staunch Medici supporters. Surely.

For it was an insult to their honour to see shopkeepers and craftsmen who had taken up cudgels and knives, fighting Lorraine men in the streets to avenge the murder of Giuliano while they simply marched past. And after bypassing the next tussle they came across, and lending a show of force to chase the enemy away at the one after, they drew their swords and attacked the Lorraine men at the subsequent melee, and then cheered with the Medici citizens as the cowards fled into dark alleys.

The streets of the Walled City were like a maze in many ways, with streets that wound back upon themselves, or branched off suddenly into thin alleys and dark stairways, and then came out on sunny plazas before disappearing off into different thin streets again. The best houses tended to be those with the widest streets in front of them, where horses and carriages could parade, but many noblemen and city councillors lived in apartments that were from the outside nothing more than a deep set door in a plain stone wall. Behind some doors were opulent courtyards, but behind others were small dingy rooms, and it was not apparent from the outside what might be behind each door. That was one of the constants of the Walled City. It hid its secrets well. No man could claim to know every nook and dwelling well, and only out on the public streets did a man need to have his allegiances on display.

Several of the victorious citizens of street scuffles offered to accompany the Medici men on their tour of the city, and the commander could not think of a good reason to refuse, so they set off, growing in number as they passed more Medici supporters. And as their numbers grew their sense of purpose grew. Anybody out and about this evening had to be looking for trouble, they reasoned. After all, the shops and warehouses and factories had been closed up tight all day, with their wooden shutters down, and any honest citizens and housewives and children were hiding behind locked doors. So every person they saw they challenged, as if they were the city guard themselves. "What is your name, citizen?" /

"What is your business?" / "What are you doing on the streets?" / "To whom do you owe allegiance?"

And for every citizen they clubbed to the ground and kicked, or every moustached Lorraine man they chased away before them, the more just their cause felt and the more certain they were that this was what they had been charged to do. Had they not a duty to enact some form of vengeance, they began asking themselves. Had they not a duty to repay Giuliano's murder at least ten-fold?

Thus, with blood running high, when they rounded a corner onto one of the many plazas of the city and came upon two small groups of citizens lined up like schoolboys, taunting each other and throwing vegetables and stones, they didn't hesitate. They simply broke into a run, drawing their swords because they were on a battlefield. The citizens who had been throwing their insults and petty missiles in support of the Medicis looked on in shock as the Medici militia stabbed and beat the Lorraine supporters, spilling the blood of the merchants and school teachers and labourers that they knew by name.

"No, no," some of the Medici supporters called, or, "You must stop this." But their cries were drowned out by the sudden clutter of boots and shouts of outrage as a band of armed Lorraine men appeared at the far side of the square and came running at them with drawn swords. These men had been winding their way around the city all evening, keen to punish any false slurs against the Lorraine name and send any rabble scattering who supported the House of Medici. They too had found their cause more righteous each time they had chased a band of Medici supporters away, and they too had found the only means of supporting their Duke's dignity and their own was in drawing their swords and baying for blood.

They had been winding their way down a particularly thin alleyway, which forced them to go single file, when a hooded man had stepped out in front of them and said, "Is this a centipede I see? It surely cannot be, for it has no sting to it."

The leader of the Lorraine men put his hand on his sword hilt and said, "Do not taunt us or we will respond with something more heavy on your head than words." But the hooded man only laughed at that, and said, in a strange Germanic accent, "You are all girly men!" The leader of the Lorraine men drew his sword and the hooded man turned and ran.

They had chased him back into a wider street where they could hurl their curses at him three or four abreast, but he was easily outdistancing them. "Hurry, hurry," the leader of the Lorraine men urged as he led his band around a corner, where the hooded man had fled, and entered the plaza and saw armed Medici militia attacking civilians.

The hooded man was forgotten and citizens of both sides ran and limped for cover as the conflict suddenly turned into a pitched battle around them. Wounded people cried for help to the absent city guard, or to the tightly shuttered houses around them, but nobody would be coming to their aid, it was clear. They slipped and stumbled on the bloody flagstones and dragged themselves away, leaving the armed men to fight each other. And if not for the fact that equally-armed men tend to do less damage to each other than armed men attacking unarmed men tend to, the bloodshed would have been considerable that evening. But after the initial clash of swords both militias found themselves withdrawing to either side of the plaza, dragging their dead and wounded with them.

The victory and the losses seemed about even, so neither side was willing to be the first one to withdraw from the battle field entirely and concede defeat. But neither was each group as keen to attack the other as they had been keen to attack civilians. So it was, when the city guard finally arrived on the scene and found the well-armed and bloodied Medici and Lorrain men lined up like school children, casting vegetables, stones and insults at each other. Both groups were satisfied to disperse when ordered to, without challenging the guards' authority, despite greatly outnumbering them, and they marched off along different streets to inevitably find citizens not aligned with their house, and start their outrage all over again.

VII

"Why don't you say something?" the Duchess hissed at her husband. But he just sat there quietly at a long table, surrounded by his councillors, who were arguing and bickering with each other as to how they should best act. He turned to look at his wife. She wore a long red robe with white trimming – quite a contrast to his sombre dark coat with pearls stitched into it – and it almost made her look beautiful. The men around them talked loudly, knowing it was just as important that she heard their opinions and advice as the Duke did, as they would eventually be dismissed from the chamber and the matter would be settled between the two of them. Those who advocated war with the Medici house stood closest to her, knowing that would be her preference, and those who advocated a more peaceful settlement, gathered around the Duke, knowing it would be his preference.

The Duke seemed uninterested in all their opinions though, toying with a small glass-covered brass object on the desk in front of him as the voices buzzed around his ears. "This is tarnish to the silvery name of

Lorraine, to accuse of us of being behind this attack. We must act decisively to restore our honour." / "Honour is best served by acting honourably." / "This tastes of a power struggle across the Medici's dinner plates, and if we act quickly we can dominate the city." / "It was sacrilege to pluck a man from life's garden in the cathedral. You must distance yourself from anything associated with it." / "The murderers may be a plot by a lesser house to start a war between the Lorraine and Medici Houses that they will benefit from." / "We must be decisive." / "We must be cautious."

"For the sake of the ancients," the Duchess suddenly snapped, "Would you stop playing with that toy!" And the room fell silent. Each of the men looked to the Duke for a sign that they should leave, but all he said was, "It is not a toy, petal of my rose, it is a scientific device of Leonardo's that can control the weather."

"Don't be absurd," his wife said pointedly. "Nobody can control the weather."

"No more than they can control the birds in the sky or the creatures in the sea?" he asked. She folded her arms and glared at him. "Let me show you," he said. He turned the device around and showed her the dial on the front. "These markings indicate high pressure and low pressure. And when a storm is coming the air pressure is lower than it is during calm weather when the air pressure is higher." He looked up at his wife but still she glared at him. "Have you not felt a change in the air when a storm is coming?" he asked. "That is the air pressure changing. If you boil water and capture the steam in a glass chamber you can measure the increase in pressure even as the steam builds up."

"So?" his wife asked.

"So watch carefully," he said. He turned a brass dial at the base of the device and the dial moved to low It took a moment, but the councillors did feel the air in the room change. It became heavier, as if steam was being released into the room from some hidden device. They looked at one another uneasily. "Does it smell like rain?" the Duke asked. Several of the advisors admitted that it did, while the Duchess said nothing.

"Now," said the Duke, "if I turn the dial the other way." He turned it and the change in the room again took a moment but there were murmurs of surprise all about him as the air became drier and cooler.

"It is like magic, your grace," said one of the advisors.

"It is science," said the Duke.

"I understand it not, and I like it less," said one of his oldest advisers. "I have always preferred the strength of observation and reason."

The Duke looked up and met his wife's eyes. "And what does observation and reason tell us we should do right now, do you think?"

Her lips curled into a mocking smile. "It tells us we shouldn't be sitting here in this chamber, playing with toys that have no practical use while we are attacked by our enemies."

The Duke waved his hand in the air and the councillors and advisors then beat a hasty retreat from the room. The Duchess rose to her feet and made a grab for the device in front of her husband, but he pulled it back towards him. "You are a man with no metals in his backbone," she hissed. "My father warned me you were a straw man."

The Duke sat impassively. He had heard it all before. She had married beneath herself. He owed all his success to the wealth she brought to the marriage. The Walled City was her prison. She should have never left her native land. He let her talk on for some time and then said, "Yes, my rose amongst roses. I know all this. As I know that your family and most of those of your homeland are undoubtedly all dead of plague, and you are only alive because after leaving me to go and live with them, you then fled back to live in the Walled City with me."

"Enough!" she said and banged her palm angrily on the table. "Don't taunt me."

"I don't taunt you, violet of my heart, I just want you to calm down."

"What good will calming down do?" she asked. "Will it change anything? Will it stop our men being slaughtered in the streets like sheep by the Medici butchers? Will it help our cause any? We should act now while our blood is up."

"While *your* blood is up!" he corrected her.

She spun around and turned her back to him.

"We don't even know who was behind this attack yet," he said.

"Why does it matter who was behind it?" she said, spinning back to face him. "We have an opportunity to move against the Medicis while they are in disarray."

"While they are armed and expecting another attack?" he asked.

"Coward," she hissed.

The Duke said nothing and toyed with the device in his lap a moment.

"I will not be held responsible for a war inside the Walled City," he said patiently. "Not while I have the means of preventing one and still defeating the Medicis."

"But you are squandering an opportunity to crush them," she said.

"We will defeat them anyway. They are no longer able to bring their ships into the harbour while Leonardo's whale men can block them."

"Nor have we been able."

He shrugged. "We have the odds of success in our favour. Our stocks of spice are sufficient. We are better placed than they are."

"You would rather count tin soldiers than knock them down."

"I would rather not risk our business interests in a war than would benefit nobody."

"Nobody but the victor!" she spat.

"Please, petal of my rose," he said, though he was thinking, *thorn* of my rose, "If we go claw to claw with the Medici household it will be a decision we make together, based on a need, not an opportunity."

"What is the difference?" she asked haughtily.

He thought back to nearly two decades ago, when he had the opportunity to marry several women, but had a need to wed her. "The differences are small but important," he said.

"You play with words," she said. "You play with these devices. You play at being a man of commerce and you play at being a Duke."

"I am the Duke," he said firmly, stroking his thin moustache, "Which you sometimes seem to forget."

"You never let me forget," she said. He knew what she wanted to say next, which she had often said when she was in one of her furies – if he was to die suddenly she would take over the ruling of the house and things would be done her way. He had no doubt of that. He met her stare and said slowly, "Observation and reason say we will not move with force against the Medicis until we know more or until we have a need. We have other means at our disposal to take advantage of their weaknesses. Cosimo without Giuliano is like…" He paused. The most apt metaphor was the Duchess without the Duke, but he said, "A sword wielded by a blind man."

"Who only a fool would attempt to dance with," she smiled. He glared at her and she returned his glare with a look of contempt and then stormed from the chamber. He sighed and looked down at the device in his hands. She would calm down eventually, though he would do well to keep his distance from her at meal time when she'd have sharp implements at hand. He wondered if she might take matters into her own hands and summons a deathseeker to attack the Medici household. It would be foolish. They would be wary of an attack and it would only confirm their beliefs that the Lorraine's were behind Giuliano's death. He turned the dial on the device once more and then back again. It was indeed an ingenious invention, but he'd rather Leonardo create him one that could control the tempestuous moods of his wife, rather than those of the weather.

VIII

"We are at war and you will make me war machines," Cosimo Medici said, standing up from his seat and pointing an angry finger at Galileo. He was not used to being defied. "No more toys," he said. He gestured around at the clockwork mechanisms that filled the side tables that he had once delighted in. A wind-up bird that could sing. A hand-turned screw that could raise water up from a basin and then have it cascade down, turning water wheels to make a windmill turn, sending out a rainbow of colour. A glass for viewing small objects that made them larger.

"They are not just toys," Galileo said defiantly. "They are machines of science. Each of these can be produced at a larger scale and benefit the citizens of the city in some way. Each one adds to our knowledge of the world."

"There will be time for knowledge of the world later," Cosimo said. "First we need to defeat the Lorraines so that we can have peace once more."

"I seem to recall we had both peace and the Lorraines for a long, long time," said Galileo.

Cosimo fumed and withdrew his pointed finger into his hand, making a fist. He now wished that he had dismissed his advisers from the chamber. He did not want them to see Galileo defying him like this while he sat there in ceremonial battle armour, and he did not wish them to see him losing his temper with the man. They well knew his worth and tended to trust his counsel. But today they should not. "You tell me that you seek the knowledge of the ancients," he said. "You tell me that will make us great. And yet the ancients possessed mighty war machines."

"And that is why they faded from our memories. Their wars cast us into a thousand years of darkness. Almost all their knowledge has been lost to us. Their ways of building. Their ways of healing. Their ways of understanding the world. They buried their greatness with war machines."

"We will be different. We will only use them to restore peace."

"The peace that could exist without them."

"The Lorraines tried to assassinate me! They killed my beloved brother Giuliano. How can you stand there before me and deny this?"

"So you obtained a confession from the attacker?" Galileo asked.

Cosimo turned away and shook his hands in the air. "If not the Lorraines, then who else?"

"That is the question we should be devoting our energies to, rather than declaring a war that is not based on any sound evidence."

"Evidence?" said Cosimo. "You insist on evidence? I know it to be the Lorraines. I feel it in my breast that it is the Lorraines." He banged a fist upon his metal breastplate and looked to his advisors to see if they supported him in this, but not a one met his eye. He felt like he was at school, with his teachers asking him to debate some point of logic and sitting there in judgement of him. Even Galileo's apprentice was following the arguments of each man carefully, he could see, hiding back there near the chamber door. He felt he was being judged harshly in his own governing chamber, where his word should have been law. But it was his own decree that no man would be punished in this chamber for speaking his mind. He paced back and forward like an animal in a cage.

Galileo said nothing for a while and waited for Cosimo to return to his seat and then said, in a soft and fatherly voice, "I have always mistrusted my feelings as leading me in directions they wanted to go rather than in directions that the evidence dictated. That is one of the lessons I've learned from the ancients. One of the basic tenants of science. Evidence is the only truth we can rely on."

"In the absence of such evidence I must rely on my instincts," said Cosimo. "They have always served me well in the past, in business, in matters of employment – such as seeking you out and offering you a position."

"I would like to think it was based on the evidence of my successes and your successes in business in turn," said Galileo, with a bow.

Cosimo the Great could not deny that and so ground his teeth in response. Then he said, "But you defy me and you infuriate me."

"For infuriating you I apologise," said Galileo, "That has never been my intent."

"Then what is your intent?" Cosimo demanded.

"To help you make the best decisions possible."

"You suggest I am making a poor decision?"

"They are your words, not mine."

Cosimo ground his teeth again. Many evenings he and Giuliano had enjoyed such bantering with Galileo, trying to keep up with the way he jousted with words and demanded sharp thinking of this. But today such behaviour was uncalled for.

"I will ask you once more," said Cosimo, bringing his voice back to a low but firm level. "Will you make me war machines?"

"And I can only reply that it would fly in the face of my duty to you, my Lord, to the citizens of this city and the very future of civilisation. It would throw us back into the darkness. I may as well throw open the gates for the plague victims to enter the city."

Cosimo glared at Galileo. He needed him to know it was a very dangerous game he was playing with him. But the old man seemed not to care. "I could have you crushed," Cosimo said, in a low dangerous voice.

Galileo bowed to Cosimo, acknowledging his power over him, but then said, "But who then would make your tools of commerce, let alone machines of war? My apprentice

Lorenzo?" Lorenzo looked up and felt his mouth go dry. He had no desire to become a pawn in this battle between his masters. "Come forward, Lorenzo!" Galileo commanded.

Lorenzo walked forward slowly, keeping his eyes down at his feet. "Can you make our lord war machines? Like those the ancients had?" Galileo asked.

Both men were looking at him. The advisors were looking at him. They all believed they knew what his answer would be. He was suddenly an orphaned ward again. No different in their eyes than the nameless boys who mucked out the stables and swept the floors. He could almost see the opportunity before him being held out on a silver plate to him. All he had to say was the truth. "Yes, I can make you armoured carts that do not need horses to pull them. And I can make you clockwork crossbows that shoot at five times the speed a man can shoot them. And I can make you devices that a single man can use to tumble the huge stones off a wall or tower." He only had to say it and he would be an apprentice no more. He would be seen as a great man of science in his own right. He would no more be the boy in-between floors. He would be welcomed to the upper floors of the palace. And he only had to tell the truth for it to happen.

But he could not stop thinking of the Medici men toppling the tower where Lucia lived and burying her in the stones of her own chamber. How could he assist Cosimo in attacking the Lorraines when Lucia was a Lorraine? And he could not bring himself to betray Galileo again. With his face burning with shame he kept his eyes at his feet and said, "No, my Lord. That knowledge is lost to us."

"Enough," said Cosimo, "You are both dismissed!" The old man and his apprentice bowed low and withdrew from the chamber.

It took some time for the first advisor to gather the courage and step up close to Cosimo's seat and say, "Perhaps there is wisdom in avoiding going to battle. There would be losses to us as well. Perhaps we should consider other ways to end this war?"

"Deathseekers?" asked Cosimo, the word a bitter one in his mouth.

"Think more of it as fighting fire with fire," said the advisor.

Cosimo turned his head up to admire the ornate gold ceilings decorated with frescos of the ancients, their great cities and great civilisation. Then he nodded. "We have men inside the Lorraine household. Let them know what needs to be done."

IX

Lucia awoke as the pillow pressed tightly against her face. She tried to scream, but the air remained in her lungs. She kicked and punched her arms, feeling a strong man looming over her, impassive to her blows. She tried to turn her head and draw a breath, but the pillow was pressed over her face too tightly. Then she felt the sharp point of the dagger probing her rib cage for a point to enter and stab into her heart. That gave her strength, and she raised against her attacker with her whole body, throwing him off. The pillow fell from her face and she squirmed to the far side of the bed, ready to scream, expecting to see the attacker falling upon her again.

But he stood there transfixed, his eyes turned up to the heavens, the dagger held out beside him. Then he dropped it to the ground. She could not comprehend at first, and then she saw the tall man behind him in the dark cape and hood. He was clean-shaven and held her attacker from behind with a blade against his neck and the other hand gripping his wrist, shaking the dagger free.

She looked at the moustached face of her attacker and recognised him as one of the servants who worked in the yard. This deathseeker was a man of their household – although clearly not a man of their house. And clearly not a man of great fortitude, as she could smell the urine stain that was filling his hose and running down his leg towards the floor.

"Please, signor," the man muttered and then gasped. His eyes rolled up in his sockets as the point of a thin blade emerged from his chest. Lucia gasped too. And threw a hand over her mouth.

The man in the dark cape and hood withdrew the bloodied blade and put it to his lips, as if it were a finger, and said, "Shhhhh." Lucia kept her hand tightly over her mouth. There was a scream welling inside her, but she did not know if she were in mortal danger still, or had just been saved. Who was this strange man and what was he doing in her bedchamber?

Then before she knew quite what to do, the hooded man said, "If only he'd said 'pretty please'." And then he scooped up the body of her attacker and stepped over to her window. He turned back and looked briefly at her wall mural in the dark, and said, "You're going to want to leave some of the wall around the city." Then he was gone. Out the window. Impossible. She sat there in bed for a moment longer, her heart racing like a bird trying to break out of a cage, and then pursed her lips and took a step out of bed. She felt her legs wobbling, as if they were going to collapse under her, but she took a deep breath and walked unsteadily across to the window. She peered out cautiously, not quite sure what to see – but there was nothing. The men were gone. She looked down the tower wall and looked up to the rooftop above. Where had he gone? How had he gone? Who was he? He had saved her life. If he was working for her father he would have said so. And he certainly wouldn't have disappeared out the window. The same way Lorenzo came to her. He was too tall to be Lorenzo. How could he have climbed down the wall with a dead man in his arms? Her head was giddy from the confusion of it. She wanted to go back to bed and lie down and close her eyes again and wake up and discover it was all a dream. But she knew it wasn't. She could still smell the dead man's piss in the room. And there was a single spot of blood on the floor where he had been stabbed by her mysterious saviour.

And she could still feel the point against her chest where the knife blade had touched. For just a brief moment she felt her legs wobbling, like they might collapse under her, but then she was filled with an anger that gave them strength. How dare anybody try to kill her in her own bed chamber? How dare they presume to make her a pawn in the battles between the Medicis and the Lorraines? She lay back down on her bed and wondered again about her mysterious saviour, certain that Lorenzo was behind it somehow. And resolved that when she awoke in the morning she would take up her paintbrushes and end this stupid war between the two Houses by painting over all their towers, replacing them with parklands and gardens where the citizens of the city could be free to enjoy their own lives.

X

Cosimo wished he had insisted on holding his brother's service in one of their small family chapels instead. It was too dark and too hot in the crypt under the cathedral. And he wanted to be alone with his brother, not crammed into a damp-smelling hole like this with too many family members and lackeys all about him. But protocol dictated a public funeral. Protocol dictated that Giuliano's mourners be allowed to see his coffin and weep and wail over it, whether their tears be genuine or not, while he stood there proud and brave.

So he stood at the back of the throng, on a slightly raised platform, watching the jostling crowd in the too small space, with his aged mother at his side. She was a little deaf but still sharp of mind, and had never forgotten he was her first born. He held her by the arm and, leaning close to her, said, "I am sorry to have brought you to such a miserable place as the funeral of your second born son."

His mother muttered something and dabbed at her eyes with an ornate cloth. She had already lost two sons to sickness while they were young and one daughter to a riding accident. He and Giuliano were all that remained of her five children and she had often said they were each the man they were only because of the other. But Cosimo knew what was really in her head. The two boys were raised together, attended lessons together, were trained in fighting together, and it had always been Giuliano who was the better of them. But he was not the first born.

"Look at them trying to outdo each other in showing how much they loved him and how much his death fills them with grief," he said to his mother softly. "But they don't know grief! I could fill the entire cathedral with my sorrow. I could fill the whole city until it pressed at the walls and threatened to break them under its weight. I could fill the known world with my sadness."

She patted his hand in reply. He looked at her face, the tears welling in her eyes, and said, "I will have artists paint frescos and sculpt statues that capture my grief." Then, "And a hundred years hence people will look at them and say, 'Never has man known such grief as this'." His mother turned to him and put a hand to his face. "I will show them what real grief is," he said, taking her hand from his face and holding it tightly. Then his mother turned towards several of the people who approached them with their heads bowed to show their respect. Cosimo gave each a curt nod and watched them trying to work their way back through the press of bodies. "Giuliano deserved better than this," he said, leaning closer to his mother. "He deserved a service in the cathedral above." His mother nodded her head a little, as if agreeing, but knowing that it would have been against custom to do so.

Cosimo watched his mother closely and then said, "He was always wiser than me. He knew what courses of actions were ill-considered and which were not. He had a better eye for strategy than I ever did." And then, in a whisper his mother could barely hear, "He would have made a better head of the House than me, wouldn't he?" His mother patted his hand again, not acknowledging if she had heard or understood him, and she smiled and nodded to another well-wisher who had come up and bowed to them. "But it was not in Giuliano's nature to covert it, was it?" Cosimo said. Then softer still, "When we were boys I told him I would kill him before I let him accede to the head of the House before me. And he just laughed as if it had been a jest, telling me rather to kill those who stood in front of me."

He watched his mother greet another grieving couple, cousins of theirs, and he said softly, "If the situation were reversed and I lay there dead and Giuliano stood here alive, would you tell him that he was the favourite? That he would be a better leader of the House than me?" But his mother did not answer the question. He put his lips closer to her ear and said, "Everyone always loved him more than they loved me. He was the one who remembered everyone's name and children's names. He was the one who would readily help those in need, rather than grudgingly. They fear me and respect me, but I don't think so many would weep so at my death, do you?"

His mother still did not acknowledge what he said and it started angering him. "If I was dead, what would you tell Giuliano, that he would succeed without me? That he does not need me the way that I need him?" His mother leaned a little away from him now, as if she did not wish to hear this, but he pulled her back close to him and said, in a low hiss, "It was Giuliano who wished our father dead. Not me. He said I would never become leader of the House otherwise. He said we should pray regularly for his early death. Perhaps he prayed and planned for mine too, but that is not the way things have turned out, is it?"

In the emptiness of Giuliano's absence he found the angry words would not be stilled. "What if I had slain Giuliano?" he asked, pulling his mother tightly to him. "What if it was me who had hired the assassins to strike him down, simply to prove that I could live a life without him, only to find that I could not?" She lowered her head and he hissed, "If he was here now he would advise me to stop talking so. He would tell me that if it was anybody else than you I was blabbering to I would have to kill them afterwards. And I would have. He knew who needed killing and when."

He felt his mother trying to pull away from him and then felt the platform they were on jostled from behind. There seemed to be more people in the crypt now. The air was hotter and he could hear murmurs of concern amongst the mourners as they were pushed and squeezed against each other. His mother, now being jostled from the other side, tried to shake her arm from his, but he was holding onto her tightly.

"This is a fitting metaphor for our grief," he said. "Let them keep coming and they will crush one another."

Now he could hear yelps of alarm from those about them and he saw one woman fall to the floor. She screamed as she fell and the piercing shout had the same effect that the sight of an assassin's knife being raised in the air would have had. Everyone was suddenly pushing and shouting, trying to make their way to the stairs before they could be dragged by the deathseekers' hands to the ground and trampled. They had all carried the thought of deathseekers into the crypt with them and now had created it as something real. The fragile moment of considering the fate of Giuliano in the afterlife was replaced with the more immediate consideration of their own fates in this life. But the more people panicked the more fell and were trampled upon. Their own fear had become manifest to attack them.

"This should've been my funeral," said Cosimo, shouting, now, to his mother. "This is how I would like to be remembered." And then the platform was upset by the pressing crowd and he felt his mother's arm being pulled from his own. He fought against the crowd now, pushing people away from him, reaching out for his mother as she sank into the mob. And it seemed to him, for just a moment, that she was withholding her hand from him, rather to be trampled by the mob than to be at his side. "Mother," he called out. "Don't leave me."

And then he had her hand and pulled her back to him. People flowed around them and he regained his feet. Then his mother looked into his face and placed a hand against the side of his face. Slowly she bent his head to her bosom, the way she had always done when he had come to her as a boy with some seeming great injustice. "My Cosimo," she said. "My troubled little Cosimo. You'll always be my first born."

XI

"The cook's assistant has been murdered." The kitchen girl who found the dead cook's assistant told the kitchen hand who told the cook who told the steward who told the Captain of the Guard who told the Duke of Lorraine, who insisted for himself on seeing it, and then summoned Leonardo. It was inexplicable. The man had been murdered in the kitchen at some hour in the night, and lay dead over the kitchen bench, with his fat face in a bowl of soup and his fatter penis out, pointing into a soup pot.

"What does it mean?" the steward asked, as each person had asked their superior upon seeing the dead man.

"It is a warning," the Duke said. "I have seen such before. They had intended to cut the man's manhood off and stuff it into his mouth. It is a punishment for betrayal."

"Who did he betray?" the steward asked.

But the Duke only shook his head. "We have been attacked in our own house," he said. "It is an outrage." He fretted a little for what his wife would say and knew he needed to put on a face of rage while seeking good counsel from Leonardo. There were more mysteries here than could easily be answered by blaming the Medici deathseekers, and he was still pondering the possibility that one of the lesser houses was trying to trigger a war between the Lorraines and Medicis.

The cause of death was apparent enough, as the man had a short metal arrow protruding from the back of his skull. "It has been fired through the open window," the steward boldly asserted. "A deathseeker has been prowling around the house looking for any target and found this unfortunate man."

"But somebody must have been inside the room to take the poor man's tower of ivory out of his trousers," said the cook.

The kitchen girl, who had been trying to steal surreptitious looks at the dead man's member, thought it looked nothing like a tower of ivory and a more apt metaphor might have alluded to a chicken's neck or perhaps a snail. But she knew nobody wanted to be disrespectful of the poor dead man and so said nothing. At least not until she was with the other kitchen girls later that day.

"Perhaps there were two assailants," said the steward. "One who shot him and the other who did this thing. Or perhaps the man climbed in the window after slaying him and did this?"

"Impossible," said the Captain of the Guard. "The window is too small for a man to climb in."

"Perhaps a boy?" asked the steward.

"Perhaps," said the Captain of the Guard. "That would mean two attackers. They would have had a harder time getting past our guards though. We would have noticed a man with a boy."

"Then how they do this?" asked the cook.

"Leonardo will know," said the Duke. The Captain of the Guard pouted his lips a little as if he doubted that the man could determine any more from the scene than he could himself. "I think the assassin fired the arrow from a long distance away. A lucky shot. He probably couldn't even tell who he was shooting at and was hoping it was a more senior member of the household. I mean, why kill a cook's assistant?"

"And who had he betrayed?" asked the cook, a little slower than the others to keep up with the pace of the conversation. He was still wondering where they were going to put the dead man's body and how he was going to be able to cook breakfast with him there.

"Perhaps he was, um, playing the bone flute," said the steward, turning a little red at the presence of the kitchen girl. "At the time of his death."

The cook looked at him aghast. "Such behaviour is not acceptable in my kitchen!" he said.

"Nevertheless," said the steward, "It might explain things a little better than the vengeance theory."

The Captain of the Guard considered it and wondered, if a man was slain while his ivory tower was erect, might it not stay erect? He wondered who would know the answer to such things. Leonardo, probably, as the Duke said. He seemed to know every other secret of the body. Rumour has it he performed experiments on the bodies of the dead to know how they worked. But rumour also had it that he could turn invisible and walk through walls. Perhaps he was in the room with them now, if that was the case. The man turned his head and looked around the room carefully and was surprised to see that Leonardo was indeed with them. The old man was standing in the doorway, out of sight, his thick eyebrows knit closely as he stroked his long unkempt beard, carefully regarding everything.

"No," said the cook firmly. "Not in my kitchen. In the guards' house, perhaps, but not here. I would not permit it." The standing of the kitchen and his role in the household had risen as the variety of foods became scarcer in the Walled City. Not only did he now supervise the growing of vegetable gardens in the courtyard but was charged with hunting down rare treats from across the cellars of the city, which citizens would exchange for sacks of plain grain. Just this last week he had obtained two jars of pickled onions – many of which were in the soup at the dead man's feet.

"How would you enforce it?" asked the steward. "You are not here all through the day and the night."

"I would come to hear of it," said the cook. "I would see guilt in the man's eyes."

"So are you saying you can tell whenever a man has committed a sin?"

"I can tell whenever anyone of my kitchen staff has," the cook insisted. The kitchen girl turned her head a little, making a vow never to let the cook look into her eyes and also to warn the other girls who worked in the kitchens too.

"These are all guesses," said the Duke. "All I can be certain of is that someone has sent an assassin who has killed one of my household and that it shall not be allowed to go unpunished, be it a Medici or lesser house who is responsible." His wife would be told of that vow and he hoped that would placate her while Leonardo solved the crime.

And then Leonardo stepped forward. He didn't say anything but looked carefully at the metal arrow in the man's neck and touched it with his fingers. Then he looked down at the pot of soup under the table and pulled the man's hand away from his member and looked at the fingers. Then at the other hand. Then he put a finger into the soup bowl that the dead man had fallen into it, licked it with the tip of his tongue and spat it out quickly.

The cook pulled a face at the thought of tasting dead man soup, and said, "Let me at least save the pot under the table."

"No," said Leonardo. "Throw it out. Throw it all out. It has been poisoned."

"But the man has clearly been killed by an arrow," said the Captain of the Guard, "Not poison."

"Very astute," said Leonardo. "But this man is a poisoner."

Everyone in the kitchen was taken aback. The Duke, the Captain of the Guard, the steward, the cook, the kitchen hand and the kitchen girl. The Duke asked the question first. "So, tell us what you believe happened."

"This man has undoubtedly been in the employ of your enemies and had poisoned this soup bowl in front of him that was undoubtedly meant for you. See the fine bowl he has used." They all saw this and nodded. Leonardo then held up the man's fingers on each hand. "See the traces of powder on these fingers," he said. "That is residue of the poison. You can taste it in the soup slightly now that it is cold, but when heated up I'd wager it is not detectable."

"What do you know of poisons?" the Captain of the Guard asked.

"Enough," said Leonardo. Then, "The person who shot this man saved your life, your grace," he said to the Duke.

"Then who was it?" asked the Captain of the Guard. "One of my men?"

"A stranger," said Leonardo. "This arrow is like no craftsmanship I have ever seen. Can you dig it out and have it sent to my chambers for further examination, though?" The Captain of the Guard nodded dumbly.

"How long has this man been in our employ?" asked the Duke. The cook screwed up his face and tried to recall, but Leonardo said, "About two months, I'd estimate."

"How can you tell that?" asked the cook.

"That's when the household soup first started tasting of piss and when I stopped eating it," said Leonardo. The other five people in the kitchen, the Duke, the Captain of the Guard, the cook, the kitchen hand and the kitchen girl all looked at the dead man's member and the pot of soup under the table.

"You don't mean…?" said the kitchen hand.

"Impossible," said the cook.

"Unthinkable," said the Captain of the Guard.

"Outrageous!" said the Duke, knowing his wife would turn purple with rage when she heard of this. Then Leonardo rolled up the dead man's sleeve to reveal the Medici sign of six balls in a circle tattooed on his inner arm. Everyone in the room stared at in dumbfoundment for a moment. "The Medici will answer for this!" the Duke railed. "We will serve them up baked turds!" The cook wondered if that was a metaphor or if he'd actually be called upon to do such baking, and while the others expressed variations of increased outrage, it fell to the kitchen girl to ask the relevant question, "So, if this man was a Medici spy, who killed him?"

"That I cannot tell you as of yet," Leonardo said. "But clearly whoever he is, he is exceedingly skilled in the art of death, and let us hope that he proves a friend and not our adversary."

XII

Standing inside his new machine Lorenzo was a giant metal man, taller than any of the great statues in the main plaza. He was three times the height of any militia man and about ten times as strong. He stood in the metal man's heart, his limbs working the arms and legs, striding along the streets of the Walled City like one of the ancient gods. People ran from the sight of him, scurrying around his feet like rats in the gutters. Now and then a braver soul would throw a rock at him, but it bounced harmlessly off his metal chest.

He turned his head to look at whoever dared defy him and the eyes of the giant metal man shot out a concentrated ray of heated light, driven from a lens that captured the rays of the sun. As he strode closer to the Lorraines' household, men on horseback galloped out towards him, waving spears and swords. But the horses shied away at the sight of him and when rallied, he emitted a high-pitch scream from the mouth of the machine that panicked them so badly they turned and ran.

Lorenzo laughed and it boomed out the trumpet inside the metal man's mouth, echoing around the streets and alleys about him. The next line of defence was soldiers, who ran towards him. But their spears and swords bounced harmlessly off his legs as he kept striding onwards. He had to concentrate on not stumbling over the men who fell under his feet and were squashed beneath him. He laughed out loud again when arrows started clattering against the metal man's skin.

He looked up and saw the men on the roof of the building beside him and reached out a long metal arm. Where he punched the wall, the rocks collapsed, and the men hiding behind them fled. Now the house of his destination was before him. He walked to the corner of the building and looked up at the tower there. He turned his head to the magnfiers above his eyes and stared up at the window of Lucia's room. She was looking down at him in awe. He could not hear her voice, but he could see her lips moving. She was calling to him, he supposed. She knew it was him. It could only be him, coming to her.

The metal man reached up an arm that increased in length as cogs and wires stretched out extensions to the hand. It stretched all the way to her window and he saw her hesitate there just a moment, before stepping to the window sill and jumping down into the metal hand. Immediately he turned the giant about, bringing the hand down so that she was protected by the huge metal body. Lucia, his loved one, curled into a ball, pressed against him, and he wished he could feel her through the metal.

Then he felt the change happening as she leant into him. Felt her merging into his large metal body, felt her heart seeking out his. Felt the wings of the butterfly inside his chest. "Not here," he said, feeling his armour turning into flesh. He turned to stride back up the street, so the transformation could be complete, knowing they would not be safe until it had. Then the change would spread out around them, changing the whole city, restoring peace.

"What is this?" asked Galileo, holding up the sketch he had been working on.

"A giant metal man, controlled by a person standing inside it here."

Galileo looked over the diagrams carefully, then said, "Where are the counter-weights to allow the arms to lift up?"

"I will put them here and here," Lorenzo said, taking the diagram and adding them to it.

"But the machine is too heavy on top now. It will over-balance too easily."

"Not if the operator is skilled enough."

"But if it falls just once, the weight of the machine would damage any of the joints here and here, and it could not rise again to walk."

Lorenzo sucked in his cheeks. "Then he would not be allowed to fall," he said.

"Perhaps it needs four legs," Galileo offered. "Or wheels?"

"But then it would not be a metal man," said Lorenzo. "It would be half man half horse. Or half man, half cart."

"If you truly wanted it to be a man it should have a giant metal phallus," said Galileo. Lorenzo blushed a little. "And a fully operational one at that. How do you propose constructing that? And what about an arsehole? What would it shit? Metal cast offs?"

"It's only meant to represent a man," Lorenzo said.

"It could be a metal pig or goat, if that is the shape best suited to its purpose," Galileo said. "Whatever that purpose might be." That was his way of asking what Lorenzo meant it for, although he suspected that his master already had an inkling.

"It is to strike awe into the hearts of men so that they run away," Lorenzo said.

"Hmmm," said Galileo. "So would not a mythical beast be more appropriate? Something from a person's nightmares?"

"It is not meant to scare everybody," Lorenzo said. "Just those who attack it."

"So it's designed for a use that is likely to have people attacking it, is it? And this here, is that not a magnifier?"

"Yes," said Lorenzo, "to see through. And here, see, this arm can extend via several metal tubes that slide inside each other and are attached to system of cogs."

"Very clever," said Galileo.

"I've been thinking we could design a magnifier that did that too, so it would be small to carry but could then be made larger when using it."

"Very clever indeed," said Galileo. "However I think your metal man might be a little more ambitious than the laws of nature will allow for. But what else have you been working on?"

Lorenzo was a little embarrassed to show him, but his master pushed his sketches of the giant metal man aside and lifted up another piece of paper and examined it. He frowned as he looked at it carefully and said, "And what would this device be intended to do?"

"It is a toy," said Lorenzo. "This metal cylinder, when spun, creates a static charge that can be discharged from this metal arm here. Like the ones you have built, but larger."

"But this one appears to be on a vast scale," said Galileo. "And it is on wheels so it can be moved around. A device this large might be dangerous, surely it would produce a charge large enough to perhaps stun or kill a man?"

Lorenzo shrugged. "I don't know," he said. "Perhaps."

"You've made a good design," said Galileo, "But what would possibly have the strength to turn the cylinder?"

"The metal giant could turn it," said Lorenzo.

"Hmmm," said Galileo, "Perhaps. But who would be strong enough to power the metal giant to turn the cylinder?"

Lorenzo bit his lip before he could say, "My love for Lucia is strong enough to power the metal giant to knock down half the city or turn the cylinder if I needed to."

"Anyway," said Galileo, "Your ideas are fanciful. There is a lot more involved in making a large model of a smaller one than just increasing its size. The weight of something has to be considered against the strength of the building materials being used. It is easy enough to build mud castles by the river, but they cannot be built to the height of our buildings without collapsing."

"They could be powered by science," said Lorenzo softly. Galileo laid his hand flat on the table, on top of the sketches and Lorenzo could see the fingers were as grey as stone. The old man said, "This hand was once young and supple like yours."

Lorenzo said nothing. Then Galileo put the hand on his neck and asked gently, "Did you intend to give these designs to Cosimo Medici?"

"No," said Lorenzo quickly. "They were just for me. Just ideas I had in my head."

Galileo nodded gravely. "And I suggest you keep them in your head. You will have never seen them, but these are the types of machines the ancients toyed with."

"Then in seeking the knowledge of the ancients, should we not seek to rediscover them?" Lorenzo asked his master.

Galileo looked at him squarely and said, "Only if we know that we will use them more wisely than the ancients did. And can you, or anyone, ever promise me that?"

XIII

The Duke of Lorraine used to love this view of the city. He stood by the window in his study, looking down on the world from his high tower, watching the citizens below going about their daily tasks. He always imagined that each was aware of him watching them. Some would be Lorraine men and would feel that he was their benevolent lord watching over them, and others were Medici men who would try and avoid the touch of his gaze, worry what he was planning. For he was always planning something. It was like a great game of chess, this battle between the two Houses. Even those who were non-aligned could not help but be caught up in it.

But increasingly, he was finding, the joy had gone out of it. There were too many other players trying to take over the game. The mysterious death of Lorenzo Medici. The plague people at the gates, growing in number daily. The City Council, always scheming to try and assert their own power. The battles with his wife. And to add to that, an assassination attempt inside his own household. The game had become a war and in a war there had to be a decisive winner. A game could go on indefinitely, but a war needed a quick victory or both sides suffered. Already the streets below were mostly empty of anyone but armed militias and guards. The city could withstand a small army at the gates, but could not withstand warring armies within. Or worse, numbers of deathseekers prowling in the dark, patiently waiting to assassinate members of each household. That would be like an insidious plague infecting the city, working its way around inside it, sapping it of its strength and vitality. His only option would be to crush the Medicis. But he could not bring himself to do it. It would be like crushing parts of the city below him. Better to try to find a way to restore the delicate balance of things. Return to the game.

Leonardo had shown him the means to make it happen, but the one thing science could not show him was the shape of the future. That is something he would ask him to work on next, he thought. That would be a power worth having.

And he pondered, if such a device had been available to him in his youth, how different his life might have turned out. Would he have married the Duchess and suffered the sorrow of losing three baby boys who died as infants? Would he instead have found a brighter path not travelled?

He had no regrets about raising his adopted daughter Lucia, though he would dearly have like to see her married to one of his sons. There were few in the city who knew that she had been sent to be raised in the Duchess' family household as a young girl and his wife, who had always wanted a daughter, had no trouble raising the child as her own – or indeed in taking her back to her family's lands when she chose to leave the Duke that one time. He had found that he missed Lucia more than he missed his wife when they were gone, and was glad when they had come running back, their horses whipped almost to death, as if the plague were biting at their very heels.

And it was, of course. Poor Lucia was afflicted. The spice wine saved her, though some scars remained. If he had foreseen that, he would have prevented his wife taking her. Would have insisted she remain behind with him in the city. He sighed and turned from the window to examine the sketches that Leonardo had given him. This was something that would put fear into the Medicis, he believed. Would show them that his power was greater than theirs. Would surely force them to back down. If not there would be running battles in the streets. The militias were already growing out of control and the city guard had no way of restraining them.

They needed a peace treaty and needed something drastic enough to force Cosimo Medici to the negotiating table. How different the city would look then, he thought. Leonardo would be freed from the need to invent machines of commerce and conflict and would be able to exercise his great talent for artwork and would create some of the most moving and striking paintings ever seen by mankind. He would paint a picture of Lucia that would show her beautiful face and mysterious smile, which people would admire for centuries. He would paint huge frescoes of the world at peace. And he, or perhaps working with Galileo, would rediscover the lost secrets of the ancients. A new era in civilisation would emerge from the Walled City. A rebirth of knowledge and the arts, and he would open a university that learned men from all around the world would flock to.

He sat heavily in his chair and sighed again. Or was that just being fanciful? He turned and looked out the window. The day was getting on. He must return to his duties as Duke of Lorraine. He had a war to win. A war between his House and the House of Medici. A war between his desires and his wife's. It was time to step off the bright path and tread that darker path once more.

XIV

Leonardo sat by the window to catch the best light as he turned the peculiar arrow over and over in his hands. It was made of a type of metal that he was unfamiliar with. It was dark and light, but incredibly strong. The point had a vicious barb in it that had required a lot of work to remove from the cook's assistant's skull. That it had gone in so deeply suggested it had been fired with great force. That was something that he had been contemplating an experiment to test. What type of force would be needed to have the arrow puncture a pig or sheep's skull to the same depth?

The length of the arrow, however – barely over a full handspan long – meant it could only have been fired from a small device, which would limit the force that could be applied. He had studied crossbows often enough to know the size and force needed to puncture armour, and knew that such a small arrow from a similarly small device could not have had the force that this one was fired with.

He also knew that this was unlikely to be something of Galileo's doing. His rival was skilled with metal

work, but primarily in the manufacture of cogs and
so on. He had seen no evidence of him experimenting
with new metals. And that begged the question: who
had created this?

He turned it over again and looked for any signs
that it had been damaged upon impact. But there were
none of the signs he would have expected to see. A
flattened tip. A bend somewhere. This looked like it
had never been fired. He lay it down on the bench top
before him and considered the possibilities. The one
he most disliked was the thought of another scientist
in the city. It was work enough for him and Galileo
to prevent the warring between the two Houses from
getting out of hand while still providing their masters
with the wonderful inventions they perpetually craved.

He placed his fingertip against the tip of the arrow
and felt that if he pressed just a little harder a prick of
blood would certainly appear. He would have done it
just to confirm the amount of force needed and then
written it down with his other notes. Every observation
was a step towards greater understanding. But he also
knew that there was a possibility that the arrow tip
was poisoned. He left it lying on the bench top and
stood up. He had preparations to make. They were
going to be putting on a demonstration that would
impress Galileo and would make the Medicis tremble.
He would have to ponder this mysterious arrow later,
and if not, he might have it sent to Galileo and let him
consider its mystery, and taunt him into believing it
something he had developed.

XV

Lucia kept replaying the attack in her own mind and could still not decide if she should tell her father about it or not, though she was unsure exactly why. But having not reported it straight away, it became harder to tell anyone. And the story seemed more bizarre and improbable the more she pondered it. A deathseeker being attacked by another deathseeker who jumped out her window and disappeared? If her rescuer had been working for her father he would have reported straight back to him, and the Duke would have come to her to ensure that she was alright.

The only person in her mind who could have sent somebody to save her and not let her father know was Lorenzo. He had to be involved in it somehow, and if he was, then her father could never know of it. He would be as enraged that a stranger entered their household as he was that one of their servants was a deathseeker. There was also something in the way the stranger put that knife to his lips and bid her be quiet. There was something of a warning in it, she felt. Some indication not only that she needed to keep his existence a secret, but that he was watching over her.

She paced her chamber trying to recall as many details about him as was possible. The man was tall, though not overly so, and clearly very strong. The dark cloak and hood hid most of his features, but he was clean-shaven and was neither overly light nor dark in features. She had not seen his eyes well, yet felt they were dark and dangerous. Or was she imagining that? She closed her eyes tightly and pressed her knuckles into them. She had to remember things as best she could before her imagination took over and filled in the missing parts.

The knife he held to the deathseeker's neck, and then to his own lips, was curved, like an Arabic blade, but was a bright shining silver, with large holes fashioned into the blade, like nothing she had ever seen before. And she had not even seen him at first, as if he had stepped out of the shadows. And how had the deathseeker not seen him? He must have come in the window, the same way he left, but where did he disappear to? Was there a rope that she could not remember? If he had gone up to the roof the guards up there would have seen him. It made less and less sense the more she chased the details around in her head, until she knew she was creating things that had not been there, like the details of his features and where he had stood in her room when the deathseeker entered.

Perhaps she would tell her father that she had dreamed of being attacked by someone in their household. That, at least, would put him on his guard against treachery from within. They had already doubled the guards around the house and she was forbidden from walking the streets, even to go to mass, no matter the number of guards she might have taken along. Her father warned her it was too dangerous, and told her that she was far too precious to him and his enemies knew it. But he now needed to know it was also dangerous for her within the household.

But then he might insist on putting a guard inside her room. She'd insist he be outside the door of course. The window needed to be kept free in case Lorenzo found a way to contact her. If he did it would be through the window. That was her eye to the city and the only way that he could reach her. She would sit by the window at times during the day or evening and hope that he was on a Medici tower somewhere looking towards her, and would know that she was there waiting for him.

That's what it all came down to: her desire to see Lorenzo again. She needed to feel that thing that had happened to them again. But she also wondered if that might not somehow have changed in her imagining as well. There was only one way to be certain and perhaps now it was her turn to go to him. She walked across to her bed and pulled out the metal gloves she had hidden there. She would learn to use them and would climb down from her tower and find Lorenzo.

They were heavy, but not overly so. She turned them over in her hands, wondering how they worked. She rolled up her sleeves and took one metal glove and looked at it. It had many tiny cogs and wires fitted to it, and she slid her hand into it slowly. It was far too big for her, but she nearly dropped it in surprise when the tingling filled her arm, and she felt it contracting upon her arm. She watched in amazement as it melded with her flesh until she stood there with a metal set of claws on the end of her arm that she could flex and move. She felt the strength of it and immediately grabbed up the other one. These were not just claws, she now understood. They were the product of science and they were really keys. The keys to her freedom.

XVI

The Duke of Lorraine strode up the high stone staircase like a younger man, buoyed by the confidence of victory. He had spent a life in the Walled City climbing up and down tower stairs, and it seemed to get harder every year. But power was demonstrated in towers, and when he could no longer climb to the top of the many family towers, his authority would be diminished just a little. Many times his knees creaked and cracked as he climbed the steps, but he was unwilling to show any sign of it to the men around him. Leonardo had once shown him the design for a cage that could be constructed inside a tower, with counterweights on pullies, to allow a man to travel up the top and back down with ease. He would talk to him more about it one day. But not today.

He emerged onto the rooftop of the tower, puffing only slightly, to a beautiful sunny day. That was good. Too much wind or rain would have not been ideal. The tower top was ringed with men in armour, to protect him and the Duchess, who was already there waiting for him. She nodded to him and smiled. She wouldn't have missed this for the world. He hoped the armed men would not be needed though. His steward was waiting for him and beckoned him over to the tower's edge. He held up a hand a moment. He would get his breath back fully first. Would compose himself. The Medicis could wait. He took several deep breaths in and out, so that he had firm control over his voice and breathing, then gave his wife a smile and nodded to his steward.

The man tapped a pair of soldiers on the shoulder and they moved away, allowing a space for the two of them to step forward. The Duke looked across to the nearby tower where a troop of Medici soldiers were similarly assembled. Cosimo Medici was standing in the centre of them, hands on hips, wearing a fine velvet cap instead of a helmet or such, as if unafraid of an arrow or spear that might be cast at him, although the Duke suspected he was heavily armoured under his robes, just in case. He was a brave man, but tempered that with precautions. You didn't head a family like the Medicis as long as he had if you were not.

The Duke glanced down into the streets below. They were full of soldiers. Lines of moustached Lorraines facing lines of bearded Medici men. This needed to be played carefully, he thought, or they would see much blood shed today. He looked back across to Cosimo Medici and watched him raise a brass ship's trumpet to his lips and call out, "What has the murderer to say for himself that would possibly interest me?"

Of course he was interested to hear what the Duke had to say, or he would not be there. He had expected the exchange to begin with such taunts and chose not respond to them. Not today. His steward passed him a similar ship's trumpet and he lifted the cold metal and called back. "It was not us who perpetrated this foul deed upon your house."

There was silence for a moment and then Cosimo shouted back. "No. The Lorraines have never engaged in murder, have they."

The Duke felt his blood rising a little but held it in check. It was a part of the game, he knew. The first man to lose his composure would lose the game. Everything was a game inside the Walled City. But today the stakes were not just power, they were life and death. But nobody was going to die today, the Duke avowed. He could win this with no deaths.

"Upon my family's honour it was not us who perpetrated this foul deed upon your house," he called back.

"And what honour would that be?" Cosimo called in return. The Duke felt the men around him shuffle a little. They would not tolerate this for long, he knew. Not such insults to their honour. Cosimo knew it too.

The Duke was about to call back that he swore it upon his ancestors, but that would be handing Cosimo the opportunity to insult his fathers, and that might be the point at which one of his soldiers on the tower or on the streets below might lose control and call back insults, which would quickly degenerate and the men below would soon be at each other's throats with spears and swords. Didn't that oaf, Cosimo, know he was playing with fire? But of course he knew. He had something up his sleeve if he was willing to provoke a confrontation. He had carefully assessed the situation and felt he had the advantage. Never enter into a battle that you have not already won, was one of the Medici doctrines after all.

He turned back to his wife and smiled again. She smiled also. The Duke then raised the ship's trumpet slowly and called out, "I have not come here today to trade insults, but to seek a peace treaty. One long enough to provide evidence of our family's innocence in this foul murder."

"Such a treaty would need to be a century long if that is your intent," Cosimo called back.

"I would accept your suggestion," the Duke countered. The men around him jostled a little in merriment. They were glad to see their lord gaining the upper hand. But he could almost feel Cosimo's glare across the distance between them. He lifted the trumpet and shouted back. "It is unacceptable."

"Two months then," the Duke replied. He saw Cosimo look to his advisor. The two men talked a moment. Not about the possibility of a two month peace treaty, of course, but of how to next respond in a manner that allowed them to appear in control. But the Duke had played his hand carefully. A short peace treaty was a reasonable request that would be hard to refuse without appearing intent on war and unwilling to at least consider the possibility that others were the guilty parties. Cosimo called back the answer he had expected. "No. One month."

The Duke smiled. But then Cosimo called back, "And you will remove all your troops from the streets during that period."

The Duke had not expected that. "As will you?" he called back.

"And leave my family unprotected from an attack?" he replied. The Duke gritted his teeth. This Medici was quick and cunning.

"I will half the number of my troops," the Duke replied. He could see Cosimo smiling broadly. The man felt he had a victory in his hands. "But be warned," the Duke called to him, "We do not rely solely on troops for our own safety."

"What else?" Cosimo taunted. "Whales? I will tell my men to beware of them on the streets." His men gave a hearty laugh that carried easily across the distance to him. But the Duke paid no more attention to it than he would a slight breeze. The time for talking was over. He held a hand aloft and momentarily a large shadow eclipsed the sun. The men on both towers looked up in amazement as a gigantic eagle rose up behind them and circled around in the sky above them. The murmur of fear carried as easily as the mocking laughter and the Duke waved his hand at the Medici tower. The huge bird swooped rapidly, descending on the tower and breaking in the air with a mighty whump of its wings, pausing long enough to grab one of the soldiers in a clawed foot and ascend back into the sky. The soldiers on the tower top were left cowering around Cosimo, who had also dropped to the floor, losing his fine velvet hat. The eagle rose up and up into the sky and then spiralled down to the Lorraine tower, depositing the Medici soldier there.

That bit was done a little awkwardly, though, and the bird almost dropped the man to the streets below, which would have been catastrophic. He landed on the edge of the battlements, and the Lorraine men grabbed him and saved him from falling, dragging him back to safety. The bird circled the tower once more and dived away, disappearing somewhere in the city streets.

The Duke watched the men on the Medici tower slowly climb to their feet and hopelessly try and restore some sort of order. They were far too shaken, though. The Duke lifted his ship's trumpet to his lips and called out over the mutterings of men below and from the tower opposite, "A one month peace treaty then. And we shall return your man unharmed." Well, relatively unharmed, he thought. The poor man looked like he'd take some time to recover.

Then he turned, held out his hand for his dear wife. She was looking very pleased with the way things had gone. They descended the stairs, together, as if dancing arm in arm, as they had once delighted in.

XVII

Cosimo Medici had enough of dealing with the bumbling fools who purported to be deathseekers. He needed to find the one man that even the deathseekers feared. If they had only been half as good as they had claimed to be when they came into his employ, the Lorraine household would be mourning their dead. But instead all he had for the gold coins he had wasted on them was two missing deathseekers and a pie delivered to his household with a turd baked inside it.

It was another Lorraine taunt, of course, and one that he would not tolerate. It was bad enough that he had been humbled in front of both his and the Lorraine fighting men by that monstrous Lorraine eagle, and that his insolent servant Galileo would not meet his wishes, but this was too much.

He wondered if the turd came from the Duke himself. There were stories that the ancients could weave a spell to control a man if they had a part of the man's body to use. It usually referred to nail clippings or his hair, but he wondered if that didn't include a man's turds as well.

He pushed the thought from his mind, as it was only making him angry. That was its purpose of course, to fill him with rage and cloud his judgement. But he wouldn't give the Lorraines that control over him. They were undoubtedly right now planning to dispatch a deathseeker to attack him. They would surely have spies in his household as much as he had them in theirs. *Had* had them, he corrected himself.

He knew enough about deathseekers' methods to be able to avoid much of the possible danger they posed to him. He knew when they attacked, and their main methods. He knew about the poisons they could employ, that could be placed in a man's food, or even upon his clothes. He knew they could conceal blades about their body that seemed small enough to be harmless, but could kill a man by being plunged into his eye, or into the base of his brain. And, he suspected, the reason the Lorraines employed such crude assassins to attack him and Giuliano in the cathedral was to throw suspicion away from them.

He did not want to spend every hour of every day having to fear every servant and soldier who came near to him, staring into their eyes to see if they might be seeking his death. Having his meals tasted before they reached his lips. Having to sleep alone with a ring of men around him, each watching the other suspiciously. He had to gain the upper hand over the Medicis and quickly. And that meant finding the one man whose name the deathseekers muttered in awe. The assassin known as the Nameless One.

He sat in the alcove in the family chapel patiently. The Nameless One was not a man you could summon at will to your chambers. He protected his identity fiercely and it was rumoured he would even slay those who contracted him if he thought they even suspected who he might be. It was said that he was so skilled that he could slay a man and even the apothecaries would not be able to determine how he had died. Unless there were a need for everyone to see how he had been slain. There were stories that he was a noble man of one of the minor houses in the city. And there were also stories that he was a soldier who had been greatly disfigured by the plague. There were also stories that he was more spirit than man.

But it was a man's voice that whispered suddenly from the other side of the partition. "You wish my services, my lord?" Cosimo tried not to act surprised. The man had arrived as silently as smoke enters a chimney.

"You know well I do," he said. "As I suspect you know exactly what I want of you."

"The removal of the thorn from your side?"

The man would only speak in metaphor, he knew, never agreeing to actually kill a man that had been named. "Yes," said Cosimo. "The great thorn must be removed. As soon as possible, before it festers and causes infection."

The Nameless One was silent for a moment and then said, "Would not my lord prefer to have the thorn remove itself voluntarily?"

"What do you mean?" Cosimo asked.

"To have the thorn removed would simply invite another lesser thorn to take its place. And one more after that. And another and another and another. If you were able to have the thorn submit to your will, though, and remove itself, there would be no danger of lesser thorns each trying to dig deeply into your side, spring after spring, when thorns grow."

Cosimo pondered this. He was right; killing the Duke would be very satisfying, but it would lead to a blood feud that would not stop until the bloodletting had worked its way through the entirety of the Lorraine and Medici Houses. The war would be long and the spice trade would suffer worse than it did now, and then they would have no way of holding the plague back from the city. He would rather cut the Duke's throat and have him hung from one of the towers, but to have the Duke bow down to him publicly, that would be as sweet. He had been too obsessed on taking revenge for his brother to consider this. Vengeance would have been good for the family's honour, but bad for business. He needed to not just dominate the city through force, but have those who challenged him bow down to him. "How would such be done?" asked Cosimo.

"If you hold what is valuable to the thorn you will have control of the thorn."

"And what is most valuable to the thorn?" asked Cosimo.

"The most precious thing to the oak tree is the acorn," said the Nameless One. "The most precious thing to the rose bush is the flower."

Cosimo considered this for some moments. Yes, he could have the Duke humiliate himself time and time again. He could gain control of those mysterious birds and whales of the Lorraines. The spice trade would flow unimpeded, and he could be the only one with ships on the seas. As long as he held the Duke's daughter captive.

"Yes," he said. "It shall be done as you say." He smiled to himself at the audacity of it, and then asked, "What assistance can I provide you in this?" But the Nameless One was gone. As silently as he had come. Cosimo the Great rose to his feet and stepped out of the small alcove. The chapel was empty except for the sound of his guards mumbling to each other outside the door. Cosimo stood there a moment and then raised a fist into the air as if he had just won a game of chance. It was pleasing to receive good counsel for once.

XVIII

The plague people had started gathering at the city's gate before the first hesitant light of dawn, so it looked to the guards on the walls as if they had been standing there all night long. They were waiting for the city guard to lead the six-ox cart down the winding streets to the gate in the early morning light. The guards up on the gate assembled in tight formation to let the crowd outside know they were being watched. If the plague people grew too restive or rebellious the gates would not be opened.

There was a large crowd there today, several hundred people. They had been slowly increasing in size over the past week, but the City Council were too preoccupied with the conflict within the walls of the city to concentrate overly on the conflict without. Each day the Captain of the Guard would report that the number of plague victims was increasing, and that they were become more and more difficult to control, but the City Council would dismiss him with a curt admonition that if he were unable to maintain discipline over sickly beggars then they would find somebody else who could.

What was the man to do? He increased the number of men on the wall and the number of armed men that escorted the ox cart outside the gates each morning, and hoped that the lottery would be enough to keep them all in check. A chance of entering the Walled City, no matter how remote, held enormous sway over desperate men and women.

The Sergeant of the Guard, an honest man of many years' experience named Cristoforo, stood atop the gates, and called down to the assembled throng to make way for the morning's draw. The plague people down below stepped back into something resembling orderly lines. When he was satisfied, the Sergeant of the Guard made them wait just a little longer and then ordered the guardsmen to form up outside. Levers were spun and cogs turned and a door within one of the main gates turned open, then a troop of a dozen armed guardsmen stepped out and formed a semicircle around the gates, holding shields and spears in front of them to warn the plague people back. These guardsmen were doing this duty as punishment for something, whoring or being drunk on duty, and they came into the closest contact with the sick. It was that or be thrown out of the city, and so they reluctantly accepted the task.

When Sergeant Cristoforo was satisfied, he ordered the gates open and one huge gate creaked slowly inwards until there was space for the ox cart to emerge. The huge beasts waddled out slowly and the sergeant wondered, as he did each day, what they would do when they had to eat the beasts. But as more plague victims arrived bringing tribute, of course the less need there was to do so.

Sergeant Cristoforo then called down to the sick and dying to bring forth their tribute. The crowd pushed forward then, calling out and holding up their offerings. Some had a chicken or two. Some had a pig and several had sacks of grain. The Sergeant had long observed that a family might arrive at the gates with several livestock and bags of grain, but they would be robbed of them before the next morning and others would stand there holding them up to the guardsmen. It didn't matter to him. His job was simply to take the largest offerings and give the person supplying them a pass into the city.

He noticed today a fat rogue with half his face eaten away with pustules, holding two pigs, three chickens and four sacks of grain. Yesterday the man had stood there with one pig only, and the day before that he had simply had a chicken. He wondered if he had slain the owners of the livestock and food or had traded them for their lives.

There was a decree that the gates would not be opened if the bodies of the dead were left around the walls of the city, so the sick and dying had to drag the corpses of their family, friends, or just strangers, to a ditch beyond a small rise and bury them there. Or at least make some pretence of burying them. The Sergeant pointed down to the fat rogue and the man beamed joyously, stepping forward while the guardsmen loaded his produce onto one of the carts.

He looked down for newcomers to the gates, bearing produce. They were easily discernible by the way they stared incredulously at the smooth unblemished skin of the guardsmen. It confirmed everything they had heard. There was a city that had withstood the plague where they had potions to cure it. Where, if you were rich enough or lucky enough, you could be admitted.

Sometimes a family might arrive, carrying a cart of their combined produce, which they would offer up just so that one of them, usually a sickly young boy or girl could be admitted to the city. At such times Sergeant Cristoforo tried not to imagine what he would do if he were outside the walls with his own wife and three children. He was, after all, a citizen of the Walled City and that was that. The plague victims were people from other lands. They had no given rights to entry to the Walled City, as the citizens of the city had no obligation to allow those not from the city to enter it.

But when his youngest daughter had been taken ill with a temperature two moons past he had woken from a nightmare in which the Council decreed that all sick children had to be put out of the city. He was trying to save her as his own guardsmen dragged her away. Most dreams faded away from him in the moments after waking, but the terror he had felt from this one still stayed with him now. He had told his wife and she had wept as if it was not a dream but a premonition, so he had kept his thoughts to himself after that.

He scanned the crowd and found the ten largest offerings he could see and had them loaded onto the carts. "We will take more offerings tomorrow," he called to the crowd below, and before they could be become restive or ill-tempered about missing out he called, "Assemble for the lottery." This always prompted more jostling amongst the plague people, but his men were ready for it and assembled tightly around the carts while they withdrew into the city and the large gate was closed behind them.

"In two lines," Sergeant Cristoforo called down to the plague people. "Two lines or there will be no lottery."

They complied with the obedience of the desperate, standing there with a small scrap of cloth or parchment in their hands. A guardsman, facing a particularly severe punishment, walked down each line with a bowl and let the scraps be thrown in, never touching them. When that was done, they carried them in through the small door and up onto the wall above the gates. The Sergeant himself was the one who made the draw each day. He held the power over them and it gave them more reason to obey his commands.

But it was a hollow sort of power, he felt. Obedience from a mass of stinking plague victims. It amazed him, sometimes, to discover there were citizens within the Walled City who had never seen a plague victim. Had never ventured up onto the walls to stare down at the putrid mass of humanity that gathered there, like half-creatures that had once been human, now disfigured and tormented by pain and pustules. It would certainly be easier to sleep soundly at nights never having seen it, he supposed. To never have seen what might become of the Walled City if they were not able to ensure the supply of spice wine that warded it off.

He knew they had not had a ship arrive since this war between the two great families had begun, but the City Council claimed there was sufficient store in the city, as they claimed there was sufficient grain in the warehouses. But he also knew that if their stores of food were as sufficient as the City Council claimed they would not need to be taking offerings from the scabbed hands of plague people each morning.

He had heard the types of stories that people told about the plague. That it spread from your fingers and everything you touched became infected with it. If you rubbed your nose it would fall right off your face. If you scratched your arse giant pustules the size of a pig's bladder would appear there. Or if you had a piss and touched your fountain of relief, it turned black and fell off and the roads to the city were lined with shrivelled black members.

The two guardsmen climbed up to him and presented the bowls. He pulled on a thick metal gauntlet and reached into the first bowl and pulled out a scrap of linen. Those who had no paper tore off bits of their clothing and wrote their names on it. Those who could not write paid others to write their names for them, even though more often than not the rogue with the pen would put his own name on the scrap. Sergeant Cristoforo looked carefully at the smudged name and had to steel himself to call it out. It was his daughter's name. Just a coincidence he told himself, nothing more, though he feared it would prompt another nightmare as a result of it. An elderly woman wailed and sank to her knees in thanks, kissing the ground and calling upon the old gods and new for delivering her to salvation. A guardsman prodded her to her feet and she stumbled in through the door. The Sergeant turned his head so as not to meet her eyes.

Now for the second name. The lines dissolved now, as ever, as desperation overtook order. The guardsmen held a tight formation. "Order, or there will be no second name called," Sergeant Cristoforo called down from above and the crowd made something of an attempt at order. Some were on their knees praying, others were pushing forward to be closer to the gate as if it might somehow increase their chance of having their name called.

The Sergeant reached into the second bowl and pulled out a small piece of parchment. It was clean and white and the name written upon it had been done with a careful and well practiced hand. Obviously a nobleman. Well, once a nobleman, now a plague victim wrapped in rags. He called out the name, and, as sometimes happened, more than one person raised a hand, claiming it was them.

He sighed. This was always unfortunate. He had at one time toyed with the idea of making all the claimants write their name again on a piece of paper and the one that most closely matched would be let into the city, and the others would be slain in front of the others, but this was made difficult by the fact that the scrawl of most peasants looked rather similar and many of the names were written by the scribes amongst them. And of course several people invariably had the same names.

It didn't matter. The Captain of the Guard had decreed that in the case of multiple claimants the gates were simply to be closed and all would miss out. The guardsmen below knew what to do; they retreated through the narrow doorway and the cogs spun quickly so it closed tightly behind them, leaving the mob screaming and banging on the gates. Sergeant Cristoforo watched them for some moments, letting the anger die down and then he threw them all a thin crust of hope.

"There will be another lottery tomorrow morning," he called, dropping the bowls to his feet so the contents could be burned. Then he descended back down the stairs to lead the oxen and the few fortunate chosen back up the streets into the city.

XIX

Lorenzo readied himself for another leap. He had studied the rooftops of the Walled City and had the route carefully mapped out, to reach the Lorraines' house as the first dim light of day arrived. The first few jumps were the hardest, but he was getting the hang of it. Using a short magnifier he had taken from the workshop he was truncating the distance between buildings and leaping across. Only once had he picked a distance too far and had almost fallen.

It required careful work, and jumping with a magnifier against one eye and the other eye closed truly was a leap of faith. There would be a total of twelve jumps, with each one taking him closer into Lorraine-held territory, but he had charted a course that avoided the buildings that would be occupied by Lorraine soldiers, and the sight lines of the main Lorraine towers.

It was a pity that Lucia could not see him coming towards her in the fading light of day, leaping across the rooftops like one of the ancients, but he had to approach the Lorraine household from the rear if he were to reach it. He was certain she could feel him getting closer though, just as he could feel her through the flutter in his chest the nearer he got. He had already made nine jumps and could feel the apprehension in his chest building as he approached. It was like this when he had climbed the tower to Lucia's chamber. The closer he got, the more dangerous it was, but also the more thrilling it was, as he knew he was getting nearer to her with each step and hand-reach. He had entered her chamber with his arms feeling like lead. He supposed it was the effort of the climb, but he was feeling something similar now in his limbs again. Particularly, his right hand, which had a single metal gauntlet on it. Unlike the gloves that he had used to climb to Lucia's tower, this one was made of copper bands, set with and springs and cogs.

He turned his attention back to the roof top he was standing on. It was red-tiled like most in the Walled City, but the roof across the street ahead of him was flat-topped, with a small wall around it. He scanned it carefully to make sure there was no door to the roof that soldiers could come pouring out of to attack him. That would be a major setback to his careful plans. He could not see all of the roof because of a set of chimneys, but it looked clear. Then he peered down into the street below. There was nobody there to see him. The streets of the Walled City were more often empty than not these days. It was dangerous to be about if you did not have an armed guard.

Lorenzo gauged the amount of steps he needed for a run-off and then placed the magnifier to his eye with his left hand. The distance closed up and he could see the rooftop just a long leap away from him. He moved the magnifier away from his eye and watched the distance restore, and then took four fast steps and thrust the magnifier back to his eye on the last step. The roof top was right in front of him and he felt himself launching through the air and then landing heavily. He almost dropped the magnifier as he stumbled and fell with a thump, knocking the wind from himself. He clutched the precious device to his chest to protect it. If he were to break it he would not be able to continue, and Galileo would be furious with him. The only thing worse would be if it were to fall into the hands of the Lorraines.

He rolled to one side to get back to his feet and saw four guards staring at him with surprised looks on their faces. They all wore thin moustaches, and had been sitting there boredly behind the chimneys. Probably getting some warmth from them to make the long lonely guard vigil a little more bearable. Lorenzo and the guards all tried to get to their feet at the same time. Lorenzo knew he would have to jump back or onward again quickly. He was so close. Only a few more jumps. But his limbs were too slow to respond. They were stiff and awkward. He should have had time to escape while they fumbled for their pikes, but he could only wriggle away from them, trying to get to his feet again. The closest guardsman stepped across to him and prodded him with the butt of his pike. Lorenzo got to one knee and punched at him with the metal glove and its force sent the man flying across the roof. The other guardsmen immediately became more cautious. Keeping back and pointing their pikes at him. He needed more time. But he had that as well. He reached into a pouch around his neck and pulled out the chronometer, winding it as the guardsmen circled him with their pikes at the ready.

"Who are you?" one of them demanded.

"He's a Medici spy," another said.

"Or an assassin," said a third.

"Kill him," said the first. "There'll be a reward in it for us whoever he is."

Lorenzo held the chronometer out before him on the flat of his gloved hand, waiting for time to slow around him, waiting to see the guardsmen move like they were half-asleep, giving him time to jump away. But nothing changed. The first one said, "Eh… What's that?" cautiously, as if unsure if Lorenzo were offering them something valuable or was threatening them with it.

"Kill him and then find out," said the second.

Lorenzo looked down at the chronometer and saw that it was not ticking. Something was wrong with it. He must have knocked something out of alignment when he fell. "No," he said. "Wait!" But the men didn't look interested in waiting. They moved their pikes closer to his chest and he scrambled back until he touched the small wall around the rooftop. So, he thought, he could stand up and be tipped off the roof top to the streets below, or he could stay there and be run through. Trying desperately to think of something to say that would save him, all he could think of was Lucia – holding out a hand to him.

"Lucia!" he said.

"Lucia Lorraine?" one of the guards asked, and lowered his pike a little.

"Yes," he said. "Lucia Lorraine. I have an important message for her."

"Who are you?" one of the other guards asked, not lowering his pike at all.

"It's important," said Lorenzo. He could see at least one of the guards was wavering, not sure if they should kill him or not. If he could just say the right thing to him, he might be saved. But before he could say anything else a dark figure landed on the rooftop behind the soldiers. He had jumped across the wider gap to the south and he landed in a rolling motion, coming up next to the closest soldier. The man barely had time to register his presence before the figure struck him heavily in the throat and he fell with a gurgling sound. Lorenzo saw the dark figure was wearing a cape and hood as he rolled under the pike of the second guard and came up heavily under his chin, knocking his head back as he struck him. The guard fell like a puppet whose strings had been cut.

Lorenzo watched the two remaining guards looking around them as if they were being attacked from all sides. The figure moved so fast they might as well have been. In close their pikes were too clumsy to be of much use and the third guard fell while trying to bring it down on the dark figure's head. The fourth guard had the presence of mind to drop his pike and pull a small sword that he had at his belt. The caped figure stood before him, not moving and the guard advanced on him, waving his sword menacingly. "Prepare to die," the guard hissed.

"Neither of us dies this evening," the figure said and then suddenly stepped to one side as the guard slashed at him, missing, and then the caped figure reached out one hand as fast as a snake, appeared just to touch the guard on the neck and he fell to the ground. "Although," he said to his opponent, "you might look a lot less ugly and more peaceful if you were dead."

Lorenzo looked at the tilt of the fallen man's head and the way his eyeballs were rolled back in his sockets. "I think he is dead," he said.

The caped man bent down and put his fingers against the fallen man's neck. "Sorry," he said to the dead guard. "That wasn't meant to happen." He stood back up and gave Lorenzo a shrug. Lorenzo stared back at the strange figure and then at the four guards and asked, "Who are you?"

"It's always, 'Who are you?'" said the dark figure. "Never, 'How did you do that?'"

"How *did* you do that?" asked Lorenzo.

"Too late," said the dark figure. "You only get one question. I'm a friend."

"But… but… are you in the employ of the Medicis?"

"Only one question," said the figure. Then he held out his arms and said, "Ah, you don't remember me, do you."

Lorenzo shook his head. He was certain he had never met this man before.

"Well, you were very young at the time. Just a child really."

Lorenzo blinked. "I don't understand," he said.

"But I will tell you that I am not employed by the Medicis," the man said. "As I said, I am a friend. A friend of horny young men who ought to know better than to be chasing a bit of skirt across the rooftops of the city with a broken chronometer."

Lorenzo reddened a little. "You insult my lady's honour." Then he looked at the chronometer in his hand. "You know what this is?"

The figure laughed. "I know many things. Some I suspect you don't know, such as the cost of using this. Or the fact that it won't work while in your gloved hand."

"But how?"

"No more questions," the dark figure said. "I'm sorry but you will not be visiting your fair lady this evening."

Lorenzo glared at the man and said, "And who will stop me?"

"Commonsense will stop you," he replied. "You will see her again soon, but not tonight."

"How do you know this?" Lorenzo asked.

"It is written," said the man enigmatically. "Now you must be very silent and very obedient."

Lorenzo considered this. He looked at his gloved hand a moment and then nodded. Almost reluctantly.

"Good man. First take off these men's trousers and undergarments."

"What?" asked Lorenzo.

"Then throw them to the street below."

"But why?" he asked.

"Think about it. They won't know quite what to report."

Lorenzo did as he was bidden while the dark figure watched on silently. Then he said, "Now follow me."

"Where to?" asked Lorenzo.

"You've used up all your extra questions," the man said, and then in a tone that brooked no disagreement, "Come. You must leave. And put away those devices before you hurt yourself."

But Lorenzo could not help himself from asking just one more time, even though he knew he would not get an answer, "Who are you?"

XX

Leonardo raised his arms in surprise as the giant eagle swooped down towards him on the large balcony. He lowered his arms and held up a finger to chide the large bird as it came to a halt in front of him, fanning its large wings open with a whump, and then settled onto the balcony's edge.

"Inside. Quickly," said Leonardo, and the bird walked awkwardly towards the window, and then turned around, spreading its wings wide again. But it was not to fly this time. Leonardo reached up and started unfastening straps as the bird transformed back into a man strapped into a flying machine of leather, canvas and wood.

Leonardo poised for a moment, staring at the handsome young man now standing before him with arms outstretched like he was on a crucifix. Damon smiled down at Leonardo and waited for him to free him from the flying machine. He fiddled with the harness straps and fastenings, checking the hinges on the wings as he separated the man from the machine. Finally he had him out and the young man stepped free stumbling forward, his bare chest still heaving a little from either the exertion or the exhilaration of flying. He was not like this when he emerged from the submergible. Becoming a whale was certainly less exciting than becoming a bird.

He watched the young man trying to regain control of his limbs and finding them much stiffer than they had been the previous time. "Come," he said again. "We must get this inside." Together they carried the harness and wings inside the large chamber and lay them upon a large bench top there that had been built for them.

"How did it fly today?" Leonardo asked the younger man.

"I truly was a bird," Damon said. "It was glorious." He was still panting a little for breath and Leonardo watched his tanned chest rising and falling. Then he stepped in close and held out the young man's arms, feeling the strength in his muscles. Looking carefully at the colour of the skin and noting where it had lost its lustre.

"When can I fly again?" Damon asked him. "You should paint me in flight. It would be a masterpiece. How could any painting of me not be?" That such beauty and such vanity co-existed was a pity, Leonardo thought. If he was to paint the young man flying it would be more likely a picture of Icarus falling to Earth having flown too close to the sun.

"That is up to the Duke to decide," said Leonardo. "These are dangerous times and we must be careful how we tread."

"I won't need to tread," said Damon. "I shall soar."

Leonardo ignored him. He was like a small child sometimes, wanting distractions and to be fussed over. And truth be told, the older man did enjoy fussing over him. Sometimes. He ran one hand along Damon's skin and felt how hard it was. Felt the small bumps that had grown along his shoulders. Then he saw the welt near the base of his neck. He asked the youth to sit and he examined the skin carefully. It was most likely only a bruise, he decided, not a pustule forming. Probably from the flying machine. It was a surprise that Damon's arms and chest did not have more bruises from the harness. But the toll of using the transformational science was showing on him. His skin was hardening and losing colour. The joints calcifying. Like his own. "So what does the city look like from above?" Leonardo asked him quickly to distract him from his examination. He also had a great curiosity for how the world would look from such a perspective. It made him feel so limited in how he could view and paint the world about him. Understanding perspective was fine for giving depth to the buildings when you viewed them from street level, or from a balcony – but to see the world the way a bird saw it? That would be wondrous.

"It's hard to describe," said Damon, moving his arms like he was flying again. "At first it is just a jumble of orange tiled roofs. But then you start to see the streets and the towers and the church domes."

"Is it like looking down at a map?" Leonardo asked him. "Or a model of the city?"

"Yes and no," the young man said. "It is so much more, because as I move, the city changes and I can see the different aspects. Alleyways emerge as I fly over them and then disappear again, and it sometimes feels like I am still, in the air, and the city is moving beneath me."

Leonardo closed his eyes to try to imagine it. Then he asked, "And what of the countryside?"

"Ah," said Damon. "It is so different from high up." They had done much of their initial practice on ships out at sea, and flying over the countryside was as different as a four course meal was to bread and water. "It looks so beautiful," he said. "You would never imagine that it is a place of pestilence and death out there."

Leonardo nodded his head. It had been a long time since anyone had voluntarily left the Walled City to travel through the countryside. Since the plague had come, all commerce was by sea and only those expelled from the city ever left its gates. It might have looked ideal from the sky, but down closer it would have revealed farms lying fallow and untilled, fruit trees grown wild, villages empty and overgrown. The land was returning to an untamed state in the absence of healthy working men and women. There were, he knew, hundreds of the plague victims who gathered at the city gates in the hope of being amongst the lucky few admitted to the city. But if they knew why those few were granted access they might not be so keen to tramp across the countryside and stand outside the city gates pleading for mercy. Dozens died out there, and the city guards demanded that the dying bury the dead if they wished to be able to wait outside the gates for the chance to enter the city. It was cruel, but necessary, he knew. The city had to be protected from the plague.

And as long as the Lorraines and the Medicis controlled the spice trade, everyone in the city was beholden to them to protect themselves from the plague. Some had to sell their family riches to afford the spice potions, while others, like himself, were under the patronage of the Duke and had a regular supply provided to them in return for their services.

Leonardo then turned his attention to examining the canvas and wires of the harness to see if there was any damage to them. Damon contented himself with looking around the room. The walls of the large chamber were covered with wires and wooden frames and canvas sheets and sketches of the many machines Leonardo had designed or was building. Most were modelled on animals. The flying machine had been developed after extensively studying the anatomy of birds. The submergible machine after studying fish. He had a war machine that was based on the shape and strength of a turtle's shell, and another that he was working on that could dig underground like a mole. It was not as satisfying as painting, he felt, but it was some satisfaction nevertheless.

He then looked back to Damon and looked at the welt on his neck again. He knew the young man's skin intimately, from the many hours he had spent gazing at it from different angles. Painting and sketching him. He knew it as if he were viewing his body from the ground or the air above. He did not need to fly himself to know what it might look like beneath him.

"Come," he said to the young man. "You should rest, but first join me in some spice wine."

XXI

Lorenzo was a hawk in the body of a sparrow. No, that wasn't it. Lorenzo was like a bird trapped in a cathedral, flapping up against the stained glass windows, unable to see outside clearly and unable to find a way out. That was closer. He wanted to have the description right when he talked to Galileo about it all. He was never as clever with words as he was with objects and pictures. He could dissect any object and state exactly how it worked, and even improve it, but to give it the best metaphor for how it worked was a difficult chore. Perhaps he should describe it as being a machine with a working component missing?

It was probably futile anyway. He had betrayed Galileo once again, and had failed in his mission, and some of the Lorraine guards were dead which would certainly cause reprisals against the Medicis, and no matter what metaphor he came up with it, it would not lessen his crime any in Galileo's eyes. The old man would not be swayed by clever metaphors to better understand what had driven him. How could he describe his need to see Lucia again to anybody in a way that they could understand? It had become more than an obsession;, it was as if some part of his body had been ripped from him and he needed it back to continue breathing and thinking normally.

He had been wandering around the safer streets of the city for most of the day with heavy feet and heavy heart, trying to revisit the morning's events in a way that would have turned out better. Trying to accept his abject failure. Putting off returning to the Medici palace. Vainly trying to find a metaphor that would somehow make his stupidity seem more understandable and acceptable. If he ruled the Walled City he'd ban all metaphors. Or maybe he'd just have a list of ten or so approved ones that people who were unable or unwilling to state things plainly had to use for all occasions. And anybody coming up with a new metaphor would be made to build a working model of their metaphor to see how useless it was. The river running backwards. A moth in an iron cocoon. Tears of honey.

Yet the stranger who had saved him seemed better described by a metaphor than plain words. He acted as if he used scientific machines to aid him and yet Lorenzo had seen none. His manner of speech was that of an outsider, yet he knew details of the Walled City intimately. Had he used secret machines to help him? How did they work? And had he actually helped him or hindered him? He had a great desire to know more about him that was as great as his desire to see Lucia again. Perhaps the stranger could even help him see her? But he had disappeared after leading Lorenzo back down to the street level. And how to find a mysterious man in the city who clearly did not want to be found?

With that thought lingering in his mind he paused a little as he walked past a dark alley, expecting the stranger to suddenly step out in front of him. But there was nobody there. Lorenzo sighed. Of course there was no one there. If he ruled the heavens, though, that's how things would happen!

He thought once more of Galileo's anger when he learned that he taking the magnifier and chronometer. If they had ended up in the hands of the Lorraine household, Cosimo Medici would have been beside himself with fury and he would have been turned out of the Walled City at the very best, and more likely executed as a traitor and an idiot.

For the first time ever, he felt the Medici household was not a place of safety for him. It was a very discomforting feeling. He was now a person of the streets, like those others he saw scurrying along quickly, keen to avoid any trouble, fetching food or whatever commerce they needed to engage in, despite the turmoil between the two Houses. There were even a few merchants stores open, which served to remind him that while the two major Houses carried great sway over the lives of the citizens of the city, they did not dominate every aspect of everyone's lives. Perhaps he could become one of them. Never return and find a trade in a small dark shop in a thin dim alley somewhere where he would not be easily found. It made his chest constrict. He would be a boy between all over again, and his chances of seeing Lucia would be near impossible.

Several of the shuttered and closed business, he noticed, had an odd symbol painted on the doors or walls, like a bowl with a flame in it. Some guild mark perhaps, or a symbol of the church or something. He didn't give it much more thought as around the next street corner he came upon a small tavern that was doing business as if nothing were amiss, and while it was not overly-busy, patrons were seated inside enjoying a drink and some gossip. Lorenzo suddenly felt hungry, thirsty and in need of some distraction, so he decided to join them, and entered the dim room and found a seat on a bench. A pretty young serving girl took his order. He found that the variety of food was notably less here than it was inside the Medici household and imagined that the rest of the city had been increasingly suffering shortages while they went from the best wine and fowl to the second best. Wealth always found a way to overcome adversity.

He watched the serving girl as she walked over to the counter, admiring the sway of her hips. Purely in the interests of perfecting the art of close observation, and analysis, he told himself. The restricted diet sat well on her thin body. Then a figure slid into the seat opposite him.

"*Bongiorno*, Lorenzo," the man said. Lorenzo turned to look at him. It was the stranger. Still cloaked and hooded. It took Lorenzo a moment to collect himself. "I was looking for you," Lorenzo said.

"You only had to look more carefully," said the stranger. "I have been following you all morning."

"Why?" asked Lorenzo.

"To see where you were going. And the answer is clearly nowhere."

Lorenzo looked down at the table. "I have nowhere to go," he mumbled.

"That's good," said the stranger. "It means you might be more willing to consider my proposal to you."

"What proposal is that?" asked Lorenzo.

"I have to ask you something. Consider it a test."

Don't let it be a test of my skill at metaphors, Lorenzo thought. But the stranger then placed his hands on the table. Under one hand was the wicked curved knife with the ornate holes in the blade. In the other was a gold coin.

"Think of it as a matter of wife or death," the stranger said.

"What?" asked Lorenzo.

The stranger sighed. "It is a play on words. You were meant to laugh. To lighten the gravity of the moment," he said.

"I don't understand," said Lorenzo.

The stranger hissed, "You might not like this test. Because if you get it wrong I might have to cut your throat."

Lorenzo blinked rapidly. "I... What?" But the stranger only tapped the knife and gold coin on the table top. "What if I don't want to take the test?" asked Lorenzo.

"You no longer have a choice." Lorenzo looked closely at the stranger, trying to see his eyes under the darkness of the hood. Why was he threatening him when he had just helped him. Or had he actually prevented him reaching Lucia?

"Then I'd have better odds of surviving if I agree to the test," Lorenzo said.

"Good use of logic," the stranger said. "I like logic."

Lorenzo nodded his head. Slowly.

"Alright," said the stranger. "Then I will test you to see if you are worthy. If you pass the test I will let you live."

Another nod of Lorenzo's head.

"Are you ready?" the stranger asked.

Another nod of the head.

"What is your favourite number?" the stranger asked.

Lorenzo felt he must have misunderstood him. The stranger tapped the knife and the coin on the table top again. "Quickly now!" he said.

"Seven," said Lorenzo.

"A good number," said the stranger.

"And that's the test?" Lorenzo asked, wondering if the man might not be crazed.

"No. That was just a practice question," the man said. "This is the real test. Listen carefully and then answer quickly. I have the power to grant you one wish. But not just anything. I'm going to give you a choice of two wishes. But first you need to know that the Medici have sent assassins to kill your beloved Lucia."

Lorenzo's mouth dropped open. "No!" he said.

"Listen," the stranger hissed. "This is very important. An assassin has seized her and thrown her from her chamber window and she has fallen to the streets below."

Lorenzo understood now. It was a part of the test. "She is not dead," the stranger said. "But she is seriously injured. She is, in fact, paralysed. The first wish I grant you is that you can live with her, take her for your bride, but she will be forever unable to hold you in her embrace or even speak more than gurgling sounds to you."

Lorenzo felt his Adam's apple bobbing up and down rapidly. Or had this actually happened? "Your second wish," said the stranger, "is that the apothecaries have a treatment that they can give Lucia, but it must be given within the first half hour of her injury and it only has a fifty per cent success rate. If it does not cure her, it will kill her and the blood within her brain will leak out her ears and eyes and mouth and nose and she will die horribly."

Lorenzo felt tears coming unbidden to his eyes. "No," he wanted to say. He could not make that choice. But the stranger hissed, "Choose quickly now!"

He stammered a moment, but then said defiantly, regardless of the knife in the stranger's hand. "They are not wishes. They are curses. I reject your wishes. I will choose my own wish, that I was free to run to her house and stand beneath her window at the moment the assassin hurls her from it. I will catch her when she falls or I will be killed by the impact, but I will use my body to shield her, saving her."

The stranger sat there for some moments, then slid both hands off the table. He brought them back, empty, arms open wide, like a long lost relative greeting him. "Well done, Lorenzo," he said, "You were as cool and brave as a… as a …" He looked up the ceiling and walls around him as if searching for a word that had just been there before him and was now escaping up there out of sight. Finally he said,

"As cool and brave as something that was both cool and brave." He reached out one arm and punched Lorenzo's shoulder, and said, "God, I hate it when metaphors evade me. Now come."

"Where are we going?" asked Lorenzo. "To save Lucia?"

The stranger rose and, taking out the gold coin again, flipped it into the air. It landed in the cup of wine that the serving girl was carrying across the room to Lorenzo. "Yes. To save her indeed," he said. "But to do that we have to first save the city, and then we might as well save the future of civilisation while we're at it. Now come, and steel yourself, for to do this we must descend into the very underworld itself, like... well, like, like two men going into the underworld."

Then he reached over and took a handful of flat breads off the counter and stuffed them in his pockets. "We'll need these too," he said. "It can be hungry work saving the future."

XXII

Lucia skipped rapidly down the stairs from her tower chamber, unaware that she was being watched closely. She was late for lunch. Again. The handmaiden had already called her twice and told her the Duke and Duchess would not be pleased if she did not hurry, but she was not in a mood to be nagged by the handmaiden. She had been wearing leather breeches and practicing climbing on the inside walls of her chamber with Lorenzo's metal gloves. She was amazed at how much strength they gave her. She had flexed her fingers and felt the strong metal bend easily. Then she tested them by thrusting the sharp ends into a gap in the stonework of her wall. It held fast and she lifted herself gently off the ground. Then she clamped on the feet claws and felt them become her feet. She flexed her toes and then thrust them into cracks in the stonework, too, and then carefully climbed the wall of her room to the ceiling. She could never have imagined having the strength to do this. It felt like magic, though she knew it to be science. She would ask Lorenzo to explain to her how it worked when she next saw him.

Perched on the wall, she had a sudden feeling of what Lorenzo had felt climbing up to her. A mix of fear and anticipation. It made her a little giddy and she lowered herself to the floor. She waited until the feeling had passed and then climbed the wall again, upwards and then sideways, wondering how much practice she would need to be able to climb all the way down her tower to the street below.

Then she had taken the gloves off and hidden them in a cupboard in her room. She fussed over her gown and hair, as if Lorenzo would be there at the evening meal to see her, while the handmaiden knocked on her door again. "I am coming, I am coming," Lucia said. And now she was following the dull girl down the curve of the stairs, her feet stepping lightly over the well-trodden stones, one hand sliding around the centre pillar, as she hurried downwards, her long crimson skirts dancing around her feet.

So easy to descend these stairs, she thought, but when each step depended on finding a firm grip between the stones it would be a different matter. If it were dark tonight, she would try it, though. She would wear her leather breeches and a dark shirt that made her look like a shadow. The guards would be on the lookout for anyone approaching the house, but not for anyone leaving it. She felt a rush of excitement fill her at just the idea of what she was going to do. She would then hurry to the Medici household and if she revealed her identity to the guards there, and told them that she had a message for Cosimo Medici, they would surely let her in. Or perhaps it would be better to ask for Galileo, for whom Lorenzo worked.

That might be safer. It was going to be dangerous, but she had to try it.

A soft voice hissed behind her and she paused. She turned around, but there was nobody there. "Hello?" she said.

There was no answer. She took another step forward and then heard it again. "Lucia!" It sounded muffled. Could it be Lorenzo? He had found a way back into the house. She turned around and climbed three steps back up the tower. "Lorenzo?" she asked in a soft voice. "Is it you? I am here."

There was no answer. She took three more steps back to the last landing she had passed and pressed one hand to her heart. She was certain she would be able to feel him if he were close to her. "Hello?" she said again.

"Lucia?" the muffled voice replied. It was coming from behind the wall. How could that be?

"Where are you?" she asked.

"I am here," the muffled voice said.

"Where?" she asked. She paused and tried to feel the butterfly growing in her chest, but was too impatient to wait for it. There were hidden chambers all through the house, she knew, as there were in most of the larger houses of the Walled City. Lorenzo was clever enough to have found his way into the house through one of them. He must have been there for hours, peeping through one of the chinks onto the stairwell, waiting for her to pass alone. The brave boy. He would be cramped and cold and hungry. She would find a way to sneak him some food and drink. But she would find him first.

She placed her hands on the stone walls ahead of her, as if she might be able to feel his presence there. "Can you see me?" she asked. "I am right here." There was no reply for a moment and she moved her hands further along the wall.

"Lucia?" the voice said again, further away.

"No. I'm here," she said. "Don't go."

"Lucia?" the voice said again, even further away.

"No," she said. "I'm here." She banged her fists on the wall, wanting to find a way through to the chamber inside. Wanting to find a way to reach him. "Lorenzo!" she called. She didn't hear the hidden door open slowly behind her and the dark figure step out. The gloved hand clamped around her mouth and pulled her backwards into the space between the walls, and she heard the door close with a soft click, and then there was only darkness.

XXIII

The door above today's chosen plague people closed with the dull thud of a prison door. The fortunate twelve – who were only eleven today – had been led into the city along back alleys and then down into a dark cellar and told to sit and wait. So they sat, and looked around the dim interior of the small room nervously. They had heard so many differing stories about what would become of them. Some said that there were wondrous cures for the plague and they would be better overnight. Others said that the apothecaries cut off their diseased body parts and limbs and sewed on the limbs of recently dead people from the city. Others said they had a magic fruit that you ate that stopped the plague, but you had to eat some every day or it would return.

The fat rogue who had traded two pigs, three chickens and four sacks of grain, who was named Frederigo, was the first to notice there was another door in the room. It was set so perfectly into the stone work that you might not otherwise have noticed it, but he was a survivor who had gotten this far by noticing small details and knowing when to act on them. His mother had known it in him early in his life and told family that he had a heart of gold – though she meant the metaphor to mean it was cold, yellow and hard to find.

He licked his lips and looked at the other ten plague people, calculating. If he sat right next to the door he would be the first one led through to whatever lay on the other side. But if it was not to his liking, he would rather not be first. But if they did have a cure and did not actually have enough for everyone, he would rather not be at the last one in. So he rose, as if stretching and strode across the room to sit himself anew between the others. Four people would go in front of him and six would go after him. That seemed a reasonably safe bet.

He looked at the others around him and thought to himself that if he had to take them all on at once he could do it. It was the first thing he thought when stuck with a group of people. Could he fight them all? Could he beat them? Who should he attack first? Who would face him and who would flee? It had been like that all the way from Naples up to the Walled City. The countryside was in chaos, with bands of plague outlaws preying on the weak. The irony of it was that the plague would be the ultimate victor over them all; no matter how strong or how cunning or how ruthless they were, the plague would get them all in the end.

But not Frederigo! He knew how to survive. He knew when to fight and he knew when to offer gold or food for his freedom. And he knew to carry a pouch of poisoned seeds as well. That had gotten him out of trouble near Pisa. His captors were going to torment and torture him all night long until the poison took its effect on them and they were rolling on the ground shitting themselves, or falling into the fire. He had the last laugh on them. Walked around the camp and slit every last one of their throats. Even the little boy, who couldn't have been more than ten or eleven years old. He was a cruel little stoat, too, that one. The boy had jabbed him with a pointed stick over and over.

The stories of the plague cure within the Walled City were widespread over the land, but they were vague and the story changed wherever you went, but they were all in agreement on a city to the north that had a large wall and that was free from the plague. Some said it was an island. Some said it was a city floating in the sky. And he had followed the stories back and forward across the land, avoiding the bandits, listening to the stories firm up into something more credible the closer he got. But he had seen the armies of the plagued too. A vast horde of them on the march, also searching for the Walled City. And he knew he had to get safely inside the walls before they arrived.

When he'd found the city he'd resolved to get inside quickly. No matter what it took. They would cure his ravaged face and he would have women again, not just those uglier than himself. Then he would warn them of the coming army and they would promote him to the city guard. It was only a matter of planning and waiting. And now here he was, staring out the corner of his eye at the door set in the wall, waiting for something to happen. Cursing the apothecaries for making them wait. But clearly that was the prerogative of people who were not being eaten away daily by the plague.

He flexed his fingers on his right hand. They were swollen and weak. Barely able to hold a sword these days, though well able enough to hold a dagger to slit a person's throat. It would not be too much longer, though, before even that was difficult. He had fought plague people who had wrapped a blade into their deformed fingers with cloth bandages to hold it there. But he knew that if he ever reached that state it would be pointless. Might as well let somebody kill you then.

One of the men to his left was coughing, a wet spluttering cough that was probably sending up splatters of blood all around him. Everyone moved a little further away, just out of habit. The apothecaries would look at him and put him out of his misery, surely. There was no point in trying to save one so far gone. The plague ate out one's lungs and stomach to the point you couldn't eat or breathe properly. That his own face was half eaten away was a curse enough, but if he turned his head to one side they would not see it and would presume him healthy enough.

Frederigo looked back to the door and frowned. Why were they taking so long? Every passing moment meant the disease progressed a little deeper into his body. He wondered about moving again, closer to the door, when there was a creaking sound. It wasn't the door set into the wall, though, it was the door at the top of the steps that they had been brought in through. They all looked up to see a new man come down. He was tall and wore a red cloak and hat. He looked at them briefly, then crossed the room to the wall and rapped on the hidden door there. After a moment's pause it opened and he said to a figure out of sight, "Let's get a move on then."

Two men, with their faces masked, came out of the hidden chamber and asked them all to rise to their feet and to follow them. It was a bit disconcerting for the others, and Frederigo pushed the four in front of him along and then followed. There was a large chamber there directly in front of them, lit by numerous candles and with light coming in from some window up high in one wall. They could see cages along one wall with people lying in them. Frederigo's first thought was that this was a trick. They were not going to be cured. They were prisoners.

But one of the other plague people asked, "We are going to be cured, aren't we?"

"Yes," said one of the two masked men who had led them in, in a not unkind voice. "You are going to be cured of your plague. It will take a few days, though, and you will need to stay here with us while that happens to minimise contagion. Is that alright?" He asked it in such a sincere way that they could all only reply that it was alright.

"But these are cages?" said Frederigo.

"Yes. That is unfortunate," the man said again. "This hospital used to house the insane who needed to be kept in cages so that they could neither harm themselves nor others, and the City Council has decreed that all plague people should start their journey to recovery in the same cages so that we can determine that we are not admitting any dangerous lunatics into the city." Then again he asked, "Is that alright?"

And again, they could only reply that it was.

He thanked them and then asked them to follow him and he led them to a set of empty cages at the far end of the room. "You will received fresh food and some wine," he told them. "Plenty of each. It is inside each cage waiting for you."

Frederigo was a little more cautious now, but he looked across at the other wretches in the cages already there and saw none of them trying to warn him not to enter. And they looked well fed enough. He crouched down and entered the cage, seizing the bread and gourd of wine left there and quickly scoffing it down. It was good, he thought. The best meal he'd had in a long time. This would be alright, he was telling himself. It was just like this good chap was telling them. They just needed to ensure that none of them was a dangerous lunatic. It was a fair enough thing to ask, as there were more than enough madmen roaming about out there.

When they were all in their cages and eating happily, the kindly man walked down the row and locked their cages. Then he went back to one of the benches with the man in the red cloak. "Is there any improvement?" he asked them.

The two men were silent a moment and then said in a soft voice, "None."

The figure in the red cloak ground a fist into his palm. "Is it the quality of the last batch of spice, as you suspected?"

"We tried making the spice wine out of previous spice deliveries," the other masked man said, softly, "but it has still failed to halt the progress."

The figure in the red cloak paced back and forward a while. "Did you try injecting the spice wine directly into the blood stream again?"

"Yes."

"And did you try mixing it with mercury?"

"Yes."

"Still fatal?"

The men didn't answer and the kindly one turned his head a little and looked across at Frederigo, who was beginning to feel his head growing light. It was just the wine, he told himself. It had been so long since he'd had good wine that it was going to his head. It took him a while to suspect it was something more though. Something that was making his eyes slip into a impassive stare like the others already in the cages here. He tried to shake it off and listen to what the men at the table were saying. Tried to calculate which of them he should attack first. Who would turn and face him and who would run.

"Damn, that one is ugly," the kindly one said. Then he turned back to his comrades, "If the spice is no less potent, then it is the plague that has gained in potency. We are no longer able to cure it. Only slow its advance."

The figure in the red cape immediately swung his cape up to cover his mouth and nose. "Slow it by how much?" he asked.

The other masked figure shrugged. "It is too early to say for sure. But it seems the more advanced the plague the less chance there is of slowing it at all."

"What chances of plague breaking out in the city?" the man in the red cloak hissed fearfully.

"As long as none of our experiments here ever walks the city streets we should be safe enough," the kindly one replied.

Frederigo heard the words, but it took a long time for his brain to comprehend them, as the meaning kept slipping just out of his grasp. It didn't matter, he told himself finally, as he felt the drug carrying him away, it couldn't have been so important. He was going to be cured soon. Then he'd warn them about the advancing army. They'd know who they had in their ranks then. They'd know the name Frederigo.

XXIV

Galileo sat at Lorenzo's bench, looking over his designs for his large mechanical man and wondering where he had gotten to. It was unlike him to be absent for such a long period and he had need of him. His aged and calcified fingers could not do the fine work that was needed of them. He had already sent some of the serving boys out to look for him but nobody knew where he had gone. He would have a firm talk to him about his responsibilities when he returned.

Galileo wondered if he wasn't treating him too much like a young boy, when he had clearly grown into a young man in the past few years. Lorenzo was so eager to try out the products of science they were building together, but he had no notion what they would do to a young body. He could not allow it.

He looked at the mechanical man design, trying to find faults in it, but Lorenzo had reworked it from his early sketches and there was little that Galileo could say needed improving now. And Lorenzo was quite right; if they used science they could make it walk and fight as if it were a metal giant. Cosimo Medici would value such an invention greatly. Galileo lifted the sketches and ripped them in two. Then again. Then again until they were little pieces of paper that could never be easily reassembled.

This was far too dangerous a thing to be allowed. A man like Cosimo Medici would not want just one. He would want an army of giant metal soldiers. Though what would he do with them once he had control of the Walled City? March out across the countryside to dominate the wasted remains of civilisation? No, thought Galileo. Unlike Cosimo, it was his mission to contribute to the rebuilding of civilisation, not the further destruction of it. A balance between the powers of the two Houses needed to be maintained. If one gained absolute supremacy over the other it would lead to state of tyranny. He would match Leonardo's inventions, but would not allow the development of anything that would crush them.

The plague could not last forever. An effective cure would be found or it would run its course. Then they would have need of science to rebuild. They would need new ways of tilling the land and growing crops. They would need new ways of building. They would need ways to help the many crippled plague survivors work like able-bodied men. They would need strong hands and arms, and science could help them with that.

Galileo stood and walked over to the wall where the metal gloves he had built with Lorenzo were housed. He looked at the empty space where they should have hung and frowned. Then he started searching all around the chamber, opening cupboards and drawers. "Oh you impetuous boy," he muttered, finding that a magnifier and chronometer were also missing. "Where have you gone and what have you done?"

XXV

The lone figure clad in purple robes stood high above his congregation and saw fear in their eyes. That pleased him. He was their high priest and they his followers. Half his face was covered by a dark leather mask to hide his features from his nose up, leaving his thick, near-swollen lips free to speak. He raised his arms up to the heavens once more, and said that the gods and the angels who surrounded them were bringing their wrath down upon the Walled City. It was a certainty that nobody could doubt. And it would be pointless to beg for mercy, he said. They should instead ask for lightning and thunder to fully cleanse the city.

"Our city needs to be purged," he called to the ceiling above him, as if he was being listened to from there as well. As if he were a native of the Walled City himself, rather than having come to it as a troubled young orphan, years before, witness to the atrocities of a northern civil war. He had learned to talk like a native of the Walled City, though, just as he had learned to project his voice to make it seem it was

coming from several angles at once. As he had learned
to find passages in the scriptures of the ancients that
made some sense of the horrors he had witnessed.
Reinforced his belief that people were being punished
for being sinners. Learned how he could make others
believe it too.

"The foolish citizens think their walls will protect
them from the plague that ravages the Earth, but it
only ensures they will receive the full might of the
next curse sent upon them. Our city has been saved
in order to prove that we are worthy – but we have
failed in this. I tell you it will rain frogs and locusts
across the city soon, and the armies of the undead will
rise and march upon us, sparing only the righteous,
who will be marked with the blood of the angel of
the ancients."

He paused and looked down at his congregation. He
could see the fervour in their eyes. Their number had
grown slowly over many months as more and more of
the citizens of the Walled City become discontent with
the way the two Houses ruled them. They wanted
change. They wanted an end to the uncertainty and
fear that had filled the city. They wanted an end to
being besieged by the plague without and the whims
of the two Houses within. And he willingly fed their
need for such change and promised them that only
they, his followers, would be spared when the day of
reckoning came.

He made a small hand sign to an acolyte by his side
who placed a bronze bowl on the altar. The masked
priest glared at him and made another short hand sign,
not unlike a throat being slit. The acolyte whisked the

bronze bowl away and another acolyte lifted a hessian sack up on to the rough stone altar and fumbled with the rope binding it. The sack twisted and turned as the thing inside tried to escape. He reached in and pulled out the lamb by one foreleg, laying it upon the altar. The animal bleated in terror and tried to climb to its feet, slipping as the acolyte held it down. The priest made another sign with his hands and the first acolyte put the bronze bowl back on the altar. The priest glared again and made the throat cutting sign once more and the acolyte removed it and a third passed him a large ornate dagger. The priest raised it above his head and plunged it into the lamb's heart – as well as into the side of the hand of the acolyte holding the sacrifice. The lamb's legs went limp and it collapsed to the stone. The acolyte bit his tongue to prevent himself from screaming.

Another short hand sign and an acolyte produced a gold chalice and together he and the priest filled it with the lamb's blood – as well as that of the wounded man. The priest held it aloft and then dipped his finger in and drew a bloodied cross on his own forehead, ignoring the way it ran into his eyes, leaving them red-rimmed and horrific.

"So shall those who are worthy be spared," the priest said. "This mark is stronger than any wall built by man, and any who bear it shall not suffer fire nor flood nor plague nor any wrath of the gods." He descended the stone steps in front of him and his congregation gathered into a close press about him. He dipped one finger into the chalice and then painted a cross on onto an elderly stout man standing before him. Then a young woman beside him. Then a young man beside her. He walked back and forward amongst the crowd, painting bloody crosses onto the foreheads of all who presented themselves to him. "You shall be saved," he said in soft tones. "As shall you be saved."

Some fell to their knees in thanks. Others threw their hands to the low ceiling of the vault. Others mumbled prayers they had concocted themselves.

"This mark will never truly be washed off," the priest said in a loud voice. "It will remain and will be recognised after the destruction of the Walled City. But you will still be tested. 'Have you burned all your earthly possessions and trappings of vanity?' they will ask. 'Have you accepted the need for cleansing? Have you scourged yourself to rid your body of sin?'"

His congregation called back to him the answers that they had, they had, they had, their voices echoing around the cave-like chamber. Torches set into the walls flickered and sent shadows dancing around them. The priest returned to the altar now, where the bloodied corpse of the lamb lay, blood pooling around its still body, and the acolyte was wrapping cloth around his wounded hand.

"A day will come soon," the purple-robed priest said, "when the blood of the sinners who walk the streets above us shall run red in the gutters like the blood of this lamb. The streets will be full of mayhem and fire and only we chosen few will walk amongst it unharmed." Another hand sign and the acolyte with the bronze bowl stepped forward, carefully. The priest nodded and he placed it in front of him on the altar. Then he poured in a jug of oil and set a burning candle to it. Bright flames leapt up to the roof of the chamber, singeing the eyebrows of the acolyte. Those closest of the congregation felt the heat of it.

"Artefacts of the ancients themselves will be used to bring down a cleansing fire on the city," he said. "And this will be the fate of those who disregard the warnings." And he lifted up the corpse of the lamb. But he did not cast it into the flames and fill the small chamber with the stench of burning wool and cooking meat; instead, another acolyte brought forward a large book and the priest had him open it to a page filled with fine line drawings and coded words, and he smeared the blood of the lamb across its pages. Then he handed the corpse to the bandaged acolyte and took the book and held it above his head with one hand, his other waving back and forward through the flames as if as if taunting the fire to try to burn him.

"This will be the fate of all who have ever followed the false doctrine of science," he hissed and cast the book into the flames. "Now come," he said. "Cast your own trappings of doubt and sin into these flames and be spared the fate that awaits them."

XXVI

The gag in Lucia's mouth was choking her, preventing her from screaming as she was carried through seemingly endless dark corridors. When she lashed out with her feet, they connected only with stone walls and twice she hit her head as she tossed her body about. Finally she was still and let herself be carried up stairs and down stairs, always in near total darkness. Occasionally they would pass a chink in the wall where light crept in, but never much, and her abductor bundled her past, quickly, before she ever had time to see any details of him.

So she tried to concentrate on learning something about her captor. He was a short stocky man and very strong. His build was different to the cloaked stranger who had entered her bed chamber. So who was he? And could he see in the dark, or did he just know these passages extremely well? Perhaps he was another deathseeker? But if so, he would have killed her, rather than carry her away. He was dressed in dark leather that she could feel when she struck him. But he paid her no heed, as if he had been wearing armour. He was too strong to fight, he knew where he was going in the darkness, and she was his captive. So she would wait until they reached wherever he was taking her to, she decided. She would wait for her chance to escape.

The dark tunnels seemed to wind around on themselves in a maze of twists and turns, but eventually he stopped and searched along a wall in front of him for something. Another hidden door she suspected. She heard the lever turning and the grind of stone upon stone, then they stepped into the light. Her captor placed her gently onto a soft chair and closed the door behind them. Then he turned and she was able to get a good look at him.

He wore a dark leather mask that covered his upper face, but this was a city of masks and she looked at the man beyond it carefully. He had grey hairs showing around the edges of the well-fitted black leather. Then she watched the way he worked his jaw, as if practicing saying something. Finally he spoke to her, and said, in a highly refined voice, "You will be quite safe here. You need not be afraid of being harmed in any way."

"Who said I was afraid?" she challenged him. He gave a courteous bow to her. She turned her head away from him and looked around the room. The chamber was sparsely furnished but comfortable enough. There were no windows and she wondered if they were at ground level, above it, or below it.

"So I am your prisoner," Lucia said.

"A guest," the man replied.

"Guests should be introduced," she said. "Who are you?"

"They call me the Nameless One," he said.

She glared at him and asked, "What kind of a name is that?"

"A name that suits my purposes," he replied.

"But you have another name," she said. "A real name."

"No," he said. "In this chamber, I have only one name."

"I shall refuse to use it," she said.

"As you please," he said. "You are my guest and are welcome to do this."

"I shall call you the Abductor," she said.

He smiled a little. "It is also a good name," he said. "But I shall prefer my name."

"Signor Abductor," she said. "How long will you keep me here?"

"I do not know the answer to that," he said.

"Signor Abductor," she said. "Why did you abduct me?"

"I cannot answer that question," he replied.

"Signor Abductor," she said. "Can I see your face?"

"Alas I cannot allow that either," he replied.

"Then you shall not see mine," Lucia said and turned her back on him.

He watched her for some moments, admiring the shape of her neck and the curtain of hair that half-hid it. She was as beautiful as she was brave.

He worked his jaw again, and then said, "And I will call you my little bird." She did not respond. "And I will leave you here in your cage to get used to your new home," he said.

Still she said nothing. "I will come and see you later and will bring a meal," the Nameless One said and then, after a few moments, as if reluctant to actually leave her, he let himself out through a heavy door. Lucia heard the key turn in the lock and then turned around. She was alone. She walked over to the wall where they had come in, but she could find no way to open it. She stepped across to the door and tried the handle. It was locked tight. She turned and looked around the room once more. She had a feeling she was being watched. There would be peep holes into the room from somewhere in the ornate patterns around the edge of the ceiling, she was certain. He was watching her this very instant. She went across to the small bed by the wall and sat on it, folding her hands on her lap. She closed her eyes, wishing to deny him any possibility of looking into them and guessing what she was feeling.

She did not want him to see the fierce resolve in her eyes that she would escape. This had merely saved her the peril of climbing down the tower wall at night. The Medicis were undoubtedly behind this, and that brought her one step closer to Lorenzo. She breathed in and out slowly. Calming herself. Filling herself with resolve. She would play the part of captive as expected of her. But she would then show them that this little bird had claws.

XXVII

"Why don't you tell me your name?" Lorenzo asked the hooded stranger, as the stranger led him along an unfamiliar alleyway and then down a dim stairwell.

"You can call me Virgil," he said.

"Is that your real name?"

"No. But I think you'd prefer that to calling me Beatrice."

"I don't understand half the things you say," said Lorenzo.

"But that means you do understand about half, which puts you up near the top of the ladder."

Lorenzo shook his head. He was still uncertain if the stranger wasn't a little unbalanced, but if he knew that Lucia was in danger and knew how to help her, then Lorenzo was willing to follow him to this underworld he spoke of and back. At the base of the stairs there was a thick door. The hooded man pulled out an odd-looking key and inserted it into the lock. There was a whirring and buzzing sound like a small machine being activated, and the lock clicked open. "This is your last chance to turn back," he said to Lorenzo.

"What is down there?" Lorenzo asked.

"Your destiny," the hooded man replied. Lorenzo hesitated a moment and the hooded man said, "If you dare to face it."

Lorenzo bristled at that, of course. Then he paused. Was the stranger leading him along by his emotions, like he was on a leash? He knew he should don an armour of logic to protect himself, as Galileo often advised him. But since logic would dictate that he did not follow the man into unknown dangers until he knew more, he conveniently ignored the many chinks in his armour. "Why should I fear my own destiny?" he asked.

"Most people do," the hooded man said. "They spend their lifetime supposedly seeking it out, but then either hide from it when it confronts them or they fail to recognise it."

"You talk like a teacher rather than a warrior," Lorenzo said. "What are you exactly?"

"Why can't a person be both?" the hooded man asked. "Or many things at once?"

Lorenzo shrugged. He did not know the answer to that. "You said you knew me when I was much younger," he asked the stranger.

"Yes," he said. "You were little more than a babe really."

Lorenzo wasn't sure whether to believe him or not. "Did you... Did you know my mother? Or my father?"

The stranger regarded him carefully and said, "These are not questions for today. The past is past and the future is what concerns us." Lorenzo wavered a little, taking half a step back. There were too many things he wanted to know before he stepped through that door. But then the hooded man reached out and held Lorenzo by the upper arms. "Before we proceed," he said, "Tell me – what do you believe your destiny is?"

Lorenzo chewed his lip a moment and said, "What man can ever know his destiny?"

"A good answer," said the hooded man. "But too neat an answer. It's not what you believe, is it?" Lorenzo said nothing and the hooded man stood there waiting. "It is my destiny to achieve great things," Lorenzo said in a soft voice. "And it is my destiny to wed Lucia."

"And it is your destiny to save civilisation," the hooded man said. He squeezed Lorenzo's arms tighter and then said, "You and Lucia are very special. On your own you each have an amazing ability you are not even aware of. But together, ah, that's something extraordinary."

Lorenzo listened to the words as if the speaking of them was creating something. He wanted to know more, but the stranger said, "But first we are going to descend into the darkness of your soul."

"My soul?" asked Lorenzo.

"It's just a metaphor," said the hooded man. "It sounds a lot nicer than being told you're descending into the sewers of the city." He turned a lever on the door and Lorenzo heard the whir of wheels and cogs as it lifted up and open.

"The sewers?" asked Lorenzo.

"Think of it as the darkness of your sole then, rather than the darkness of your arsehole," the hooded man laughed. Lorenzo thought the word play in extreme bad taste but followed through the door and onwards, down another set of steps. Soon he could smell the stench. It was foul beyond description. Lorenzo pulled out a kerchief and held it against his mouth and nose. The hooded man did not seem to mind the smell.

And there were rats everywhere. There were rats enough in the city above, but he had never imagined there could be so many living here below them. The hooded man turned to Lorenzo and said, "Watch the rats." He said it very slowly, as if it had a hidden meaning. Lorenzo nodded. "I will." The vermin ran from them as they approached and that was when Lorenzo noticed the light. The hooded man held something in his hand that was casting a beam of light before them, but it was not the glow of a fire, it was a bluish-white glow like moonlight. But the rats ran from it as if its touch burned them.

Then, suddenly, the hooded man held out an arm to prevent Lorenzo going any further and shone the moonlight at their feet. There was a channel of filth there before them. The stench was overpowering. Undoubtedly when it rained the sewers would be flushed clean, but it had not rained for some days and the wet dark mass had been accumulating there from the many drains above.

"This is the River Styx," the hooded man said. "There should be a boatman here to ferry us across." He shone his light up and down the channel. "Never mind," he said. "We will cross ourselves." Lorenzo was starting to understand that many of the hooded man's statements were jests to himself that no one else was meant to understand. He watched him take one step back, tense and spring across the channel, landing lightly on his feet on the other side.

"Now your turn," the hooded man said, shining the moonlight at the channel for Lorenzo to see the knee-deep or worse porridge of piss and turds and occasional swimming rat that he'd land in if he slipped. Lorenzo took a step back, as the hooded man had, and jumped, though not quite as far. He landed awkwardly and one foot skidded in something wet and slippery that he did not want to identify, and just before he fell back into the channel, the hooded man grabbed him. Lorenzo felt how strong his arms were, as he easily pulled him back to his feet. "That's no way to impress a girl," the hooded man said, and turned and led their way onwards again.

It took some time to be far enough away from the stench that it did not fill his nose anymore, though he suspected the smell was lingering cruelly in their clothes and hair, following them as they went down the winding stone tunnels. There were just as many rats here, and every now and then the hooded man would kick one that was too slow in getting out of their way. "Did I mention to watch the rats?" he asked Lorenzo.

"Yes, you did," he replied.

"That will make sense to you one day."

"Why don't you tell me what it means now?" Lorenzo asked.

"Because there are some things you need to find out for yourself. Like your destiny."

"I thought you said you were going to show me my destiny."

"I am. But it's up to you to figure out how to act upon it."

"You talk in riddles."

"Would you rather riddles or metaphors?"

Lorenzo hardly had to think about that one. "Riddles," he said.

"Good man. Now we need to be very quiet as we proceed."

"Why? What's ahead of us?" Lorenzo asked.

"Great danger," the hooded man said. "And that's not a metaphor nor a riddle. It's a reality."

XXVIII

"Your grace," said the Lorraine steward. "I am sorry to interrupt you, but your daughter's handmaiden has some troubling news for you."

The Duke, Duchess and Leonardo, who were seated together in one of the upper rooms of the Lorraine household, pouring over sketches on the table, all looked up. The handmaiden tried to raise her eyes, but as soon as they met the Duchess's she dropped them back to the floor again. "Yes?" the Duke asked again.

The handmaiden stammered a few words towards her shoes and the Duchess said, "Speak up girl!" She nearly burst into tears at that, and wondered if her punishment would be any less severe if she were crying. "It's... it's... Lucia," she stammered.

"Yes?" said the Duke again.

"She's... she's... she's... gone missing."

"What do you mean gone missing?" the Duchess demanded, and the handmaiden started spilling words to match the tears now falling on the floor about her in soft splashes. She told them that when Lucia had not come downstairs for luncheon she

went back up to her chamber to tell her of the
parents' displeasure, but she was not there. She had
told herself that Lucia was surely somewhere around
the house, and was in no trouble. Then when she
could not find her she told herself that she was
hiding somewhere, but was still in no trouble. As the
day dragged on, though, and still Lucia could not be
found, she had told herself that Lucia had probably
slipped out of the house with one of the other
servants to go shopping or something, and while she
was going to be in trouble for it, she was certainly
in no great danger. Then as she asked each of the
servants if they had seen her, she came to believe
that Lucia probably was in some danger.

She glanced across to the steward who declined to
add his part in the story. She had reported to him each
time she had failed to find Lucia. At first he had said,
unconcerned, "Then you must look a little harder for
her. It is a big house, but not so big that you won't
find her."

When she next reported back that she could still
not find her the steward had shown a little concern
and asked if she had talked to all other household
staff yet, and then sent her off to do so. And when
she returned to tell him that still Lucia could not be
found, the steward finally started looking concerned
and said to the handmaiden, "You will have to tell the
Duke," he said.

"Me?" she asked. "I thought you might choose to
inform him."

The steward gave her a "do-I-look-like-I'm-mad?"
look and said. "Come. I will take you to him." The

handmaid nodded obediently and told herself, as long as he's not with his wife it will not be too bad. But of course he was with his wife. And that strange old man Leonardo who they said was a magician.

"M... m... missing," the handmaid stammered once more, still keeping her eyes to the ground, afraid to meet the Duchess' glare. But the Duchess was ignoring the girl and firing rapid questions at the steward. "Has the house been searched? When was she last seen? Has she gone outside for any reason?" The steward told them what the handmaiden had told him and the Duchess dismissed her. "Go and do something useful, like cut your wrists," she said to her. The girl scurried off, sobbing. She should have told them about the young man. But they had dismissed her before she could tell them. She fled to Lucia's bedroom and sat there on a chair rocking, as much in fear for her own safety as Lucia's.

The Duchess circled the table in fury. "It is the Medicis!" she spat. "They have abducted her. They think to gain the upper hand. We should rally our troops and march on their house this evening. We should burn them out."

"They have gone too far," said the Duke, matching his wife's anger.

"I think we should examine the facts before us before making any rash decision," said Leonardo. "Surely if the Medicis have kidnapped her somehow, they have done so to provoke such an action from you."

"We'll give them more goose stuffing than they bargained for," the Duchess said. "And they'll be the type of geese that bite the hands that feed them!"

"Yes, I'm sure," said Leonardo, "But why play into their trap? For it is surely a trap."

The Duke considered that a moment, and then said, "Leonardo may be right. This could be a trap. They might be trying to provoke us to send our soldiers against them as they have some stratagem to defeat them."

His wife banged her fist on the table. "My father would never have hesitated," she shouted. "He'd have marched at once and have been over their walls before midnight. Roasting them in their beds. He'd cook their geese to warm his feet."

"If Lucia is inside their house such an attack might lead to her being harmed," Leonardo said calmly. "Either by the Medici forces or inadvertently by your own."

The Duke nodded his head. Then he said, "You will need to build us some more machines. Something that will let us invade the Medici house without putting our daughter at risk."

"A flying goose rather than an eagle?" Leonardo suggested quietly.

"What about the mole or the turtle machines?" the Duke asked. "How far advanced are they? The mole could have men dig into their courtyard and we'd fill the household with our men before they knew what had happened."

Leonardo stroked his long white beard a little. "I have not yet been able to duplicate the machine the way the ancients had built them. They were able to build tunnels all under the city, as you know, but the experimental model I built was not so successful. The tunnel the fellow was digging collapsed behind him, burying him. They are too dangerous to use."

The Duke waved his hand in the air. "These are simply fine details for you to perfect. I will send you twenty more men to trial the thing with. You can afford to lose half of them."

Leonardo raised his eyebrows in surprise. That had sounded more like a sentiment the Duchess would have voiced than the Duke.

"I will need four days," Leonardo said.

"You have two," said the Duchess.

"Three," said Leonardo, as if he was bidding on something more material than men's lives.

"Agreed," said the Duke and slapped a palm on the table. "We must have them as soon as possible. I expect the Medicis will be wanting us to sweat a little before playing their next hand anyway, so we have a little time to prepare."

"We will pluck their geese without them even realising it," the Duchess said.

"And I'm sure that would be a goose of a different colour," said Leonardo, arching an eyebrow, not hiding his displeasure at this request being made of him.

"Your grace?" said the handmaiden, meekly; she had returned to the door with the steward.

"What is it now?" snapped the Duchess.

"There's something else," the handmaiden said softly. "There was a young man."

XXIX

The Nameless One examined himself in the mirror for some time, pondering the growing dark lines under his eyes and the increasing droop to his mouth. He stared long and hard until he could see his youth hidden beneath it. He had shed his leather clothes and mask and was dressed once more in his silk and jewelled finery.

This evening he wore a white silk shirt with a black and silver jacket and dark pantaloons. He came into the dining chamber where his wife waited for him at the table, and complimented her fine blue dress with embroidered white flowers on it. It was one of her favourites, and she always wore it when in a good mood. He smiled to see it. "You're late for dinner, my love," she chided gently.

"Yes, I'm sorry," he said. "An urgent task that needed my attention."

"Nothing difficult, I hope?" she said.

"Nothing too difficult," he replied.

"Do we have a guest in the lower chamber?" she asked.

He worked his jaw a moment and then said, "You need not worry yourself about my business affairs." She gave him a stare, as if to disagree, and then nodded her head.

"What news of the city today?" she asked him, lapsing into their regular evening small chat.

"All is calm in the city," he said.

"Was there not some conflict?" she asked.

"It is all well now," he said. He had told her of the conflict between the Medicis and the Lorraines the day before, and she had quizzed him about it, but he knew she would not remember it clearly today.

"Come and sit by me," she said. He smiled and carried his chair across to her. "Yes, my dear."

"I wish we could go for a walk after our meal," she said. He placed a hand on hers. They would not be walking this evening. The wasting disease was a terrible thing. It left a person looking healthy and whole, but ate them away from the inside. It slowly took away strength from a person's limbs and also the strength of a person's mind.

He had visited the apothecaries many times for potions, some of which seemed to help and some of which did not, but they said that it was only possible to slow the wasting disease – never to cure it. The ancients had a cure for it, he had been told. But the knowledge of that was lost to them, like so much else of the ancients' wisdom.

But he continued to urge them to try new cures. For as the disease ate away at her, he found it ate away at him too. It was making him increasingly unfeeling. Making him more careless in taking risks.

Making him less skilled at the secret trade that he was so valued for.

"Will you be going out again this evening?" she asked him.

"Just for a short time," he said. "I will not be late."

"Always business," she chided him.

"These are difficult times," he told her. "One must maintain one's interests."

"Of course," she said.

They supped for a while on fowl and vegetables, and then he said, "I have a present for you, my dear." He reached into a pocket and pulled out a little brass object of wheels and gears.

"What is it?" she asked.

He worked his jaw again and said, "Watch closely." He took out a small brass key and wound the device. Then he set it down on the table. The wheels turned and the gears clicked and the object rose and changed, rising into the shape of a bird; then it bobbed its head and opened its beak and chirped.

He watched his wife's eyes open is amazement and she put a hand to her mouth in delight. "It is wondrous," she said. "It is like magic."

"Yes," he said. "It is. But it is only the work of skilled craftsmen."

The bird continued chirping until the spring inside it had wound down and then it disassembled back into a formless collection of wheels and gears. "Magicians I think," she said and lifted up the object to examine it closely. Then she said, "Wind it up again and let me hear it sing once more."

He gave her the key and said, "It is your gift. You may wind it and have it sing for you as many times as you like."

He watched her take the key and carefully insert it into the slot in the bird and he wondered if, when he gave it to her anew tomorrow, he might hide from her how he wound it and see if she might somehow remember it from all the days she had wound it already.

XXX

"Very quiet now," the hooded man said to Lorenzo. "We are not alone anymore." Lorenzo and the hooded stranger had descended deeper and deeper into the tunnels under the city, winding their way along the maze of dark passages that had been built by the ancients. "Tread slowly and silently," he told Lorenzo. Then he did something to the light he carried and its beam softened so that it barely illuminated a few paces in front of them. "Put a hand on my shoulder," he then whispered to Lorenzo.

Lorenzo did as he was bid and felt something like chain mail under the man's cloak, but so thin it was like cloth. More mysteries. The hooded figure led him onwards one step at a time and soon Lorenzo heard moaning coming from ahead of them. "What is it?" he asked in a soft voice.

"Shhh," cautioned the stranger and kept walking onwards. Soon they entered a wide chamber. There were a few dim lanterns in nooks and Lorenzo could make out more details of the stone work and shapes in the shadows. He had taken several steps into the chamber before he realised that the shapes were men. He froze and let go his grip on the hooded man's shoulder. Was this a trap? He turned around in a circle and saw the men were were all about them. He nearly shouted before the strong hand clamped over his mouth. Then the hooded man was whispering in his ear, the mouth so close he could feel his breath. "We are safe, but you must be silent. Treat them as sleeping dragons." He lowered his hand and lifted Lorenzo's hand to his shoulder once more and led him onwards again.

Lorenzo could see the figures were chained to the walls, like this was some prison, but he could also see those figures who were closest to the lanterns. They were not people. They were creatures of some kind. They were hideous. Hugely deformed heads. Limbs missing. Faces with no eyes. And the stench. It was somehow worse than the river of human waste because it was the mixed with the smell of living creatures.

"*Mio Dio*," Lorenzo muttered to himself. "Where have you brought me?"

"Steel yourself," whispered the hooded man closely again. "It gets worse."

How could anything be worse than such monstrosities, thought Lorenzo as they stepped from the chamber into one of the tunnels leading from it. But the next chamber was infinitely worse. The figures chained to the walls were children. So many of them. But none a child as he would have described them. They were chimera creatures like existed in the tales of old. Some had the heads of dogs. Others had the features of cats. Some had stumped wings in place of

arms. Others had claws for feet. Lorenzo felt he had
crossed into a dream, or a nightmare. This could not be
real. He stumbled as he walked and nearly fell to the
fetid ground. But the hooded figure clasped his hand
and pulled him close. "Strength," he urged softly.

Lorenzo took a deep breath of the putrid air and
closed his eyes to block out the horror of it. But even
with his eyes shut he could see the creatures before
him. The hooded figure pulled his hand and Lorenzo
felt himself being guided along as if he were blind.
Eventually the stranger said, "We are passed." And
Lorenzo opened his eyes.

"What are those things?" asked Lorenzo.

"I will explain momentarily," said the hooded
figure. "But we have one more chamber to pass
through and it is the worst of them all."

"Worse?" asked Lorenzo.

The hooded man said nothing and led him along
the tunnel to the next chamber. Lorenzo wanted to
close his eyes again and have the hooded man lead
him through blindly, but he had to know what horror
could be worse. Once more the hooded man said,
"Tread slowly and silently." Lorenzo felt his insides
knotted in fear but nodded his head. The chamber was
set out with wooden shelves filled with large jars. And
in the jars were the heads and limbs of the children
from the last room. They were covered with plague
pustules and malformed, but more horrific still, the
eyes seemed to follow him as he walked across the
chamber. And as he looked at the face of one young
girl, her eyes seemed to blink. He felt his blood run
cold. It must have been a trick of the dim light. It must

have been his imagination. Then he swore she did it again. His legs would no longer obey his will to walk, even though he wanted them to run from this place.

"Look away!" the hooded man hissed sharply. "And keep walking!" Lorenzo did as he was told and soon they had passed from that chamber. "*Mio Dio*! *Mio Dio*! *Mio Dio*!" Lorenzo muttered to himself as the hooded man pulled him along. "This is a place of nightmares. Who are those poor wretches?"

"Experiments," said the hooded man.

"What do you mean experiments?" Lorenzo asked. Experiments were things conducted with weights and measures and lenses and pendulums to determine a scientific principle. These were something far other.

"The apothecaries of your city have been charged by the City Council with finding a cure to the plague that does not hold them hostage to the two Houses' spice trade wars. They have been experimenting on plague victims." His tone was so matter of fact. So heartless.

"Your disgust is written plainly on your face," the hooded man said. "You judge me as being complicit it this, but it is your people who have done this."

"They are no people of mine," said Lorenzo.

The hooded man smiled. "Well spoken." But then added, "Though strictly speaking the City Council's desire to find a cure to the plague is driven by their desire to break the control that the two Houses have over them and the city through their control of the spice trade, so anybody in the employ of either of the two Houses is also complicit in this."

Lorenzo wanted to slump to the ground and he wanted to keep walking further away from these atrocities. He wanted to find an exit that would take him back to the streets. He wanted to have never come down here. And he wanted to go back and see if the face of the young girl had really been alive and had blinked at him. "Are they alive?" he asked. "Those heads?"

"What if I tell you 'no'?" the hooded man asked.

"I won't believe you," he said.

"And what if I tell you 'yes'?"

"I still won't believe you." Then Lorenzo said, "It was an evil thing to have brought me here!"

"Was it?"

Lorenzo did not feel he had to answer, but the hooded man said, "Do you know why I asked you to be so silent? It was not in order to prevent them from harming us. It was to prevent us from harming them. If they see people walking before them it will remind them of what they once were, and that will cause them great pain and sorrow. Their lives are miserable enough without that."

Lorenzo was taken aback at that. This hooded stranger continued to surprise him. And so many thoughts filled his head. Should they be freed? Would it be kinder still to kill them? Shouldn't the citizens of the city be made aware? "I can see what you're thinking," said the hooded man. "That we should stop these experiments, yes?"

"Yes," he said.

"And you're full of anger and grief and all other things, yes?"

"Yes," said Lorenzo. "We must stop these experiments."

But the hooded man said, "Did you ever consider that if you believe in a god, or gods, then everyone on this Earth is but an experiment in the nature of the human condition? Every travail and hardship is but a part of the experiment, no more ghastly than this here."

Lorenzo didn't like the weight of that idea. It still sat like a great stone upon his shoulders. "And even love," the hooded man said. "What if even love is a part of the grand experiment being played out upon you by your gods?"

Lorenzo shook his head. "No," he said. "I feel love in here." He rapped on his chest. "It is not based on belief. It is a truth that is undeniable."

"Good," said the hooded man. "That's a belief that will hold you in good stead for the next level we are going to descend to."

"There is more?" asked Lorenzo.

"Oh, so much more," said the hooded man. "Come."

XXXI

"Hello, my little bird," the Nameless One said, causing Lucia to jump from the bed with a start. She had dozed off, despite vowing to herself not to. "I see you have made yourself comfortable in your cage."

She sat up on the bed and brushed her skirts out flat, turning her head from him. How long had he been here in the room watching her? She wanted to demand it of him, but did not want to speak to him. She looked down at her hands as if she had no interest in whether he was there or not.

"I have brought you a meal," the Nameless One said. "I hope you do not consider it too poor for your taste." She did not look up at him. "I prepared it myself," he added.

She gave a quick glance up to see what his culinary skills might be capable of and saw some kind of soup in a bowl. Probably horrendous, though the aroma that was now reaching her across the room suggested otherwise. At the smell of it her stomach grumbled noisily and she felt herself reddening a little around the neck. That her own stomach was such a traitor!

The Nameless One chose not to comment on it, though, and said, "I will leave the meal here by the door and you can eat it at your leisure. I will come and collect the tray later. Will that be satisfactory?" She still chose not to respond.

"Very good, then," he said. "And if there is anything else I can do to be of service to you, just let me know."

"You could free me," she said quickly, and then pursed her mouth to prevent any other unbidden words to escape.

"Ah, I would truly love to free you, my little bird," the man said. "But that I cannot do just yet."

"When then?" This time she did look up and saw he was smiling under his dark leather mask.

"That is difficult to say. We are walking across a very narrow bridge that flows over very turbulent waters and to rush across would only increase the chances of falling."

"My father will be furious and my mother even more so," she said.

"Of that I have no doubt at all," the Nameless One replied, and he bent down and placed the tray on the floor. She wondered if he were inviting her to attack him. Letting her think she might have some chance of catching him by surprise and taking the key from him and escaping. But she knew it would be pointless. He was too fast and strong for her. It would just be a game to him.

He straightened up again and adjusted his clothing carefully. "Well," he said. "It has been a pleasure conversing with you, once more." And he reached into his pocket for the door key. Lucia waited until he had turned the key and then said, "You have a lovely coat." He turned back to her and looked down at the garment. It was expensive black cloth, set with pearls and silver thread.

"Ah," he said. "I see you are observant for a little bird. You are deducing that I am not merely some lowly-paid kidnapper, correct?"

Lucia did not reply. "I think we might have a pleasant game here," he said. "If you can deduce seven things about me correctly, I will grant you one wish."

"Any wish?" she asked.

"Any wish within my power," he said.

She mulled on that a moment. "Even setting me free?"

"That is not within my power."

She pouted and turned her head as if she did not want to play. Then she looked back and said, "Would you deliver a letter for me?"

He thought on that. "Most probably. Yes."

"Alright," she said, turning around on the bed and facing him square on. "Let's play."

"My shoes," he said. "What can you guess about me from my shoes?" She examined his boots closely and then said, "They are well kept, unlike most of the old boots being worn around the city that can no longer be easily replaced. So you clearly take pride in conserving what you have."

He gave a low bow. "What about my voice? What does that tell you."

"You enunciate very clearly, so are obviously well-educated, and I think a native of our city."

He bowed again.

"What of my cooking skills?"

"Since I have not yet tasted your soup, I cannot say," he held up a finger, but she quickly cut in, "But since you have skills in the kitchen at all you clearly do not rely entirely on servants for your meals."

He bowed once more.

"Then what of my profession?"

Now she frowned a little. "I would guess some experience as a military man. Some time spent in one of the mysterious cities to the east, before the plague years, where assassination and kidnapping were considered art forms. I would guess many years of training as a much younger man."

"All too easy," he said. Then, "What of my heart?"

She looked at him and said with a certainty she did not fully possess, "That's the easiest of all. Your heart beats like a large drum of sorrow."

His eyes blinked rapidly, but he did not look away. "No. You have guessed incorrectly," he said and without another word he quickly opened the door and stepped out, locking it behind him. Lucia reached out a hand to stop him, but said nothing. He had said her guess was incorrect, but then why did it feel like she had just shot an arrow at a deer and only wounded it, and had just seen it run away, bleeding and confused?

XXXII

Cosimo Medici looked down at the bloody mess before him and said with certainty, "There will be more blood spilled before this is over."

He sat in a dim upper room of the house, decorated with ornate tiled floors and mosaics on the walls. The apothecary who was changing his dressings didn't reply. He had already lain the bloodied bandages on a tray on the table beside them and was now washing the wound with warm water, scented with some of his secret ingredients. "It smells," said Cosimo.

"It smells because it is potent," said the apothecary. "It will keep away infection." And as if he was instructing a young child rather than the head of the Medici household, he added, "We have been perfecting our arts for hundreds of years and many of our secrets were passed down from the ancients. Our ways are built upon long-practiced and proven cures."

"You sound like Galileo," said Cosimo. "Always talking about proof and evidence."

"Galileo is a man of science," the apothecary said. "There are many in our order who do not trust science. It is too quick to seek new ideas. Too radical in its propositions."

"I would rather a scientist who was more radical still," said Cosimo, and then winced as the apothecary pressed hard on his wound.

"Pardon me," the man said. "But a little pain is sometimes necessary."

Cosimo shrugged. "Finish your work," he said. "I have much to plan today."

"Proper healing cannot be rushed," the man said.

"Nothing can ever be rushed in this city," said Cosimo. "Except for war. That comes at a speed that few are ever prepared for."

"We do not concern ourselves with politics," said the apothecary.

"Only with the mending of those wounded as result of political battles," said Cosimo.

"That is one of our tasks," said the apothecary.

"And what else do you do that you keep secret?" asked Cosimo, wondering for a moment if there were any way the apothecaries could be made into allies for his cause.

"If there are any secrets we do not reveal," the man replied, "they only remain secrets because they are not revealed."

"So you do have some secrets? Anything that I might find of interest?"

"Every profession has its secrets," he said. "But nothing I fear that you might find useful for your current preoccupations."

"What about the plague?" asked Cosimo. "How have you not managed to find a total cure if you have the knowledge of the ancients?"

"We have their secrets of spice wine," he said.

"That only keeps the plague at bay," said Cosimo. "It is not a cure."

The apothecary pressed hard into his wound again, but this time Cosimo was ready for it. "We do not possess all their knowledge," he said.

Cosimo said, as if casually, "I wonder if I should direct Galileo to allocate his resources to finding a cure? That would be a secret worth having, wouldn't it."

The apothecary said nothing.

"Yes," said Cosimo. "I think whoever finds the cure for the plague is going to have the ultimate power in our city, don't you?"

Still the apothecary said nothing. "I'm sure science could find a solution," Cosimo said.

"That would greatly upset the status quo," said the apothecary.

"Don't tell me that you don't wish to see it upset just a little more in your favour," Cosimo Medici said.

The apothecary gave a grim smile and worked on. Then he said. "This looks like it is mending well. As you know, infection needs to be kept at bay to prevent it moving into dangerous territories. But there are some parts of the body that are difficult to cure and in such cases prevention is the best course, which means not allowing the infection to take root there in the first place."

Cosimo immediately realised that the conversation was moving into new territory. "So if a limb became infected you must cut it off to prevent infection spreading to the body?"

"We would first seek to cure it," said the apothecary.

Cosimo studied the man closely to see if he was being impudent or not. He grunted. "Anyway, I am more interested in finding ways to clip the wings of a bird than to sever the limbs of a man," he said.

"If this dagger had been poisoned," the apothecary said. "There might be very little we could do. You can cut off a limb, but you cannot cut off a head and expect a cure."

Cosimo stiffened a little, certain there was a subtle threat in the metaphor. "If a creature had two heads instead of just one," he said, "severing one head might be possible, but then the remaining head would control the body entirely would it not?"

The apothecary bowed a little. "As I said, we do not concern ourselves with politics."

Cosimo gave a single short laugh, like a bark, and said, "And I do not concern myself with healing. Except when I'm wounded."

The man did not reply and gathered up his things and said, "I will return tomorrow to inspect the wound. It is healing well, but the risk of infection still remains."

Cosimo glared at him. "A man of your reputation would not put himself in such a position as having a patient succumb to infection after healing so well, surely."

The apothecary bowed and removed himself from the chamber. Cosimo's steward, who had been sitting silently in the corner of the room the whole time, said in a low voice, "I will make sure we have a new apothecary from now on."

"Good counsel," said Cosimo. "I don't like the man's tone. The apothecaries have grown far too powerful and disrespectful. They forget they are servants of the city, charged with its welfare."

"And they wish us not to forget that only they can make the spice wine that keeps the plague at bay."

Cosimo nodded. "Look for a young apothecary," he told the steward. "One who might have an eye for a pretty woman. Or a boy. Or a taste for jewellery and gold. Let's see if we can't find a way to encourage them to share their secrets."

The steward bowed. "It shall be done."

Cosimo turned in his chair and looked up at the large portrait of his father sitting astride a horse with the family crest of six balls in a circle over his head. The portrait dominated the room, grander than any of the mosaic scenes of the ancients. When Cosimo used this room he preferred to sit beneath it in a way such that anybody coming into the room had to face both men. His father's arrogance and power would sit upon his shoulders like a mantle. Cosimo wondered what his father would do if he were still alive? Would he have Galileo tortured to make him make new war machines? Would he find a way to shoot the giant eagle out of the sky? He would certainly have had the apothecaries of the city working for him by now. He turned his chair away again. He preferred to have his father's disapproving eyes glaring at others in the room rather than himself.

"Fetch a parchment and pen," he commanded the steward. "It's past time we wrote a letter to the Duke of Lorraine and told him that we do not fear his eagle because we have a certain little bird in a cage."

XXXIII

"I am going to tell you once more to tread slowly and silently," said the hooded man in a soft voice, "as we are not alone, and this time the danger is to us."

"More monstrosities?" asked Lorenzo.

"Of a type," said the hooded man. "Now not another word until we are safely past. We must become masters of shadows. That's what you called me once. The Shadow Master."

"When?" asked Lorenzo. "I have never met you before."

"It was a long time ago," said the stranger. "We will talk more of that later." Then he pressed a finger to Lorenzo's lips to cease the inevitable questions and to let him know how deadly serious he was in this and then turned his soft light in front of them again.

Lorenzo had a feeling that they had walked beyond the borders of the Walled City already, but they had made so many twists and turns and gone down so many steps, that perhaps they had just gone deeper below the city. Each step took him further into a feeling that he was now in a mirror city down here.

There were perhaps as many tunnels as there were streets above and for each tower in the city there was a shaft or descending set of steps here. But this mirror city lacked people to reflect the many who lived above.

They walked along in the darkness until Lorenzo heard voices ahead of them. A chanting-like groan that at first sounded like some weird cavern echo, but became more distinct the closer they came to it. It was a chant and refrain from a group of people, as one might hear in a mass. But this one was not subdued and tonal like those uttered in the cathedral above; this was bordering on hysterical. The hooded figure slowed, then he extinguished his torch beam and held out a hand to lead Lorenzo along in the darkness. Already, however, he could see the flicker of light ahead of them. The warm glow of torches and lanterns. And yet Lorenzo felt a chill run along his spine.

The voices were now echoing around them, distorting in the tunnel so they could not easily be understood. He tried concentrating on the voices to pick out any meaning, but he could only catch individual words. Then he looked up and found the hooded figure was gone. He looked around but could see no sign of him and felt the soft icicle fingers of panic in his insides. Then a hand reached out and touched him. He looked and saw the hand was attached to an arm and the arm attached to a body that was standing in the shadows of a stone column. His companion was indeed the Shadow Master, he thought, melting into the darkness like that.

He pulled Lorenzo close to him and suddenly he could see and hear everything. They were standing in a passageway overlooking a large chamber beneath them, like they were upon a balcony. It was closely set with pillars that provided both an open view and a hiding place for observation. And down below them were perhaps forty robed men, dressed like monks, but in rough hessian, kneeling in supplication to a figure at an altar. That man, dressed in robes of soft violet, was masked with the top half of his face obscured by a rough leather mask. He had descended into a mysterious world of hoods and masks, Lorenzo thought.

The man, standing in front of the crowd like he was their priest, had blood smeared across his cheeks and held a curved knife aloft over his head. "The time has come," he called out to the men kneeling before him. "Time to cut off the head of the beast! Time to free the city from sin and blasphemy. Time to ascend to our rightful places."

Lorenzo wanted to ask the Shadow Master what the man meant. What was he talking about? Who were these people? What kind of a secret service were they holding here? Why was he daubed in blood? But he kept his tongue as he had been bidden and the congregation below called back to their priest, "It is time!"

"The ascension is near," he told them.

"It is time," the congregation replied again.

The purple priest then held his dagger high over his head once more and muttered something that could have been a prayer, or could just as well have been an evil incantation, and then slowly and deliberately he lowered the dagger, held out

his other arm, wrist up, and carved some strange
sign on the skin of his arm, drawing blood. It was
not possible to see what he had carved, but Lorenzo
thought it might have been some variation on a
cross. Then the priest held the tip of blade into the
fire of a candle beside him.

"Blood and fire shall be our creed," he said. Then he
made a hand motion and an acolyte stepped forward
with a bronze bowl. The priest made another hand
motion and the acolyte stepped back quickly, to be
replaced by another acolyte, bearing a wooden chest.
He laid it on the altar before the priest who held his
knife over it and said, "One sacred blade amongst
many makes all blades as sacred." Then he opened
the chest, not without some assistance from the
acolyte, and Lorenzo could see, looking down, that
it was filled with daggers. The purple priest pushed
his own dagger down into the chest and then called
the congregation forward. They came obediently.
Each man took one dagger, like they were playing
some parlour game, turning it over in their hands,
as if wondering if it had been the one that the priest
had used.

Lorenzo tried to see their faces, to see if he knew
any of the men down there taking part in this
bizarre ritual, but they were turned away from him.
When each man had a dagger in his hands, they all
proceeded to carve a symbol into their own forearms.
Then at a hand sign from the purple priest the first
acolyte brought the bronze dish back to the altar and
lit a candle to it, standing well back. It was filled with
oil and a bright flame leapt from it and Lorenzo knew

it as the symbol he had seen on many of the shop fronts in the city.

Then the priest figure took off his mask. Lorenzo tried hard to see his features, but he was now standing side on to him. One by one the congregation, or army or whatever they were, stepped forward and looked at the man's face with a look of astonishment, and then dipped their daggers into the flames, mumbling some incantation before returning to the centre of the chamber.

Then Lorenzo felt the Shadow Master pull at his arm. He was reluctant to leave, wanting to see what other madness the men below him were going to perform, but the other was insistent. They moved along the back wall of the tunnel and were soon around a corner. "We must leave this cavern of twisted reason and fear," he said to Lorenzo, still softly.

"Who are they?" Lorenzo asked, in a whisper. "Who is that man leading them?"

"Who do you think he is?" asked the Shadow Master, softly.

"He sounds like the High Priest."

"You can call him the puce priest," said the Shadow Master.

"What does that mean?" asked Lorenzo.

"It could mean he left a red sock in the wash with his robes, or it could mean he is a madman."

"What?" asked Lorenzo. "Why did you always talk in these strange riddles?"

The Shadow Master faced him squarely and said, "Never forget, the greatest fight should always be against those who dwell in darkness and oppose enlightenment. Now we do not have much time. We must hurry. There is still more I must show you," the Shadow Master said. "But this time, something both terrifying and wonderful."

XXXIV

The Duke looked up at his wife and wondered if he had ever hated her more than he did now. Many nights he had dreamed of reaching out in bed and placing his hands around her neck and squeezing and squeezing until her eyes bulged and she gasped for breath, but then he would be shocked by the violence of it, and roll away until the feeling passed from him. But now, he thought he might be able to actually do it.

He could reach out to her and touch her, the way she had just reached out and slapped him. His cheek still stung from it and he suspected one of her many rings might have even drawn blood, but he was not going to put his hand to his face and find out. He just glared at her. He wanted her to feel his anger and hatred. He wanted her to fear him. If he leaned forward just a little he could slap her and send her tumbling to the floor. But he also felt she had grown too distant for him ever to reach. There was a vast chasm between them and its cause lay on the table in front of them. A short note with no crest or seal on it, stating that their daughter, Lucia, was enjoying the hospitality of the Medici family and as an honoured guest would receive the best of treatment until her stay with them was concluded. They hadn't even bothered using metaphor, increasing the insult.

As soon as he had read it, the Duke's heart had sunk deeper into his chest. He had suspected it was the Medicis who had her, but to come out and say it so boldly showed an arrogance that he had not guessed at. It implied they would harm her if they chose to. The Duke's first impulse had been outrage. A desire to rally his men and assault the Medici house as his wife had demanded, but that soon faded and he now wanted to enter into negotiations to get her back.

But the Duchess had surprised him with her reaction. She had read the letter and then dropped it to the table where it lay. "They have overplayed their hand," she'd said coldly. "They would never dare pluck a single petal from the flower. We shall not even reply to their letter, and we will win the upper hand with our silence."

"How you can be so certain they will not pluck a petal?" the Duke had asked. "They are desperate and vengeful men. They think we were the ones who blew out Giuliano's candle and tried the same on Cosimo. They feel they have a blood right."

But she'd waved her hand in the air. "You know nothing of how they think," she'd said. "You are incapable of imagining how such men think because you do not dare lie with lions like they do. They have made a tactical error that will only be made worse by harming her. They have no proof that we blew out the Medici candle, only a suspicion. But we now have proof that they were behind the picking of our blossom. They clearly sent that young man to steal her away."

"You would risk our dear flower's safety for the benefit of holding a higher card?" he'd asked. "What happened to your great desire of assaulting the Medici household with our soldiers and Leonardo's inventions?" Though in fact he knew his wife was liable to make extreme changes of mood. She would be driven by a passion one day and then by cold and calculating schemes the next. It made her a formidable adversary.

"We shall still see their house fall," she had said. "But we will not need to send our tin soldiers alone to do it. If we have this letter posted all over the city the citizens will turn against the Medici as sure as the tide turns against the strand, and come to our side in any conflict."

"But many of the citizens are chained to the six circular balls of the Medicis."

"This will give them a reason to break that allegiance," she'd said, pointing a finger at her husband. "They will come to our side and will help us tear down the House of Medici stone by stone."

"At the risk of our daughter's safety? Possibly her life?"

She had waved a hand at him dismissively and he'd felt that chill thought of what it might be like to place his hands around her sleeping neck and squeeze. "It is not Lucia's life you care about," he said. "Is it because she is not our blood child or is it more about your honour? You would have had me rush out of the household and attack them in my day clothes when it was the honour of our House that had been insulted, but if we can turn that to an insult to their House you are content to sit and wait."

And that was when she had slapped him. A swift blow that he'd barely seen coming and had taken full on the side of his face. She'd glared at him and said, "I may not have grown that child in my womb nor suckled her at my breast, but she is my daughter nevertheless, and don't you ever tell me that I am a mother who would put her own child willingly at risk."

The Duke glared back at her and then said, "You are a mother who would put her own child willingly at risk." She raised her hand for another slap, but he stood quickly and grabbed it. She raised her other hand to slap him and he grabbed that too.

"You are too weak to restrain me," she said, struggling, kicking at him with her legs.

"I am strong enough," he said, wrestling her around so that he could spin her arms about her body and turn her away from him, holding her tighter.

"Coward," she hissed, spitting. But he had turned her around now and the spit flew past him. "Witch," he said. "Clown!" she taunted. "Harpy!" he replied. Then she pushed her body back at him and banged him into the table. It weakened his grip enough that she was able to pull free. She whirled on him and bared her nails like an angry cat, reading to strike at him and rake down his face. He thrust his face forward, daring her to. Instead she reached out a hand and grabbed him by the hair, twisting it painfully and pulling his head towards her. He put both his hands into her hair and twisted it as viciously, pulling her face to his. They snarled at each other once before their lips met. Then they were kissing passionately. The way they had kissed when they first met. Before the years of courtly behaviour and business etiquette had turned them into strangers. Before the long years of parenting had replaced their tumultuous love for each other with a more stable love for their daughter.

With her missing, and in danger, it was like that had been sucked out of the space between them, drawing them violently together. They fell to the ground and lay there in a tight embrace, panting and kissing, husband and wife, hands in each other's hair and around each other's throats.

XXXV

"Come to bed and we can make the majestic moth together," the Nameless One's wife said to him. She lay in their bed, with an imploring look upon her face. He looked at her for a moment and then said, "Of course."

He took his time undressing though, as if it were vitally important that each item of clothing be folded just so. "Do you remember when we were younger and spent a week on that small farm in the hills?" she asked him. She often let her memory roam back to their youth. Back before everything. But they were painful memories to him as they were so wonderful.

"Yes," he said. "It was a blessed time."

"We made the majestic moth together endlessly," she said.

He nodded his head, recalling it. It was warm and they were alone in the farmhouse and had dismissed the servants whenever they were able and spent the day in each other's embrace. "Truly blessed," he said. But it was a different time too, he thought. He had been much younger and she had been, well, she had been the woman he had married. Had been young and vibrant and full of wit. This evil disease had left but a shadow of his wife. A woman who was like her in so many ways, but also not quite her.

Finally he stood there naked and she held out a hand to him. The way she had when they were younger and alone in that farm house. He wanted to take her hand, but he also wanted to weep at the sadness that was filling him. "Come," she said.

Wordlessly he climbed into bed beside her and lay down next to her. "Stroke my hair," she said, and he did. "Hold me," she said, and he did. Her good hand touched his bare chest and he closed his eyes and tried to remember the feeling of being in the farm house with her. Any glimpse of a naked part of her body had filled him with passion. He had wrapped his arms around her tightly and they'd flown on the breeze like a majestic moth, to all corners of the house, settling on a couch in the sunshine, or on a rug on the floor.

He screwed his eyes tight to try to recall it now, but he could not feel the lightness filling him. She ran her hand lower down his stomach, but he was still failing to respond. He tried to think of her when she was younger. And then he felt himself stirring. She grabbed hold of his ivory tower and felt it rise in her hands. "Come," she said again.

He had to do the rest of the work. Her limbs were too weak. She could but lie there and let him enter her cave of wonders. Let him climb the heights of the mountain of desire. Let him try to carry them both away in the flight of the majestic moth. But all he could feel was his weight upon her. She had been the one who'd filled him with lightness. She had been the soft wings that had beaten for them, bearing them aloft. And now she was broken and he felt his mortal weight pushing her into the mattress of the bed each time he plunged inside her.

And he felt the passion leaving him. Felt himself getting heavier. Felt like weeping aloud for the frustration of it. He cupped one of her mountains of the goddess in one hand and then found an image of Lucia's bosom in his hand filling him. Her body beneath him. And he resumed his climb up the mountain. He imagined it was her he was embracing. Imagined her arms and legs were metamorphosing into the limbs of the butterfly. Imagined the wings were spreading out beneath him. Then he felt the lightness filling him. Felt the wonderful weightlessness come upon him.

He wanted to hold the moment as long as he could. It had been so long since he had felt it again. But he continued climbing the mountain, faster and faster, floating higher and higher until he reached the pinnacle of lightness. He moaned aloud, suspended in that moment of apogee, and then felt the soft sadness of the falling start to fill him. He lay his body down upon her and felt her push back at his weight. He rolled to one side and opened his eyes. She was staring at him and had a curious look on her face. What had she felt? Did she know he had just betrayed her in his mind?

"Was that good, my love?" she asked.

He worked his jaw and then said, "Let us rest now." He closed his eyes so she would not see the sadness welling up in them. He reached out one hand and cupped her mountain of Aphrodite again. Tried to think of his wife in that farm house, but could not prevent himself thinking of Lucia lying there beside him, her soft moth wings slowly folding back into her body as she lay there, breathing softly beside him.

"Yes, let us rest and dream of happier times," his wife said.

XXXVI

"Many more of them have come overnight," said the guardsman to the Sergeant of the Guard. "I used to try to count them, but have given up."

Sergeant Cristoforo looked out over the mass of the plague people that huddled around the gates and he nodded his head in agreement. "I will inform the Captain of the Guard," he said, "And he will inform the City Council. Again." The guardsman thought that if he had not been standing in the company of the Sergeant he would say that the Council were no more likely to pay the news any heed than pigs were likely to start speaking.

"One or two of the City Councillors should come down to the wall one day and see for themselves," the guardsman said. And Sergeant Cristoforo thought that if he were not standing in the company of a common guardsman he would say that was as likely to happen as pigs were likely to start singing hymns.

"The Captain should offer them an invitation to that one day," the Sergeant agreed. And both men thought that if they were not in the company of each other, they would say that it was more likely that pigs would start pissing wine.

"Do you think there are other cities, like us, that have withstood the plague?" the guardsman asked the Sergeant.

"They say there are," he replied. "They say that there are cities across the seas that have resisted it."

"Are they but stories? What if the whole world is dying of plague but for us?"

"My wife's brother was the *capitano* of a Medici vessel," Sergeant Cristoforo said. "He told me that the cities they sailed to in the heathen lands to buy the spice from were free of the plague. They did not even know its value for warding away the disease. If they had, they would have charged ten times the price or refused to sell it, perhaps."

"Does your brother-in-law ever think of staying in one of those foreign ports?" the guardsman asked. "I have heard of ships that have sailed away and never come back."

Sergeant Cristoforo shook his head. "Those ships have been lost at sea," he said curtly. "Captains choose their crews with care and the men in the employ of the great Houses would never betray them."

"Of course," said the guardsman quickly. "I was not implying any dishonour on your brother-in-law's part. It is just a story I have heard."

Sergeant Cristoforo looked out over the hovels and the shelters that the plague people had built around the walls of the city and thought it was time they sent out a detachment to clear them away again. But there were so many of them now. What would happen if the plague people turned on the guardsmen? They would be overwhelmed quickly. They needed more men.

"What is his ship?" the guard asked.

"It was the *Windseeker*," Sergeant Cristoforo said. And then before the guardsman could ask any more, he said, "It was lost to the maelstrom recently."

"I am sorry for your loss," the guardsman said.

Sergeant Cristoforo nodded his head. Just a little. He would rather his brother-in-law had fled to a foreign port and set himself up as a merchant or a slaver or anything other than to have died just in sight of the safe harbour of the Walled City.

The two men stood there in silence for some time, staring out at the uncountable numbers of plague people there before them. The Sergeant knew that if you stood there too long you started seeing individual disfigurements, and then started seeing each figure as a man, a woman or a child. That meant it was time to go below. He would wear armour over his eyes to fortify his senses against it. He would have liked to ask the guardsman if he ever saw them like that, but it was not a question that a Sergeant of the Guard ever asked a guardsman.

"I hear stories," said the guardsman, "Of a great army of the plagued who are roaming the land like vermin, overwhelming each city they come to, be it free of plague or not."

"Just stories," said Sergeant Cristoforo.

"They say that this army is so large that when it moves across the land it is like one of the plagues of rats from the era of the ancients that moved like a giant black cloud many leagues in length."

"Just stories," said the Sergeant again.

Both men stood in silence a while longer. Then the guardsman said, "I have heard the plague will last eight years and will then leave the lands."

"I have heard that too," said the Sergeant.

"How many years now has it been?" asked the guardsman. "Five?"

"Six," said Sergeant Cristoforo.

"Two years then," said the guardsman. "We can last two more years."

"Of course we can," Sergeant Cristoforo replied. As long as the war between the great Houses did not continue that long. As long as there was no army of the plagued out there. As long as ships were able to continue trading without losing too many to the maelstrom. Then he turned to the guardsman and asked, "What do you see when you look out upon these wretches below?"

The guardsman shrugged. "I am a guard. They are the enemy trying to get into our city."

Sergeant Cristoforo thought upon that a moment. Wondered if thinking of them as the enemy made the task of standing here on the wall more bearable. "So would you attack them and drive them away?"

"I would."

"Would you put a case to the City Council that to defend our walls we must kill them?"

"No," said the guardsman, and spat over the ramparts. "No point in killing them. They are dying already. We just need to stand here and wait."

It was an interesting logic, thought the Sergeant. Then he asked, "But what happens when the number of plague people outside our walls is greater than the number of people inside the Walled City?"

"But that has already happened," said the guardsman. "That's when I gave up counting them."

XXXVII

The Nameless One had been standing outside Lucia's door, watching her through one of the spy holes for at least a quarter of a small candle's length. He wondered if the letter he had sent to Cosimo Medici had been an error. He must find out. When he finally gave a quick tap on the door and stepped inside he was surprised to see how startled she was. He had been watching her so closely, surely she had felt him there. Surely.

But perhaps she was just good at masking her feelings from him? Not all masks were made of leather, he knew. He had watched every breath she had taken and watched the way her long hair moved when she turned her head. Surely she suspected she was being watched and was showing him how beautiful she was. Some of his guests had sat on the bed with their head in their hands for the whole duration of their internment here. Others had lain on the bed and cried, or hidden under the covers. But not this young woman. She was brave. She was willing to stand up to him. He admired that. And more. Of course more.

But what did she think of him? He had to know. "How is my little bird today?" he asked her. "Do I detect a sense of sadness in you?"

She stared at him coldly. "Do I detect a little conceit in you?" she asked.

He smiled. "Perhaps it is just that the little bird wishes for a warm scented bath, or some fresh air. Anything can be arranged," he said.

"Birds do not have warm scented baths," she replied. He pulled a mock sad face as if he was going to miss a treat. "Neither do reptiles," she said, "So we can both go without."

From anybody else he would have grown angry at that insult, but he smiled again. "And what type of reptile might I be?" he asked. "A dragon?"

"A lizard," she said.

"Yes. One who can disappear into the walls, and when its tail is trapped it still escapes."

"A snake then," she said.

"A silent foe that lies in wait and strikes with deadly accuracy."

"A scorpion," she said.

"An armoured warrior that fears nobody."

She stopped. "You are not a reptile," she said. "You are a rodent."

"But what type? A rat that lives beneath the city and emerges when it pleases? A mouse, that can move into a kitchen and steal cheese so stealthily that it is never seen nor heard?"

She clamped her mouth shut, refusing to play any more of his games, and the Nameless One shrugged and walked along to one of the few pictures on the wall and moved it a little one, way and then a little the other, as if it had been crooked and he needed to straighten it. Then he turned back and asked, "And what kind of bird are you, my dear?" But she would not answer.

"I will tell you," he said. "You are a most rare bird. Probably there is no other like it in the world. One of the most beautiful birds even held in captivity. Undoubtedly the bird has a beautiful song too, but this is the sad thing about this bird. When it is in captivity it will not sing. It deprives all who would capture it and hear its beautiful song the pleasure of its music."

Lucia narrowed her eyes and stared closely at him. "But I think the bird just needs to realise that it is not in captivity," he said. "The bird needs to realise that it has freedom, but within the limits of a new master."

"This bird will sing for no master," Lucia said. "This bird only sings when it finds dead reptiles and rodents to feast on."

That was too far. The Nameless One tried to control his temper but felt his face reddening. He clenched his fists by his sides, working his jaw a moment, and asked carefully, "Do you know what I am offering you?"

"No," she said. "I do not."

The Nameless One came and sat down on the bed beside her. She moved away a little. "I am a very lonely man," he said. "I'd give all my wealth for a chance to live in solitude with a song bird to keep me company."

"Then buy one in the markets," she said.

He shook his head a little and then reached up and touched her hair. "Think again," he said. "Do you know what I am offering you?"

"I don't care," she said.

He reached for her hand, but as soon as he touched her she pulled it back, as if bitten, and then slapped him on the face. He made no move to stop her. Let her hand connect with his jaw and he even closed his eyes a moment as if wanting to prolong the feeling of her touch.

But then he stood slowly and looked down at her, feeling the heat from the blow, feeling the heat of his anger filling him again. He reached out quickly and did grab her hair, pulling her a little off the bed. Then he saw the angry plague scars on her neck there and let go quickly. He stood up and remained completely still for a long time, the sound of their breathing suddenly loud in the room. He was aware that she was now watching him as he had watched her. Carefully monitoring his every small move to see what he would do next.

"You have made me very angry," he said eventually, in as calm a voice as he could manage. "I am at times a violent man and you do not want to make me angry. You would do much better to make me happy. I am a very generous man when I am happy."

"I don't care," she said again, though much softer this time.

"Do you know what would make me the most happy of men?" he asked. Perhaps she guessed, but she did not say so. "It would make me the most happy of men if you would ride away into the hills with me and sing your bird songs to me." And I could pretend I was twenty years younger once more, he thought. I could pretend life was other than it is. Even if for only a short time.

"I do not wish to leave the city," she said softly. "I do not wish to sing for you."

"Consider it carefully," he said. "And don't respond so readily with haste and hot words. The city is falling into a war that will end badly for all involved and we may be the only two who can hope to hear a bird's song rather than the drums of war." When she said nothing still, he added, "Or the drums of death!" Then he turned and stepped back out the door. Returned once more to the peep holes to see how she would react. Would she drop her head to her hands now, or throw herself onto the bed, or just sit there and glare around the room, hoping to defiantly meet his eyes somewhere?

XXXVIII

The City Councillors had never felt more like impotent old men. Well, there was that one time of the mid-summer's feast when the dancing girls had been arranged, but they had collectively vowed never to talk of that again. Apart from that evening, they had never felt more like impotent old men.

There had been a time when their word was not just law, but it was a law that was trusted and followed by the citizens of the Walled City. But that had not been for some time. The only power and authority they now held was at the Medici and Lorraines' bequest. They had less troops in the City Guard than the two families had. They had less money in their coffers than the two families had. And they held less sway over the citizens of the city than the two families had.

It would have been good to point the blame at some city statute or some individual, and say, "That is what caused this. But we can turn it around." But in truth they were all guilty of trading away their powers. For small favours. For gems. For spice wine. For a private dinner with the Duke or the Medici. For a pageant or a portrait or a fresco. All small vanities really.

The current Head Councillor, an elderly man called Signor Pacciani, who had particularly embarrassed himself on the night of the dancing girls, waved the slip of paper in his hand at his fellow councillors as if it were a large sword, and said, to bring them to order, "The City Guard reports the number of plague people at the gates has increased again. We must make a decision as to what is to be done."

The men around the table looked at him, waiting for him to make a suggestion. It was his turn in the chair, after all, so all responsibility for failure should be his. The City Council rotated leadership every two months, which was ideal in better times because it allowed no one to scheme too much or demonstrate too much corruption, and it also meant that almost no decision was in the hands of a single leader as the implementation of any decision generally took more than two months. But since the plague people had arrived it seemed a good excuse for the Head Councillors never to have to make a hard decision – just wait out their turn and pass the problems to the next Head Councillor.

"What do you propose?" the man to his left, Signor Narducci, asked. When he was Head Councillor, Narducci had overseen a failed scheme to bribe the plague people to leave the city walls.

"Well perhaps we should turn the City Guard on them," the Head Councillor said.

The men around the table made as if they were considering this, but it had already been discussed at previous meetings and they knew the idea would not work, for if the plague people resisted and they lost guardsmen they would be even more powerless to the two families than they were now. "If only we could have the two families fighting the plague people instead of amongst themselves," a man to his right, Signor Fabbri, said.

Everyone around the table looked across at him and frowned. It was not his turn in the Head Councillor's chair for another two months and he had no right to be making such suggestions before his turn. "Yes," said the Head Councillor. "That would be a wonderful thing to see indeed, as would seeing the city rise up into the sky and float away to another place where there were no plague people."

"But this city is the only place in the known world where there are no plague people," said Narducci.

"The problem is not one of taking the city to a new place, it is one of *sending* the plague people to a new place," said another man, Signor Spezi, further around the table. "Perhaps we can put them on ships and take them over the seas?" The Council frowned at him too. He would not be Head Councillor for at least six more months. "We could leave them in the ports where we trade for the spices," he said.

"Except that we have no ships sailing due to the war between the families," said the Head Councillor. He looked across the Council Secretary to make sure that his comment was being recorded. He smiled and turned back to the Council. "It seems to me that any solution is going to be based around finding a way to stop this escalating war between the families."

"What do you propose?" the man to his left, Narducci, asked once more. The Head Councillor stammered a little and said, "Well. Obviously we just need to convince them to make peace." He watched the other members of Council snigger into their beards and turned to the Council Secretary and made a small hand signal to indicate that his response should not be recorded. "What I mean is that we need to invite the members of the families to a Council meeting where we can discuss in confidence issues of the war, and what to do about the increase in plague people and decrease in the effectiveness of the spice."

"Do you suggest we hand over all our remaining power to them?" Narducci asked. The Head Councillor made the small hand signal to the secretary again and said, "Of course not. I am suggesting that we let them know of their responsibilities to the city. We let them know that we alone cannot solve the pressing problems before us. We let them know that we need their cooperation to make the city and its citizens safe."

The Council considered this for a time and nodded into their beards at the possibility of the idea, until Narducci again asked, "How do you propose to convince them it is in their interests to attend such a meeting?"

"A war is not good for trade," the Head Councillor said, glaring at the man. "Any fool can see that."

"But winning such a war would be outstandingly good for trade," Narducci replied. "And which of the two families would not gamble on a chance to gain a monopoly – especially if they believe they can win it? Surely any fool can see that!"

The City Council leader frowned and resolved to save up some really difficult challenges to throw to Signor Narducci when it was his turn in the Head Councillor's chair. Pacciani wanted to cry at the man, "Then what should we do?" but it was his turn to be the one to propose what to do. He folded his arms and looked down the table, hoping some divine inspiration would occur. Instead a man at his side tugged at his sleeve. He looked at him, peeved, and saw he held out a document to him. He sighed. It would be another note from the City Guard informing him that the numbers of plague people had doubled overnight. Or it would a message from the apothecaries that the spice wine had lost its effectiveness entirely and plague had broken out in the city. Or it would be a message about an uprising of those in the catacombs, which was another topic that the Council had made a collective vow never to mention.

He opened the document and read it. Then again. Then he stood and held it over his head. Not like a sword. Like a battle axe. An axe wielded by a Head Councillor who was finally able to stop the war between the families and able to restore stability to the city and power to the Council. "I have a proposal," he said aloud. "One I think you will all find to our benefit."

XXXIX

Cosimo tried another bite of the quail on his plate, but it tasted bitter and he spat it back out. Even the wine tasted like vinegar to him. They had not had quail for a long time and he imagined it had been carried back alive on one of his ships, when they were still getting into the harbour, at great cost. He should remember not to have it thrown to the dogs then. He sat in the dining room alone, waiting for his mother to join him. He had already ordered the servants from the room so that none of them could see the look of disappointment and defeat on his features. All because of a single-line message.

He had been sitting at his meal planning his next stage of attack on the Lorraines, confident that he had the upper hand. He had laid out salt shakers and glasses and cutlery around the table to represent the Walled City, and he was manoeuvring the pieces around to how he would isolate the Lorraines and force them into fewer and fewer towers and then have them submit to him entirely, along with their new scientific discoveries. The giant eagle and the whales that followed their commands and whatever other inventions that man Leonardo had devised for them.

Several of his scribes had been searching the city for sketches that Leonardo had done, certain that he was leaving clues in them that they could decipher and so understand what he was planning. He had visited them in one of his libraries and seen them all gathered around a table with six or seven sketches laid out before them. They were scanning the backgrounds for details that were clues. They believed the man hid his secrets in his sketches and paintings. Secret visual codes that only the most astute mind would be able to decipher. His way of leaving his secrets for the future, rather than recording them in books where they could easily be accessed by his enemies. This way, only the most intelligent and deserving would ever know them.

He wondered if Leonardo was proving as difficult for the Lorraines as Galileo was proving for him, refusing to create weapons of war and destruction. What good was science if you did not use it to achieve your aims, he thought. What good were paintings and sketches if they did not share their meaning? Painting the faces of the nobility of the Walled City onto the faces of the ancients in the paintings and frescos was easy enough, and having different meanings in visual symbols – such as whether a horse's feet were all on the ground or one was in the air telling you whether the rider in the portrait had died in battle or not – these were all well understood by most people, but hiding secret information in a picture seemed arcane. And when he asked the scribes to tell him what they had discovered, and then listened to how they interpreted the faint and weak lines they found as having particular meanings, or the way a hill stood in relation to a river, or the turn of a finger on a hand, he began to suspect they were so desperately looking for secrets that they were creating them themselves.

He had looked at the sketches and paintings and had seen hills and rivers and hands, yes, but no hidden codes in them. But, he wondered, if he'd spent all week in that room with the scribes, might he not start to see them too? As one who spent hours studying a dining table battleground might start to see victory over an opponent where in fact there was none. He sighed heavily and wished Giuliano were able to advise him. He looked down at the single-line message in front of him once more. It simply read: "The bird is no longer in hand."

That was a secret code that he did understand and needed no interpretation or puzzling over by his scribes to find a deeper meaning. Lucia had somehow escaped from the Nameless One. And that changed everything. Lucia had been his bargaining chip. With her in his grasp he could have manipulated the Lorraines into giving him concessions. They would not have turned over control of their wealth to him all at once, of course, but he knew that if he made small demands, one at a time, it was likely that he would have achieved what he wanted.

First he would have had their soldiers refused any access to the streets of the city. Then he would have had restrictions placed on their ships so that only his had unimpeded access to the city's port. Then he would

have had the Lorraines publicly admit that they had
been the ones who had assassinated Giuliano, and that
they were willing to make reparations to him. They
would have given up spice concessions. Handed over
some of their ships to him. Little by little he would have
whittled away their wealth and power until they'd
stood before him, pleading for what little they had left.

And if at any point they'd refused, he would tell
them that Lucia had fallen ill, and he worried for her
life, or that she had expressed interest in marrying
some old and fat dung collector. They would squirm,
the Duke and that witch of a wife of his, but they
would comply. But only as long as he held Lucia.

He cursed the Nameless One for allowing her to
escape and he wondered whether she had already
returned to the safety of her family's house and was
telling them what had happened to her. Or was she
somewhere in the city in hiding? Perhaps he should
have his men out searching for her?

The Nameless One should have given him more
information. He didn't even know where the man
was to contact him, or admonish him or punish him.
Then he wondered if he might somehow be in the
employ of the Lorraines, playing one off against the
other? Taking Medici coin to kidnap the girl and then
taking Lorraine coin to return her? He could trust no
one! His advisers and scribes were fools; Galileo was
stubborn; and sell-swords and mercenaries, like the
Nameless One, were only obedient to gold. He pushed
his meal away and stood. Where was his mother? He
needed someone he could trust to talk to about this.
The only person in the world he trusted now.

He walked around the table putting the implements on the table back into their places. He did not want her to come and find him at play, as if he were still a small boy, spreading out his toy soldiers and forts across the floor of his bed chamber. He wanted to throw the message from the Nameless One into the fire, but thought it best to show to his mother first. He hoped she was in a clear mind today. He could do with some good counsel, as long as she didn't tell him to sit down and eat his meal, as she'd used to repeatedly when he was a boy. He should have one of the servants take his meal away, so he didn't have to explain to her that the message he had received had made everything sweet suddenly taste bitter to him. And he imagined that for the Duke and Duchess of Lorraine, who would soon have their daughter back, everything that had recently tasted bitter would suddenly taste very sweet once more.

He turned around suddenly as his mother came into the room, one of her nurses supporting her by the arm. "Mother," he said and held out his arms to her. She looked at him and then at the table and said in a chiding tone, "Cosimo! You're a naughty boy. You shouldn't leave the table until you've finished your meal."

XL

"Stop!" said Lorenzo. "No more."

The Shadow Master stopped and looked back at him. "What is it?" he asked.

"We are going deeper and deeper into the Earth and further and further from the world above where we should be to save Lucia from the dangers you say she is in." He had been trying to estimate how long they had been down here under the city, and thought it must have been after dark already when they came across the cavern of the madmen mass, yet still they went on.

"Sometimes the most direct path is a circuitous one," the Shadow Master replied.

"No," said Lorenzo. "No more dark tunnels. No more abhorrent creatures and madmen. How will any of this help her?"

"All will be revealed," the stranger said. And now Lorenzo felt anger rising in him. "No," he said again. He did not have a good feeling about what lay ahead of them. "Not one step further until you answer some questions." And Lorenzo pulled out the copper glove and slipped it onto his hand, feeling it constrict and merge with his skin. He bunched his fingers into a fist and held it up to show the stranger.

The man turned fully back to look at Lorenzo. "Ah," he said, ignoring the gloved fist entirely. "The point of emotional overpowerment. That is to be expected."

"What do you mean?" Lorenzo demanded, shaking his fist at him. But the stranger reached out a hand and wrapped it around the glove and Lorenzo felt it somehow coming loose from his hand. "What are you doing?" he asked and pulled back, but the glove came off and the stranger put it into his clothing somewhere. "When the senses take in so much that is new and unknown," he said to Lorenzo, "sometimes the only reaction possible is to fall back upon an emotion that is easily conjured. Anger. Rejection. Much better than denial at least."

Lorenzo blinked and shook his head. "You mock me. I follow you willingly down into this pit of darkness and misery and you refuse to tell me why. Refuse to tell me where we are going. Thrust shocking scene upon shocking scene in front of me and expect me to just take it in like a school boy might take in his lessons, unquestioning."

"That is a good analogy," the man replied, with a wry smile. "A school boy learning something he had never dreamed of, his mind needing to expand to take in a new understanding of the world that at first seems too strange to comprehend."

"Enough of riddles and secrets," said Lorenzo. "I only have one thing of interest. I want to save Lucia."

"And I want you to save civilisation as well," said the stranger.

"It is not my concern," said Lorenzo. "Lucia is my only concern."

"Well shall see," the stranger replied and turned away from him.

"Stop," said Lorenzo and grabbed at him, his hand feeling once more the fine armour under his tunic.

"Yes?" he asked, turning back once more. Then, "Why don't you ask the question you most want to ask?"

Lorenzo barley hesitated. "Who are you?" he asked.

"Yes. That is the one," he said. Then, almost mockingly, "But why don't you tell me who it is that you think I am."

"You are an enigma," Lorenzo said.

"A poor answer," he replied.

"I think you are dangerous," Lorenzo said.

"Only to my enemies," he replied.

"I think you are not of our city."

"And yet I am here now."

"I am not sure I can trust you."

"And why not?"

"You are the Shadow Master," said Lorenzo bitterly. "You play in the realm of secrets and shadows."

"Yes," he said. "That is all true. So enough of secrets and shadows, as you say. Now it is time to be the master of illumination and understanding." And he turned something on the small torch in his hand and it glowed brightly, lighting up the entire chamber around them. Lorenzo felt his mouth drop open. Felt his breath fade out of him like a candle going out. He turned his head this way and that, trying to take it all in. He had been preparing himself for something more shocking than that which he had so far witnessed. But this! Nothing could have prepared him for this!

"With this," said the Shadow Master, "You alone have the means to save your loved one and you shall save your city and shall save your civilisation. For this is the secret of the ancients."

XLI

Cosimo Medici looked back across the long table to the Duke and saw his eyes wandering over the many maps on the walls. Typical, he thought, not focussing on where the danger was before him. Or was it an act to seem casual about admitting his defeat. For Cosimo was convinced the Duke had requested this meeting in order to admit defeat to him. Which meant Lucia had not yet returned home, and he could truthfully swear he did not have her in captivity. He smiled and tried to catch the Duchess' eye. He would particularly enjoy humiliating her.

The Head Councillor, Signor Pacciani, seated at the top of the table, rapped the table-top and called the meeting to attention. "Firstly, in accordance with the agreement for this meeting we will turn the locks on the doors so that there is no possibility of outside forces entering. Are all agreed to this?"

Cosimo shrugged as if he didn't care. The Duke looked to his wife and then nodded. The city guardsman at the door proceeded to lock it. Cosimo did a quick count of those in the room. Four bearded

Medicis, four moustached Lorraines and ten City Councillors and city guardsmen. The letter had been very specific about this, and as long as the Lorraines abided by these terms, he felt they were fair. This meeting was a surrender, after all, but they had to maintain some illusion of dignity. He was generous enough to accept that.

He then looked across to the large mechanical model of the world in the corner of the room. It was an intriguing piece of machinery, and looked like something Galileo might have built, with bright bronze cogged wheels within cogged wheels within cogged wheels. He imaged the inner wheels would turn more rapidly as they were smaller and the larger outer wheels would turn slowly, rotating the whole globe at the pace of one rotation a day. It was probably fanciful to imagine that the planet was a giant machine, run on cogs within cogs, but it was also not impossible to believe.

He looked across the table and saw the Duke was now staring at the mechanical globe too. He probably coveted it as much as Cosimo did. He frowned. He could imagine them coming to blows over it. The Duke's reach was probably larger than his own, but Cosimo's grasp would be stronger, and he'd wrestle the man's arms from the globe. The Duke's witch of a wife would join in undoubtedly, trying to restrain him while her husband took control of the world. Then their advisers and guardsmen would join in, with the City Council calling vainly for order, and then they would be spilling blood. But that would not do. They had all just taken a vow that no blood would be spilled in this room. That was one of the conditions for the meeting.

Cosimo turned his attention back to the table. He would ask one of the councillors to demonstrate how the globe worked before they left the Council chamber. If the meeting went well, that was.

The Duke also turned his attention away from the globe of the world. He was thinking that the logical thing to do would be take the many maps of the world off the walls and make a skin for the globe showing how all the parts fitted together. No need to see all the cogs beneath. More important to see the overall shape of the continents. The ornate wooden walls of the chamber were covered in closely-fitting golden frames, each with a map of a different part of the world, portrayed in golden continents on dark blue seas. He suspected that some of the maps were actually more imaginative than real, for so much of the world was unknown, but they were said to be based on surviving texts of the ancients and it was believed the ancients had mapped the entire world. He shrugged. That was a question for another day. They were here to address a peace accord and ensure Lucia's freedom. He placed a hand on his wife's and gave it a small squeeze. He knew they had the upper hand today, otherwise Cosimo Medici would never have requested this urgent midnight meeting. His wife said it was not prudent to agree at such short notice, but the Duke's curiosity was aroused.

The Duke looked across at Cosimo and met him eye to eye. He wanted to see him blink and turn away. Wanted to see his indecision or lack of courage or whatever it was that had led him to propose this peace meeting. He had written that he wanted to return things to the state they had been before. They both knew that meant a submission, but he had to save some face. The Duke would allow him that, even though his wife wanted to crush him and humiliate him. They had to ensure Lucia's safety, after all. There would be time to crush and humiliate him later. And more.

The Head Councillor then looked to both families and said, "Next let me acknowledge that you have both agreed to place your palms open on the table, regardless of what decision the Council makes as to how you should bend your knee and open your purse to the City."

Cosimo and the Duke both broke their gaze at the same time and stared at the councillor. "What is he talking about?" the Duchess whispered into her husband's ear. He shook his head a little. "And we are pleased that you have agreed to have your armies lay down their swords and axes, and allow the City Guard to be the only men thus seen on the streets once more," Signor Pacciani added.

The Duchess put her hand on her husband's arm, giving him a warning squeeze. He looked back at Cosimo Medici, but he was staring at the councillor still, a look of rage growing upon his face as his steward leaned across to whisper something in his ear.

"The Council have discussed this matter and feel the bend of the knee and the depth of the open purse must be extreme to deter such follies in the future," Signor Pacciani said. "And to reassert the primacy of the Council as that which governs the order of how letters are placed to spell out peace throughout the city."

Cosimo Medici now looked across at the Duke. He was not going to remain here and be made a fool of for the Lorraine's pleasure. This was too much! They must have their daughter back safely and had come upon this ploy as a way of mocking him. He would make them pay for this insolence. But the Duke just looked back at him and said, "Do you mock us?"

"You mock yourself through this thin excuse of theatre," said Cosimo.

The Head Councillor looked up. He was following a closely written speech and kept one finger on the line he had been at so as to return to it. But looking at the two angry men before him, he had a sudden feeling that he was not going to get to read any more.

"Me?" asked the Duke. "You are the one who wrote to me pleading for a meeting."

"No," said Cosimo. "You wrote to me!" And his steward cast a letter onto the table. The Duke could see the Lorraine coat of arms on the top of it. The Duke's wife snatched it up. "A clever forgery!" she declared, and snapped her fingers. Their steward lay down another letter with the six balls of the Medici coat of arms on it. The Head Councillor was having trouble keeping up with what was happening. "But you wrote a joint letter to the City Council," he said. "You asked us to moderate this meeting. Said you desired peace." And he wondered if he had misunderstood some of the complex metaphors in the letter.

The Duke's wife whispered one word into his ear. "Enigma!" Their personal code word for a trap. He looked around the room but nobody was making a hostile move against them. The city guardsmen seemed as confused as anyone. Then one of the lesser councillors, a man named Sforza, with eyes that never seemed to be both staring in the same direction, stood up and slowly walked across to the large mechanical globe of the world. He reached his hand inside it and turned something with a loud mechanical click.

Then the many framed maps on the walls inexplicably swung open on hinges. Everyone in the room except Signor Sforza stared in surprise as men in hessian hoods leapt out of the spaces behind them. Each was armed with a dagger and they fell upon the city guards first, stabbing them viciously and easily overpowering them by their superior numbers and the element of surprise. Then they lifted their bloodied daggers and advanced on those seated at the table.

XLII

The Nameless One had dreamt of death and it filled him with fear. He paced up and down the corridor outside Lucia's room, as if it was his own prison, trying to decide what to do. In the dream he had put a pillow over his wife's face and smothered her, and then ridden away into the hills with Lucia to live a new life with her where there was no plague or wasting diseases or ageing. He had woken in a sweat and reached across to touch his wife, afraid that he had actually done it. Afraid he would find her dead.

Then he had jumped out of bed and fled to the corridor. He had to confront Lucia. Had to end this. But the closer he got to her chamber the more his resolve left him. He knew that when he was with her he would choose her. He should go and climb back into bed with his wife and wake her and tell her that he loved her. Embrace her and make love to her and not think of anybody but her.

He stood there in the hallway, halfway between his own chamber where his wife was, and Lucia's chamber, and stared into a mirror. There were three of them along the wall here. Each showed a slightly different image, depending on the flaws in the mirror work. He looked at the troubled face before him in the first mirror. It was him, but not quite fully him. He had heard of eastern scientists who had found a way to free a person's reflection from a mirror. He wished he had the knowledge of that, for he would free one of the three reflections here before him, and one of them could go back to his wife while the other went to Lucia. He moved to face the second mirror and looked at the next reflection. It was subtlely different from the first. The face distorted a little in slightly different ways. What might this reflection be like if freed? Would it be crueller? Weaker? Which should go back to his wife and which on to Lucia?

He had a sudden desire that one of his reflections might climb from the mirror now and challenge him. Tell him he could not go back to his wife, or perhaps that he could not go on to Lucia. That would make things easier. He would refuse to be told what he should do and would pit his strength against this other him. He would challenge him and refuse to be denied. That would decide the choice for him. He would finally be facing somebody just as strong as himself, who he could only beat by superior will and determination.

He looked again at the second mirror. In his mind this reflection was a little uglier than the other two. This is the man he would like to fight. There seemed a cruel twist to his lip. He would grapple with him and overpower him, throw him to the ground. Or might this other him actually defeat him? He should know the answer to that, he thought, since he had been wrestling with himself since kidnapping Lucia.

He slumped down against the wall and put his head in his hands. He was a prisoner of his own making. Whatever he chose to do now would haunt him. It was enough to make him laugh. He had murdered men and committed atrocities that had never worried him. He had taken pride in how he had killed them. He was an artist of assassination. But now he was haunted by an act of violence that he had not even committed.

A more superstitious man might think it some kind of retribution for his past life. He stood upright again and stared at his own face in the mirror once more. He needed to steel himself for a difficult decision. He needed to be strong and brave, but he felt that he could never be braver than either his wife or Lucia. And that shamed him. He looked at a weak ageing man in the mirror who was playing at still being young. Who dreamed fanciful dreams that turned around and became nightmares.

He stepped to the third mirror and looked at that reflection. What did he see in that face? He fancied he saw a man who was somehow better than himself? That's who was needed now, he thought. Someone more able to make the right decision, and strong enough not to waver. Surely there was some science that could allow him to trade places with that reflection of himself. That would free him of the responsibility of having to do what he needed to do to free himself of this torment. He looked down at his hands again and flexed the fingers. He was still strong enough to do this.

He turned from the mirror and strode down the hallway. When he got to Lucia's chamber he allowed himself a momentary glimpse through one of the peep holes. She was still sitting up on the bed, like she had not slept at all, waiting, ready to defy him again. He clenched his fists and opened them again, striding up and down in the thin corridor. He needed to be as brave as her for this. He stepped away from the peep hole and unlocked the door, stepped into the room and walked straight across to where she sat on the bed. He grabbed her arm and lifted her to her feet. She looked closely into his face and he saw no fear there. Then he saw her lift her hand. She had a weapon in it. He recognised it. It was a spoon. The spoon he had left her. He could see she saw the mockery in his eyes and a blaze of anger filled hers and then he saw something quite amazing. The metal spoon began bending and reshaping itself, melding with her very skin and becoming a long talon.

He felt the slash across his check and he fell back, as much in surprise as to protect himself. Then she turned and thrust the metal talon into the secret door in the wall and struggled with it. He could have reached out then and grabbed her. Could have held her from behind. Forced her onto the bed. Seen what strange thing she had done to her hand. He could do anything he chose to.

But then, almost impossibly, she had the door open. He saw her disappear into the tunnels and heard the tinkle of metal falling to the ground. He looked down and saw two halves of a bent and broken spoon where she had been standing. "Go," he said in a pained voice, trying to still the frantic working of his jaw. "The little bird has her wish. You can go free."

XLIII

Lorenzo's head was spinning. Barely had the Shadow Master let him explore some of the secrets of the ancients in the large cavern, than he was pulling him towards a small chamber, telling him, "We are out of time. Come."

But Lorenzo could not. He wanted to spend hours walking around the vast machines around them, trying to understand how they worked. They were enormous. They were of a scale he had never imagined. Stone blocks and copper pipes and metal cogs were everywhere. It was like he had shrunk to the size of an insect and was walking around the insides of a vast and complicated machine. And all around them were statues of the ancients, like in the city above. But these were not mounted on pillars. They were standing about them, like people who had become petrified where they worked. What did they signify?

But the Shadow Master did not give him any more time to ponder it. He dragged him into the small chamber and Lorenzo saw there were controls of some kind on the wall in front of them. The Shadow

Master manipulated them a moment and then said, "Ready yourself."

"For what?"

"A life altering experience. And you'd better put that spring-punch glove of yours back on. You might need it.

As ever, Lorenzo didn't quite understand what he meant, but then he felt his body growing. Not like he was turning into a giant, it was more like he was stretching, becoming thinner and thinner and climbing higher and higher. "It is disconcerting the first time," said the Shadow Master. Lorenzo looked down at his hands, but they were already far, far down below him somewhere. He looked and saw the Shadow Master's face had become so thin it no longer resembled a face.

"What is happening?" he tried to say, but found his mouth and tongue were too misshapen to get the words out properly. He looked at the walls of the small chamber and tried to look to its top and bottom. The top was still there above his head but the bottom was far out of sight, way, way down there where his feet were.

"Close your eyes," said the Shadow Master. "It will help counter the disorientation. We will arrive shortly, and when we do you will need to be ready."

"For what?" Lorenzo tried to ask him again, his mouth grown longer still than it had been a moment before.

"For anything," he replied. "Expect the best but prepare for the worst."

"I don't understand," Lorenzo tried to say.

"It will all be clear in a moment," the Shadow Master told him, "as long as we have the timing right."

"And if not?" Lorenzo was starting to get control of his mouth again. That was almost distinguishable.

"Too early will be forgivable, but too late will not be." Then Lorenzo shut his eyes as he had been advised. He moved his arms and hands and they felt just normal to him, no longer stretched impossibly thin and tall. "Ready?" the Shadow Master asked.

Lorenzo opened his eyes. The chamber was normal sized again, as were they both. He felt a little giddy and disorientated. "Now your chronometer," he said. "Get it out and be ready to activate it." And then he drew his sword. It was a strange shape. Long and thin, with a slight curve and an even width along its length. Then the Shadow Master kicked at the wall in front of them. Nothing happened. "That wasn't meant to happen," he said. "Let me try that again." He moved a little to the left and kicked once more, and this time the wall swung open in front of them like a door. Lorenzo looked out in shock. The hessian-clad men from the catacombs were climbing out of holes in the walls and falling upon the people in the room before him, stabbing them brutally. Then he realised they were in the Council chambers. He knew it from the many maps on the walls and the huge model globe of the world. And then he looked closer at the people in the room. Those at the table were the councillors. And there was the Duke and Duchess of Lorraine. And Cosimo Medici as well. He shook his head a little as if it might clear it and help make sense of this all. "Now would be a very good time to activate the chronometer," the Shadow Master said and leapt out into the room. Lorenzo looked down at the device in his hands and then back at the Shadow Master, who was moving as if time had been slowed already. Lorenzo could only watch in amazement as he fiddled with suddenly clumsy fingers to activate the chronometer, forgetting to not hold it in his gloved hand. The man whirled like a demon, whipping his cape behind him so fast it cracked like a whip, and each time he spun past an assassin, the robed figure fell as if by magic. But Lorenzo could see the blood spilling on the floor from their insides or throats. The Shadow Master's sword might have looked thin but it was obviously deadly sharp, severing limbs and disembowelling men with seeming ease.

It took a moment for the attackers to realise he was amongst them, and he had killed half of them by that time. The men at the table were trying to defend themselves from attack, which only made it easier for him to whip past the assailants from behind. He saw one man raise a dagger over the Duchess of Lorraine and smile before his head flew from his shoulders. The Shadow Master's sword then whipped left, a flash of light striking down two more attackers.

One of the robed men got a lucky blow in, striking the Shadow Master with his dagger, but, seeing it coming, he actually opened his arms as if to invite it. The dagger broke on the armour beneath his clothes as if the blade was made of card and then the robed man's legs fell out from under him as the full length of the Shadow Master's blade ran through him before he could understand what had happened to his blade.

And then it was over. The attackers were all dead.
The men at the table were still in shock, looking about
them in astonishment as the Shadow Master stepped
back into the small chamber. Lorenzo stood there with
the chronometer in his hands. He had not managed
to activate it. "I'm... I'm,,, I'm sorry," he said, holding
it up between them. "No matter," the Shadow Master
said. "It was really just to measure how fast I was. Less
than ten heart beats, I'd think."

"It was... it was..." Lorenzo said.

"Amazing, wasn't it? You were amazing. No,
perhaps courageous is better."

"Me?" asked Lorenzo.

"Of course," he said. "I don't exist. Remember that.
And when you explain things, you'd better make it
good." Then, as fast as he had moved amongst the
assassins, he whipped his hood and cape off, had them
around Lorenzo's shoulders and had pushed him out
the door into the chamber. Everyone in the room
turned to stare at him. He looked down in his hands,
but the chronometer was no longer there, having been
replaced by the Shadow Master's curved, bloodied
sword. He heard the door close behind him with a click
and imagined the Shadow Master was stretching back
down to the cavern, way beneath them.

Lorenzo pushed the hood back from his head and
surveyed the carnage about him. He held up his
gloved hand to knock any guard across the room who
might try to attack him, but no one did. There were
dead and wounded men everywhere. A few of the city
guardsmen were still alive, although badly wounded,
and most of those at the table were uninjured, though

clearly shaken. They looked at him, as if unsure if he was going to attack them or not, and he dropped the sword to the floor and lowered his gloved hand and detached it, then held up his empty hands to them. The Duke was nursing a wound on his hand. The Duchess seemed untouched and his master, Cosimo Medici, was staring at him fixedly. He could see one or two of the guardsmen grabbing for their pikes and he wondered if this was going to become another one of those "that wasn't meant to happen" moments when the Duchess said, "You saved our lives. Who are you?"

"And how did you do that?" asked the Duke.

"Tell them nothing," said Cosimo Medici, suddenly recognising Lorenzo. Then he heard a banging on the outer door and one of the councillors hurried over to unlock it. Things were going to move very, very quickly now, he thought and he was saved from having to explain himself until he was back inside the Medici household. And then, he knew, however he explained himself, it would need to be very, very good indeed.

XLIV

"What are you doing?" Leonardo demanded, and Damon turned around slowly and looked at him, his eyes glaring beautifully in the candle light. He had awoken to hear a strange noise in the workshop and had come to investigate. "I am going to fly," Damon replied joyously.

"No, it is too dangerous," said Leonardo, hurrying over to the youth, who was already half-strapped into the harness.

Damon shrugged. "The affairs of the Houses are not my concerns when I am an eagle. I will fly way beyond the city, over the countryside, or up above the clouds. It is dark now and no one will see me when the sun rises."

"No, you must not," Leonardo said firmly, placing one aged hand upon the youth's forearm.

"You are not my master," Damon said.

"I think I am," Leonardo said with a harsh tone to his voice.

"You are not my master anymore," Damon amended.

Leonardo then noticed the dried-blood cross mark on the youth"s forearm. "What is this?" he asked.

"It is a mark of my faith," said Damon, pulling his arm away from the old man.

"What faith is that exactly?" asked Leonardo, cautiously. But Damon would not answer and continued fixing the harness about his body.

"Come now," said Leonardo, "enough of this. Take the harness off at once.

"You should build more of these," Damon said. "Enough for a flock of beings. I would lead them up out of the city and we would fly away over the lands to build a new world high in the mountains. Or atop the clouds. We would escape the wars and pestilence of the Earth."

"You and your master?" Leonardo asked.

"Yes," Damon said. "And his flock. They must be made to understand that they do not need to skulk under the city in the catacombs anymore. They have a glorious destiny ahead of them if they choose the shape of angels."

"Birds," said Leonardo. "You become a bird, not an angel."

"No," said Damon. "It only appears a bird to your eyes. From my eyes I know I am an angel."

Leonardo closed a fist over the strap that Damon was trying to fasten across his chest. "This is dangerous," he said to the young man, placing his other hand on his chest. "Metamorphosis is a largely unknown science. You know how it transforms your body, but you don't know what other changes it can bring."

"This is not science," said Damon. "Science is heretical. This is divine but you think it science."

"Who has told you this?" Leonardo asked.

"My master."

"If I am not your master, then isn't the Lord Duke your master?"

"He is not my master."

"Then who is?" Leonardo asked cautiously.

"You will know him when he ascends over the city like a giant angel. You will build the harness that will transform him into his rightful form."

Leonardo took his hand off Damon's chest. He now saw that the glare in the youth"s eyes that he had at first thought beautiful had a tinge of madness to it. He had been blinded by the young man's beauty and not seen what was before him.

"What has this new master promised you?" Leonardo asked.

"We will be saved the sufferings of this Earth," Damon said. "We will see this city destroyed by plague and war and we alone will escape it. The sinners will all be punished."

Leonardo tightened his grip on the harness strap and said, "You must stop this at once. You must take this harness off." But Damon jerked the strap from Leonardo's hand. "You are not well," said Leonardo. "You must come and lie down. Let me fetch some potions to calm you."

"No more potions," he said. "Angels do not need potions."

"I insist," said Leonardo, grabbling hold of the harness strap once again and attempting to undo it.

"No," shouted Damon and swung wildly at the old man. His arm and one wing struck Leonardo, sending him falling heavily to the floor. Damon did not hear his head strike the stones heavily and did not see his eyes roll back in his head, as if staring sightlessly. He continued to put on the harness as if he was alone in the chamber. He had a destiny to fulfil, to show his master and followers that they were not defeated, that they could still achieve their ascension. He only had to show them the way.

XLV

The dead bodies were laid out in rows along the floor under the framed maps of the world that they had appeared through. They had been placed on hessian mats, like the cloth their hoods had been cut from, to prevent their blood from staining the tiles beneath them. On one side of the dead men, the Duke of Lorraine stood with about two dozen moustached men at his back. On the other side, Cosimo Medici stood, with a similar number of bearded men behind him. The Head Councillor worried that at one wrong word they would all rush at each other with weapons raised.

Cosimo and the Duke walked up and down the row of men, warily looking at them. They were surprised to recognise several of the men. Ghislieri the merchant. Cervini the stone mason. Farnese the minor noble. All good men of the city.

"What madness has driven them to this?" the Duke asked. But the only man who could perhaps have told them, the councillor Sforza, lay amongst the dead, having taken poison when he was seized by the city guardsmen at the Head Councillor's orders.

Cosimo Medici shook his head in amazement at the simple but brutal way each of the dead men had been slain. "It seems a little too neat that they are all dead and we have no one for questioning." the Duke had protested, upon learning that the man who had saved them had been in the service of the Medicis.

"These men do not easily talk," Cosimo replied, thinking back to the survivor of the attack on him in the cathedral that he had tortured for information.

Looking at the parade of dead men, Cosimo or the Duke would occasionally reach out a foot to turn over an arm with a booted toe, looking for tattoos or other marks, finding the same bloodied cross-shape cut on each one's forearm.

"So, are you now satisfied that it was not the Lorraines who snuffed out your brother's candle in the cathedral?" the Duke finally asked.

"It seems I might have been, uh, a little hasty in presuming your breath was behind it," Cosimo said.

The Duke smiled, knowing the poor excuse for an apology was probably the best he was ever going to get. But Cosimo Medici went one further. "And do you also agree that it is probable that it was not the Medici who were behind the loss of your daughter?" he asked the Duke.

The Duke looked across the chamber to his wife and seemed a little pained, but then said, "Yes. I admit it also. Perhaps we too were a little hasty in making the logical presumption."

"Wait," demanded the Duchess, striding across the room and confronting Cosimo. "How did you know our daughter has gone missing?"

"Ah," said Cosimo. "Your household is a leaky bucket of whispers." The Duchess scowled at him, unconvinced. But the Head Councillor took the initiative and clapped his hands together and said, "Well that's the first step towards peace. Admitting that you don't need to be at war anymore."

"Oh, we still need to be at war," said Cosimo. "With whoever was behind this cowardly attack on us."

"Yes," agreed the Duke. "Somebody seems to have been manipulating us to attack each other. Somebody with an interest in seeing us weaken each other."

"The minor houses?" suggested Cosimo.

"The City Council?" suggested the Duke.

The Head Councillor waved his hands in the air quickly, "No, no, I assure you, the Council has no desire for the city to descend into conflict." The Duke nodded and looked to his wife with a wry grin. It took the Councillor a moment to realise that the Duke was making sport with him.

"And why have these men assumed the robes of monks?" asked Cosimo. "Do they wish to have us believe there are actually holy men behind this? Perhaps stirred up by the rantings of the High Priest?"

"We should ask the young man," said the Duke. "Where is he?"

Cosimo had tried to have Lorenzo whisked away by his men, but the Head Councillor had demanded that he be kept for questioning and the Duke had firmly agreed. The Duke had also demanded to know, "Who was that man who saved us?" And Cosimo, trying to maintain the upper hand, had said, "Just one of my minor bodyguards." He had looked closely at the

Duke's face to see if that had impressed him in any way, but he had not responded other than to say, "He is almost as accomplished as my own bodyguards."

The Councillor had the guardsmen bring Lorenzo into the chamber and he looked down at the dead men – supposedly his handiwork – and felt sick at the sight of them. They just looked so utterly dead. Not like somebody who had recently passed away in their bed looked, who might somehow awaken at a touch. These men died in pain and with blood splashed across their bodies. "Do you know who they are?" the Councillor asked him.

"Yes," said Lorenzo. "They are followers of a mad cleric."

"Who?" asked the Duke.

Lorenzo had spent some time deciding what he should tell when questioned, and what would be best left unsaid. "I don't know. He was masked. But I heard him telling these men that all followers of science are heretics and should be killed. He has assembled a small army of fanatics down in the catacombs to help him take control of the Walled City."

"You have been into the catacombs?" asked the Head Councillor warily, wringing his hands a little.

"Yes," said Lorenzo, after a pause.

"Then we must act quickly and decisively," Cosimo said. "These madmen must be rooted out and destroyed."

"It is forbidden to go into the catacombs," said the Head Councillor. "The punishment is banishment."

"And would you banish the boy here who recently saved your life?" Cosimo asked him. "Or would you issue a decree that all assassins who lurk down there are banished, and we will all shake hands and share a bottle of wine, considering our problems fit to be kicked under the table?"

The Councillor squirmed.

"We must lead an army down under the city and destroy them," Cosimo said.

"I don't think that would be wise," said the Head Councillor quickly. "They would be in their element. There are miles of tunnels. Or so I have heard."

"We must flush them out," said the Duke.

"Then let us use science," said Lorenzo.

"Explain yourself," demanded Cosimo.

"They condemn those who follow science and fear it, but Galileo and Leonardo working together could develop a means of ridding the catacombs of them without putting any more men in danger."

The Duke and Cosimo considered this and then nodded their heads. "Agreed," said the Duke. "Yes, agreed," said Cosimo. "They could flood the tunnels with sea water, drowning them all."

"That might affect the foundations of the city," said the Head Councillor.

"Then they could suck all the air out of the tunnels so that they might collapse in on themselves," said the Duke.

"Or they could develop mechanical soldiers," said Cosimo, "that would not need light nor nourishment and could go through the catacombs and slay all those they found down there."

"Or animal-men," said the Duke, "that could dig through the earth." He looked at Cosimo's amazed face and decided to say no more.

"Could not a way be found to drive just the fanatics to the surface," asked the Head Councillor, "And do no harm to, well, innocents who might be down there?"

"What innocents?" asked Cosimo.

"The Duke's daughter, for one," said the Head Councillor. "Did you not say she was in the hands of the fanatics?"

"Yes," said Cosimo, after a pause. "I imagine she must be."

XLVI

The puce priest's men came back in one and twos, licking their wounds and lamenting the loss of so many of their brothers that had fallen before the mystery attacker. The survivors, who had witnessed the slaughter and survived by choosing to stay hidden within the wall cavities rather than leap out and join in the attack, all seemed to have a different story to tell. One said there were several attackers who overwhelmed them. Another said they had walked into a trap. One said they were so weary after their long climb to the surface and up inside the council building that they had no strength in their arms to defend themselves. Another said it was all proof that the plan was ill-conceived.

The puce priest felt their anger and discontent like arrows being shot at him, and despite his first instincts to dodge them, he stood before the altar and called down to his followers, as leaders of lost causes have called for centuries, "Yes, there were several men waiting for you. Yes, they used strange weapons devised by science to overcome you. Yes, you should have prevailed. But you were betrayed! We have a traitor in our midst."

The anger and discontent immediately moved away from the priest to those about them. Each man looked at the man beside him and wondered if it might be him who had betrayed them. "Fear not," the puce priest called down. "We have a way of discovering who the traitor is, through trial by fire."

"Yes," his followers called. "Show us who the traitor is. Trial by fire."

The priest continued the theatre by beckoning to one of his acolytes with a hand signal. The man, who had already been stabbed inadvertently by the priest, stepped forward and cautiously held out a dagger in his bandaged hand. The priest gritted his teeth and made the hand signal again. "Trial by fire," he hissed at the man. The acolyte stepped back and came forward again with a candle. The priest closed his eyes a moment and tried another hand signal, then he said in a loud voice, "Bring me the bowl of flame." Another acolyte, the one with singed eyebrows, hurried forward with the bronze bowl and then filled it with oil.

The priest beckoned to the first acolyte again who brought forth the candle. He had the man light it from one of the torches and touch it to the oil. Flames leapt up like an angry spirit dancing and whirling before them. "The flames shall reveal the traitor," the puce priest said in a slow deep voice, letting the fire illuminate his face. "We shall find the traitor and burn him out and the flame will cleanse us of his infection."

"Yes," called his followers. "Show us who the traitor is." And again the priest beckoned to the acolyte with the bandaged hand. The man looked carefully to see what his master was asking him to bring to him, but it seemed he only wanted him. He stepped forward and the priest took his hand and held it tightly. "In this manner shall we discover the traitor," he called and waved his and the acolyte"s hands through the flames.

"Yes," his followers called again.

The priest repeated himself, "In this manner we shall discover the traitor." And he waved their hands through the flames again, more slowly this time. The acolyte was grinning like an idiot, enjoying being a part of the spectacle, and the high priest waved their hands through the flames a third time, slower still. This time the man's bandages caught. The priest watched the look in his eyes as he saw his stupid grin turn to horror. "The fire cannot be deceived," he called.

The acolyte now pulled his hand back and tried to beat at the flames, and the puce priest took the remains of the pitcher of oil and threw it onto the man's hand, as if helping to extinguish the flames, but they now leapt higher, running up the man's sleeve. The acolyte was now screaming and flapping his arms, fanning the flames. The priest reached up and took off his mask and said to the acolyte, "Stare upon the face of the betrayer!" Then he stood back from him, as did the other acolytes. The man stumbled forward towards his brothers, looking for assistance, as the flames spread across his rough, hooded tunic. His screams were horrific now, as the flames seared his flesh and boiled his blood inside his body.

His brothers pushed to get out of his way as he stumbled amongst them, until one of the men spat

the hated word at him. "Traitor!" The others took it
up too. Then one man plunged at the acolyte with
his sacred dagger, stabbing him in the back. Another
stabbed at his chest. Then another at his stomach. The
acolyte fell to the floor of the chamber, rolling on the
ground until he had all but extinguished the flames
and then lay still, the smouldering cloth soon damp
in his blood.

"We are cleansed," the puce priest called out to his
followers. "We shall still prevail over the sinners. And
this time nothing will stop us."

XLVII

Rats scuttled past Lucia's feet. She was no longer so afraid of the dark in the tunnels, even though it was as cold as a lonely winter's night and as black as a sullen nightmare. The rats, however, were a different matter. Especially when she stepped on one and it squealed and squirmed under her slippered foot. She expected one of them to bite her at any moment, drawing blood that would attract other rats. But she kept her head high and kept on walking. She was not going to give into anything as inconsequential as fear.

She had run from the Nameless One's place, down the tunnels, as if she knew where she was going and could make her way safely back to the family house. But of course she quickly became lost. She knew she had to find stairs that would lead her upwards, towards the surface. If she could find any exit anywhere she would emerge into the city and could then find her way home. But almost all the stairs she found went downwards. And the further down she went the darker it seemed to become.

The first rats she saw she simply jumped past. The first that seemed to challenge her she kicked defiantly out of the way. But as their frequency increased and her bravado decreased, their screams seemed to be telling her that she was in their world, they were not in hers. She moved ahead slowly, at times having to mask her mouth and nose from the unbearable stench where sewer outlets ran, and she kept going. It might have been easier to turn around and try and find her way back again, but she refused to even consider it. Moving forward was the only way to outpace her fears and get home again.

So, she was edging her way along a particularly dark section of tunnel, holding one hand out to touch the damp walls to guide herself and sliding her feet along carefully. If there were steps ahead, she did not want to tumble down them. She felt a sudden urge to curl up into a small ball and wait there until somebody found her, but stepped away from that thought. Logic told her if she just kept moving onward she would come to some place better than this. She would find some light. She would find something.

She wished she hadn't lost the spoon that had melded into her skin to become a taloned finger. It had broken when she was prying the door open and separated from her skin as mysteriously as it had merged with it. She turned her hand over and over in the dark and tried to see if it was changed or harmed in any way. Lorenzo's climbing gloves had clearly been a product of science, but how had she done the same thing with the spoon? She would have to ask Lorenzo if using the gloves had changed something in her. He would know.

She wished that she didn't have to do this on her own and that he had some ability to find her. There must be some science that he could use. Some way to hear her voice, or feel where she was. Their flesh had joined. That was something he could use. She held that idea close inside her, like it was something sealed tightly inside a small locket, giving her some secret hope.

But as soon as she had tucked the idea away she knew that she was just being fanciful. More likely she would need to find her own way out of these tunnels and would then encounter him on the streets of the Walled City. Fate would be kind to her and place Lorenzo in her path, if she could just find her way up into the city. That seemed a fair thing to wish for. A realistic thing to expect. Especially in exchange for not succumbing to the dark and dangers of the tunnels. She tried hard to recall that feeling of Lorenzo's flesh passing into hers and the warmth that had filled her. That feeling that they were on the verge of spreading a warm light out across the whole city.

And then, as if her thoughts had somehow created it, she did see a faint light ahead of her. Her heart beat a little faster. Was it a way out? Was it somehow daylight? She edged closer, seeing the outline of her hand a little clearer before her face now. Seeing the dim walls. Seeing the stones beneath her feet. Seeing the scuttling dark shadows of the rats. She gathered up her courage and gave one a sound kick. "Out of my way, ratface!" she said.

She came around a curve in the wall and found the source of the light. It was a lantern of some kind, but had no candle in it. It glowed a faint green. She reached out and took it off the wall. This was some kind of science. Perhaps something distilled from fireflies. Lorenzo would probably know.

She held the lantern up high and saw that she was at the junction of four passageways. The lantern was here to guide people. That meant one of the three passageways ahead of her would undoubtedly lead her back to the surface. She could have wept at the simple logic of that. She only had to walk on and find the next lantern and that would be the path out of here. She looked at the three passageways and chose the one on the right, asking her heart and her head to work in conjunction to guide her.

She walked ahead steadily for a short distance and found another lantern on the wall. She allowed herself a small smile. That was good. That meant she was on the right path. Then she heard faint noises ahead of her. Not rats. Something else. She slowed and listened carefully. Was it people? Was she so close to being saved?

She took a few more cautious steps. Then slowed. For she realised that in her haste there was another path that the lanterns could be leading her on. One that went deeper underground. She stood there for some moments pondering. Reason did not help her here, so she tried to feel which would be the right way. But she could equally feel and fear that the way forward was right and was wrong. She took a few more cautious steps and came to another set of stairs. These led up. That was good. They ascended about a dozen steps or so and then there was a curve in the passageway. She edged around it slowly, the noises ahead of her louder now.

She passed into a chamber that had other dim lanterns in nooks in the walls and they illuminated statues about her. But then she saw them move. She stopped and swung around, waving the lantern about. They were not statues. They were people. Chained to the walls. And the stench about her was that of humans, not rats and sewage. She gave a small shriek and the figures about her stirred as if woken from a spell. She kept turning, looking at them and looking away again. They were nightmarish people. Horribly deformed. Some had no faces. Some had no limbs. They looked to her and reached out their arms, trying to touch her. Their arms were covered in plague sores. "Help us," said one of the figures, holding a grasping hand out to her. She stepped back from his reach and as another figure grasped her by the hair, she pulled away from him and lifted her hair, revealing the plague scars. And the man in front of her, or whatever it was, began crying. "You are one of us," he said. Hearing that quite unnerved her. She stifled another shriek and ran past them.

But then she was in another chamber, infinitely worse. All around her were children, also tied to the walls, but they were half human and half animal. She could see the heads of dogs and cats and limbs of animals and birds. They turned their heads and looked at her and she could not walk on. She felt her knees buckling and had to fight not to fall.

One of the cat-faced children mewed at her, pitifully and a dog-faced child whined. She felt her breaths coming in shorter and shorter gasps. Felt panic overwhelming her, as if they had surrounded her and were going to keep her with them forever. "So pretty," said a voice to her left. She spun and saw one of the children, a young girl with the legs of a goat or something, was looking at her and her face was full of pain. "So pretty," she said again and reached out a hand towards Lucia.

She was running from the chamber now holding a hand against her mouth, tears filling her eyes, and only stopped when she stumbled and fell to her knees. It took her some moments to get back to her feet and she felt her whole body trembling. What nightmare was this? It had to be a horrific dream that she was going to wake from shortly. She would even welcome waking in the home of the Nameless One to find this was not real. But the pain in her knees from where she had fallen told her this was real. The smell in her nostrils told her. The quiver in her arms told her. All her senses told her.

And now she also knew she had come the wrong way. She needed to turn around and go back the way she had come. But she could not bring herself to pass back through those horrific chambers again. "Oh, Lorenzo, please find me," she muttered as if a prayer. "I need you. Please find me." But again, she knew she had gone too far into this netherworld to be easily found by anybody. She gathered her courage and walked on, trusting her belief that to keep moving forwards was the only way to escape this increasing horror. And then, presently, she saw another faint light ahead of her. This one flickered like a real flame. That meant people. That meant somebody was down here searching for her. It might even be Lorenzo. She opened up that small locket of hope insider her and ran towards the light.

XLVIII

Lorenzo was sitting between the Duke of Lorraine and Cosimo Medici as they planned for war. And they were asking his advice. For who else was there to turn to? They had sent for Galileo and for Leonardo and messengers came back to tell them that Leonardo had been attacked and was unconscious and Galileo was missing from his chamber and there were signs of a struggle. The madmen had undoubtedly abducted him too.

"If they fear our science so much," said Cosimo, "then that is how we will attack them"

"But if these madmen have my daughter, as you suggest, then she must be saved," demanded the Duke. "I will not risk the loss of a single hair from her head."

Cosimo rubbed his chin. "Are you prepared to strike a deal with these fanatics to have her released? That will put the power into their hands."

Lorenzo watched the way the two men worked together, neither willing to commit too much of their preferred tactics to the other, trying to find weaknesses in the other, as they supposedly cooperated. "There is always a way," said the Duke. "But we must learn more about them first."

"We do not have the luxury of time," said Cosimo. "We must act now and be decisive."

The Duke glared at him. "It is easy to demand action when you do not have the lives of any family at stake."

"Have I not already lost a dear brother to these madmen?" Cosimo asked.

"An action that you were quick to blame the House of Lorraine for."

Cosimo fought down his reply and said, "That was an error and I believe I apologised for it. But I was grief-stricken and it clouded my judgement."

"Do you imply that my judgement is also clouded because they have my daughter?"

"We must act quickly if we are to act at all."

The Duke said nothing for a moment and then Lorenzo said, "If science is their weakness, you must be willing to share your secrets."

Cosimo frowned at Lorenzo for speaking on his behalf, but then considered it and looked to the Duke. "Yes," he said. "You will have to show the boy what Leonardo was working on."

Now the Duke frowned. He asked, "And to whom in my household will you show what Galileo has been working on?"

"I will share what I learn with both of you," said Lorenzo, cutting through the increasingly hostile air about them. Cosimo Medici gave him a quick, warning glare, letting him know that he was still a Medici man, and should not presume to make such statements without his approval. "There is no other way for this to work," Lorenzo said, returning his stare.

Cosimo ground his jaw. The youngster was growing as impudent as his teacher.

But the Duke quickly said, "I agree." Cosimo ground his teeth again, and then nodded his head.

"Both Houses must put their trust in me," Lorenzo said.

"That is a big ask," said the Duke. "You are a Medici."

"In this you can consider me also a Lorraine," said Lorenzo.

The Duke scowled. "What do you mean?"

"I will save Lucia because I love her."

"You dare!" said the Duke almost rising from his seat in indignation.

"Yes, I dare," said Lorenzo softly, not meeting the Duke's eyes.

"Yes! He dares," said Cosimo, smiling at the way the youth had now unsettled the Duke. "Clearly our young man has both courage and motivation we have not anticipated."

The Duke thought on this and then nodded his head. It was true, any upstart who would dare tell him to his face that he loved his daughter had courage, and if he was infatuated with Lucia he would go out of his way to ensure she was not harmed. "A young man capable of surprising us may be just what we need to surprise these fanatics," he said at last. Then he remembered what Lucia's handmaiden had said about there being a young man in her chambers. He would have to get to the bottom of that when he had the boy alone.

"Then take him to Leonardo's chambers at once," Cosimo said, "and show him what secrets the old man was working on, and with those of Galileo he may formulate a way to quickly and easily defeat these madmen, cleanse our city of them and save your daughter."

The Duke nodded and waved a hand for one of his men to escort Lorenzo to his house. "I will not disappoint you," Lorenzo said as he went.

"The confidence of youth!" Cosimo mused, after he had gone.

"The audacity of youth!" said the Duke.

"And if he fails, are we agreed that the blame will fall solely upon his head?"

"Of course."

"And will we ready our soldiers to invade the tunnels and flush out these vermin with fire and water and steel and whatever else it takes?"

The Duke stared at Cosimo and met his defiant glance with his own. He knew what stakes were involved here. And knew he would have to answer to his wife on whatever he decided. Then finally he said, "Yes. Whatever it takes."

XLIX

Lucia followed the passage towards the light of the dim flickering flame as if it was sunlight. But as she rounded the next corner she almost ran into two men walking towards her. Her first thought was that she had been found and would be rescued, but then she saw the knife and the hard features on their faces, and the one with the flaming torch reached out and grabbed her wrist. "Got you," he said.

"You'll have some explaining to do," said the other, regarding her carefully. "What are you doing in our tunnels?"

Lucia dropped the lantern in her hand in trying to struggle free and then managed to pull her wrist free from the man's hold. "Come here," he said lunging for her, but he was slow and she was not prepared to give him a second chance. She turned and fled, trying not to stumble on the stones beneath her feet or run into one of the walls. The brightness of the flame had reduced her vision in the dark and even the sparse lanterns on the walls did not provide enough light for her flight. Twice she ran into the walls, spinning her around as she ran, only her held-up arms protecting her. She heard the men calling out to her and running after her as she found herself now seeking the darkness that she had so recently fled from.

She was running through the chamber of chimera children before she knew it and then into the second chamber, when she stumbled again. She fell sideways, but arms grabbed her before she could hit the floor. She looked up to see who had caught her, but saw the shadowy shape of a malformed head, and knew it was one of the creatures chained to the walls here.

"Let me go," she said, trying to pull herself free, but other arms had her now. Hands covered in plague sores grabbed at her clothes and she heard one rasping voice say, "You belong with us."

She slapped at the hands that were grabbing for her and then felt the chamber fill with light. The men had caught her. The pitiful souls against the walls threw up their hands to cover their faces from the heat and the light of the torch and shrank back, turning themselves towards the dark stone walls.

Lucia was free for but an instant before one of the two men grasped her, this time with two hands, forcing her arms behind her back. "No running and no screaming," he hissed into her ear. "May the plague tickle your privates," she said, in anger and frustration.

Both men laughed and then forced her to walk in front of them, leading her back the way they had come. The light of the torch showed the walls here were ancient, and in places in poor repair. There was mould, and cobwebs, across many areas, but at least she saw no rats, though she heard them ahead of her. They clearly feared the flame.

"Where are you taking me?" Lucia asked at last, turning her head towards the men behind her.

"You'll see presently, my lady," one of them said.

She wondered if they knew who she was. If they were Medici men, they would not treat her ill and would ransom her to her father. But if they were not Medici men, and were bandits or criminals of some kind, they might treat her worse if they found out. Soon they had reached another chamber. This one was filled with torches and a two dozen men, all robed in rough cloth monk's attire. She was bundled over and sat on a stone seat next to another figure. He was tied with ropes. She looked across at him and said, "I know you. You are Galileo."

"And you are the Duke's daughter," he said softly, "though I don't think it will benefit you to make that be known amongst these men."

"Who are they?" she said. "What do they want of us?"

"They only want ill of us, I fear," the old man said. "And they are madmen all."

"Silence," called a loud voice from the front of the chamber and Lucia looked up and saw the priest standing there. He had his arms spread out wide, with a dagger in one hand and candle in the other. He looked at her and then looked to Galileo. "The trial will now begin," he said.

L

The Nameless One's wife awoke at the touch of his soft kiss and looked up to see him standing there holding a pillow over here. "What is it my love?" she asked.

"Lift your head," he said, and then slipped the pillow under her neck. "That will be more comfortable for you."

"You are so good to me," she said. Then, "Your face. You have a cut on it."

He gave her a small smile and turned he head away from her. "Just a scratch. Nothing to be concerned about."

"Why are you still dressed?" she then asked him.

"I must go out for some time," he said.

"Oh no," his wife said. "Not now. Stay with me, please."

"I wish I could," he said. "But I have some urgent business."

"Always so many things to do," she sighed. "Can it not wait for another day?"

"There is a wrong I must right," he said, placing one hand on her head and stroking her forehead.

"But there is so much that is wrong with the world," she said. "You cannot right it all."

"That's true," he said. "But I can at least right the wrongs that I have done."

Now she smiled. "What wrongs have you ever done?" she asked.

"Aha," he said. "There should be some mysteries left in a marriage."

She held out her hand and took his both in hers. "Surely there are very few left to us after all our years together," she said. He nodded his head. "Yes. Very few. But I have one for you before I go."

"What?" she asked.

"A surprise," he said. "A present."

She sat up a little and he removed one hand to withdraw a small box from inside his jacket. She took it and turned it over and then opened it. "What is it?" she asked, lifting out a small brass object of cogs and wheels.

"Let me show you," he said. He took out a small brass key and wound the device, and the wheels and gears clicked and turned and the object rose and changed, rising into the shape of a bird once more. His wife looked at it in amazement as it bobbed its head and opened its beak and chirped. "It is like magic."

"Yes," he said. "Like magic." Then he pressed the key into her hand.

"Will you be gone long?" she asked.

"Not so long," he said. "I will have one of the servants prepare a sleeping potion for you and when you awake I should be back again."

She patted his hand. "You are so good to me." He said nothing and stared into his wife's face until he couldn't bear it any longer and then said, "I wish I had been better." Then he stood up and was gone, filled with the unshakeable belief that doing this one good thing would somehow make up for everything that he had done in his life in the service of wealthy houses. And that this one act of independence would allow a foolish old man some peace in his last years.

LI

Lucia understood that Galileo was fighting for his life, and yet he acted as calm and collected as if he were talking to students or friends. The puce priest had allowed the ropes binding him to be unbound so that he could stand and address them all, outlining his defence. If he had been a soldier they might have given him a dining knife and then asked him to defend himself against a dozen men armed with swords. Or if he had been a younger man they might have demanded that he engage in a tug-of-war against ten men. For she could see that the men in hessian hoods and robes had effectively blocked up their ears against his logic.

Galileo had begun by asking the priest for a clear outline of the charges against him, and when told that it was heresy for practising science he nodded his head slowly and then said, "I would like to respond to these charges in the form of a conversation between two friends. One of them, let us call him Salviatti, is interested in understanding the nature of the world around him. The other, let us call him Simplicio, has learned everything he knows of the world from the books he has in his library." Galileo turned around to ensure everyone in the chamber could hear him. "The two friends are discussing the forces of nature, floods and maelstroms and storms, and find they have very different explanations for their existence. Simplicio states that according to his texts these acts of nature are caused by the Devil, whose drive in life is to make the lives of mankind miserable. Salviatti, however, states that he believes that such events are caused by the gods of the ancients, as a means of testing mankind. Now, it is apparent that both explanations cannot be true, so we have to find the one that is most true. Do you accept this?"

He looked around at the men about him again. The puce priest stood at the altar with his arms crossed. He considered what Galileo had said and then nodded his head for him to continue. "So, how do we determine which of the two friends has the truth of it? We could attempt to make observations to help us, but they would probably not be very illuminating and for every text we found that supports one theory, we might find another that supports the other, correct?"

Nobody said anything. Lucia looked around at the stony faces about them and felt he might as well be addressing the rocks themselves.

"But what if there was a third possibility?" Galileo said. "Not that neither was right, but rather what if both statements were able to be true at once? What if there existed a state whereby one reality could exist and another reality could exist with it?"

Lucia watched the priest shift his feet uncomfortably. "What if we could find a way of allowing these two truths to exist together? Would that not provide both a means of preventing the conflict between the two friends, and also a means of finding harmony in many conflicts that exist between people?"

He waved his arms around him, as if producing an object into his hand, and then said, "Imagine a candle, like the one your priest holds. We understand that there is one way to light it to illuminate a room. But if we change the way we think about it and turn the candle sideways we can light it at two different ends. It is still the same candle, but the light it gives out is suddenly twice as bright and will change the way it lights up a room, allowing us to see more clearly, while casting two shadows." Lucia saw some of the men in the room frowning at the idea.

"And if we agree that such a possibility was a beneficial thing to seek, we could also imagine that there might be a way of similarly allowing the conflicting realities we see before us to coexist. And if we accept that, we should also accept that those doctrines or dogmas we have adopted, and those new realities that science allows, should be able to coexist in harmony too?"

Lucia had been long told by her father that Galileo was an evil scheming man of cunning genius, with no moral qualms, and yet she found the man both humble and eloquent and felt that amongst any other audience they would surely be moved to at least see some point in his arguments.

"For whatever knowledge we have gained of the world is only gained because we have been given the ability to gain it. How can science be heresy if it discovered through our God-given abilities to discover it? How can the existence of different understandings be wrong if we agree that it is good if both Simplicio and Salviatti agree with each other, and do not have to go to war over their different beliefs?"

Then he turned to the puce priest and said, "Your beliefs and mine can coexist with each other, and I believe that accepting this fact is the first step towards restoring the harmony to our world that will allow us to overcome the pestilence that ravages the land. Would you abandon that possibility?"

Lucia felt she should clap her hands in support of the old man, but she watched the priest's face carefully to see his reaction. She was unsure what these crazed people were going to do with her, but was certain her fate was linked to that of Galileo. She watched the priest carefully scrutinising the faces of his followers, trying to see if Galileo's words had swayed any of them. Then he turned to Galileo and said, "Your words are dangerous tools that you use to enslave those with lesser conviction than ourselves. But they only serve to condemn you as a heretic."

"Who are you to condemn me?" Galileo demanded, and the puce priest smiled and reached up and removed his mask. Galileo gasped in surprise to see his own face reflected back at him.

"I am you," the priest said. "And through your own words, you have admitted to practising science and so condemn yourself. You shall now proceed to the second trial. Trial by fire!" He made a gesture with his hand and the acolyte with the singed eyebrows once more brought forth the bronze bowl and the oil.

LII

The army of the plagued roamed across the countryside like a horde of locusts, following stories of a city of plenty, where there was no contagion, and where fine wines and foods could still be found. Where the women were unblemished and the men weak from good living.

They army had begun as a large group of vandals and outlaws, stealing and eating what they could and burning what they could not. It left its dead and dying as it went, but attracted new recruits. Lone individuals or bandit bands that were pulled along by the army's growing momentum. It grew so big it could never stay in one place for more than a few days, ravaging what crops and livestock were to be had, acting like a contagion itself, burning property and infecting the fields and forests, leaving behind pustules of festering and burned out ruins. And the infected corpses of those too weak to keep moving.

The plague army had no leader, and anyone who tried to take command of it was either supplanted by the plague or by the army itself, and crushed underfoot, so it moved like a headless serpent, thrashing sightlessly about and refusing to die. Spilling dark poison as it went. Writhing this way and that.

But it always followed the stories of the city of plenty where there was no plague. It ingested these stories, growing them until they became mythic in proportion. Rivers of wine, and warehouses of grain, and wagon loads of pheasants and ducks and quail, and beautiful women and unarmed men in a lightly defended city – just to the east, or a few leagues to the west, or perhaps to the south or north.

The plague army might have destroyed itself eventually, disintegrating back into smaller bands, riven by infighting and hunger, as it moved back across countryside it had already ravaged. But then they saw the angel in the sky. It was just like in the stories of the ancients, the beautiful, white-winged creature guiding them onwards like a bright star in the night. Leading them up through the pass in the mountains and over any obstacles placed there in their way, towards the Walled City.

LIII

Lucia watched in horror as the acolytes held Galileo fast and the priest gripped his hand, waving it back and forward slowly over the flames. Galileo's eyes were like a frightened horse, and he stared into the flames as if transfixed. But neither man was showing any pain. Yet.

The men around her pressed closer and Lucia wondered if she could slip away. Wondered how far she might get. Wondered if it was completely unreasonable to expect a miracle still at this moment. Now she saw the look of pain on Galileo's face. The priest looked pleased as Galileo struggled harder. She wished she somehow had the power to stop this. To bring the roof of this cavern down upon these madmen. She willed it to happen and held out her palm towards the priest at the altar as if the strange power that had allowed her to meld with metals would help her now. And she saw, to her surprise, the ceiling behind the altar start to crumble. She willed it harder. Pushed her palm as if there might be some force coming from it. Dirt and stones started raining down upon the acolytes.

And then something completely and unreasonably miraculous *did* happen. The priest and the acolytes fell back from the rubble as a giant creature emerged into the chamber. Two huge, dark eyes scanned around as Lucia wondered what type of monster she had summoned. It pushed its way fully into the chamber with two large claws and then she recognised it for what it was – a mole. A giant mole.

The acolytes ran in terror and confusion, and only the priest stayed his ground, pulling Galileo in front of him to protect himself. The other followers were in a panic, not sure whether to attack the monster or run from it. A few of the bravest ran at it with daggers, but its huge claws cut open their stomachs before they could stab it.

"Burn it," their high priest called above the noise. "Burn the abomination." One of the braver acolytes grasped a torch and ran at the creature. The mole's hair caught alight and then others started seizing torches and threw them at it too. "Drive it back to hell where it came from," the priest called. Soon it was ablaze and thrashing about wildly, but, instead of retreating, the giant mole suddenly stood on its rear feet and started shedding its skin, like a snake might. Lucia stared in wonder as the mole's chest opened up to reveal a young man inside. It was Lorenzo! He had turned into a giant mole and had burrowed through the earth to save her. She felt a rise of something warm inside her chest. They were going to be together again. They could stop all this madness. But she could see, though, that he was struggling to free himself from the harness that bound him. He had one arm loose, but as the mad followers realised it was a man there, not a monster, they waved their blades and advanced on him.

"Lorenzo!" Lucia called and jumped to her feet to run towards him to help him. To protect him somehow. But then everything seemed to change. She felt a slowness overcome her and saw Lorenzo move at a startling speed. He was free from the harness and moving amongst the acolytes wielding a sword that seemed to stretch and bend, reaching out to cut down the men that attacked him. But he was not slaying them. He was cutting at the backs of their legs behind the knees, crippling them. He moved from one side of the chamber to the other, his limbs blurring too fast to easily follow. Men tried slashing their daggers about them, hoping to strike him, but he dodged them and was then behind them cutting them down. Then he was beside her, cutting her bonds, but when she reached out for him he was gone, back into the fray. Soon there were no acolytes left standing, and Lucia felt the air about her change again and saw Lorenzo looking around him, walking at a normal speed, making sure there were no attackers left.

There were only two men left standing, Galileo and the priest, who stood near the altar. Lorenzo looked across to them and held out his sword in a warning gesture. Then he stepped over to Lucia. "Light of my heart," he said.

The warmth in her chest grew larger, and she was certain that was a term that he had used with her many times before, though she knew she was hearing it for the first time only. "Light of my life," she replied.

He smiled and she reached out and grabbed him. Kissed him. This boy who would climb high towers and tunnel through the earth for her. How could she not? And she felt for a moment that surely the touch of their lips would transform them both into some creature that would fly them back to the surface. She could feel the pressure rising inside her chest, flowing into him as something of him flowed into her once more. Felt something transforming them. But a sharp cry from Galileo to Lorenzo broke the kiss and they turned their heads to see the puce priest forcing the old man down one of the tunnels ahead of him at knife point.

Lorenzo looked back at her, and she saw the distress in his eyes. She could see the painful choice he had to make and she knew she had to make the decision. "Go," she said. "Save him first."

LIV

The priest pushed Galileo down the tunnels ahead of him, cursing himself for not having slain the old man at once. This was not how it should have been! His vision was coming undone. The heretic Galileo had to be behind this all somehow. He had conjured that cursed man-beast abomination using his science! He should be flung into a pit of flames to see if his foul arts would serve him then. But, he mumbled to himself, he needed him for the moment. He could still turn things in his favour. His divine mission would not be thwarted.

Galileo stumbled as the priest pressed him ever onwards, first pushing him too hard and then pulling him back to his feet to stop him falling, hissing into his ear each time, "Faster." The tunnels ahead of them branched in many directions, with the lanterns on the walls illuminating the way only faintly, but the priest never paused at each new turning, pushing the old man steadily ahead of him. Now and then he threw a quick glance back over his shoulder to see if he could see the man-beast pursuing him, for he was surely coming after him, and he wondered if it might be easier to just cut the old man's throat and leave him. Or better still, he might slash the back of Galileo's legs as the man-beast had done to the priest's own followers, and that would slow him in his pursuit while he stopped to help the old man along.

But there was time for that yet, he thought. So many options, like the branches of the tunnels, and he needed to make sure he was choosing the right ones. This was surely a test, he told himself. A test of his worthiness. He had to show he had the strength of will to rise above these setbacks. That thought filled him with renewed confidence and he urged Galileo on faster still. He knew just what he had to do now. It was as simple as ignoring all the wrong turnings. They were distractions. They were put in his path to test him. But he would not be deterred.

Galileo stumbled again, and fell heavily to the ground. The priest put his knife to the back of Galileo's neck and said, "Stand up or die."

"I suspect if I stand up I will die anyway," the old man replied. The priest growled and hauled him back up to his feet with great effort. And when he pointed him forward again, he saw a flickering light ahead of them that he had not seen there a moment before. He hissed in the old man's ear. "Silence now." He pushed Galileo forward more slowly and soon could hear the moans and calls of wounded men writhing on the ground. The priest stepped out into the chamber cautiously, looking at his followers bleeding on the ground, grasping their wounds.

"They have been tested and found wanting," he said softly. "They were not worthy."

He scanned the chamber carefully for the man-beast. He was not there. But the young woman was, staring down the tunnel he had fled along. He smiled. She did not even see him there, she was so preoccupied with expecting to see her man-beast returning with him and Galileo from that direction. She was not even looking around to see if one of the wounded men would somehow find the strength and will to crawl across to her and enact some vengeance on her.

He strode across to her quickly and seized her by the hair. She was so startled she screamed, but he had his dagger at her face and said, "Silence!" She closed her mouth. Now another choice had been placed before him. He could only take one of the two non-believers with him, but which one was it to be? Who was the most valuable? Who would ensure his success and who would not? He looked from Lucia to the scientist. The old man was puffing from the exertion of hurrying down the tunnels. He could not walk much further. The girl was young and light. He could even carry her if he needed to. But the old man was the Medici's scientist. He could be a bargaining tool. And the young girl was... Yes, who was she? He tugged at her hair to turn her face to better see her in the fire light. She looked at his face and he saw the surprise there as he recognised the face she looked at. Her own face. And then he knew her. She was the Duke's daughter. He smiled again. His path was now very clear.

Without letting go of Lucia's hair he dragged her back across towards Galileo and said, "For your sins." And he stabbed him with his knife. He felt the blade enter the old man's stomach easily and saw him slump to the ground. It was so easy he would have liked to pull him to his feet and do it again. "No," the girl called but he pulled her head back and put the blade to her throat, and said, "And for your sins." Then he noticed for the first time the scars along her neck, as if she had survived having her neck cut many times already. That thought shook him a little, as did the stubborn look on her face. She should have been whimpering for her life, but refused to. He wondered if she had arcane science at her disposal too, and almost loosened his grip, but then he saw the fear in her eyes. And he smiled. It was just another test of him. "We'll see how well you survive another cutting of your neck," he said. "Unless you are very, very quiet." Then he turned and pushed her before him, down another tunnel, the bloodied knife dripping by her throat.

LV

Lucia wanted to turn her head around and see Lorenzo there behind them, his sword drawn, striding quickly to overtake them. But she was just as certain that he would not be there. He was off down another tunnel searching vainly for the priest and Galileo. The priest jerked her hair, turning her head forward again. She wanted to call out to Lorenzo, to let him know which tunnel they had gone down, but she feared the mad priest's wrath. He had killed Galileo and would surely kill her just as easily if she angered him. It just wasn't fair, to have to expect another miraculous rescue, she thought. She would do better to wait for her chance to escape.

This high priest was muttering some strange curses at her, or at Lorenzo, or at himself, as they went on, and he ignored her when she protested that he was hurting her. He just pushed her along, going down several tunnels that were lit with the small lanterns and up several winding stone staircases. They were small and awkward, and with the priest holding her hair it was hard to precede him. She had to twist her body into difficult positions to be able to climb, and the thought filled her that it might be her best chance to escape. She could fall backwards on top of him as they ascended and her weight would knock him backwards. With luck he would bash his head on the stairs and his body would protect her from too much harm. But she might fall onto his dagger. She might injure herself worse than she injured him. And even if she broke free, could she find her way back along the tunnels to Lorenzo?

She decided that as they were going steadily upwards, they would undoubtedly emerge in the city somewhere soon. That had to be good. She would wait until they were in the city and then she would find a way to escape him. She would endure the tugging of his fat fingers in her hair until then. She had escaped the Nameless One and she would escape from this priest too.

They were in a level tunnel now and had just turned a corner when Lucia bumped straight into someone, and felt hands grabbing at her. She gave a short scream, at first thinking it was one of the disfigured plague people again. Then she wondered if it might somehow be Lorenzo. But now she saw the face in front of her. It was the Nameless One. She blinked and tried to push him away. He had to be in league with the priest and his madmen. And she would be his captive again.

But then he dropped his hands from her, took a step back and drew his sword. "Release her," he said to the priest. It was not said as a threat, but in a tone of one who expected no refusal.

"Who are you?" the priest asked. "I have just saved this young woman from the grasps of madmen. I am going to take her back to the safety of her father."

Lucia tired to protest but felt the dagger press into the back of her neck in warning. "My name is not important," the Nameless One said. "But my mission is. I am here to ensure no harm comes to her." The priest did not move. "And I am not a man to be trifled with," the Nameless One said. "Release her at once."

"My apologies," said the priest, "You clearly know her identity then, but how do I know you are acting in her service? You might be taking the Medici coin and I should not like to release her into your care to see her enslaved again."

The Nameless One looked at Lucia and said, "I wish to see her free."

"Can I believe you, old man?" the priest asked.

Lucia saw the Nameless One lower his sword a little as he said, still looking at Lucia, "I speak from my heart."

"How can one believe a masked stranger?" the priest asked.

"You are masked too," said the Nameless One.

"Then I will reveal my identity to you, and you can decide who should possess her." Lucia felt the lantern come close to her face as the priest reached up to remove his mask. She saw the look of astonishment on the Nameless One's face.

"No," he said. "It cannot be."

"Take her," the priest said and pushed Lucia towards him. He pushed her hard so that she stumbled. The Nameless One was fast, though, and turned his body to catch her fully with one arm, the other still holding his sword. She looked into his eyes and thought that in the darkness she saw a terrible sadness in them. Then his mouth opened in a gasp. She felt his grip on her tighten and then loosen as his legs buckled beneath him. She fell with him, first to his knees and then to the ground. He lay half on top of her, one hand still on his sword, his face so close to hers that she could see blood and spittle on his lips as he tried to say something to her. But she never heard it. The priest grabbed her hair in a painful grasp again, and pulled her to her feet. "Fool," he hissed waving his newly-bloodied dagger at the Nameless One. It had gone up under his ribcage and into his tortured heart.

Lucia tried to turn her head back to look at him, willing him to climb back to his feet and pick up his sword again. To not be dead. But the priest twisted her hair viciously and pushed her forwards again. And then a quiet rage filled her like she had never known. She vowed that the Nameless One would be the last person this priest slew. He would not kill her and he would not kill anyone else. She knew what she would do, if she could just be granted the opportunity.

LVI

The night glasses that Leonardo had devised made it easy to for Lorenzo to find his way along the tunnels, but they didn't help him in finding the right direction to take. Eventually he backtracked, following the cries of the wounded men, using the hearing horn that Galileo had developed. He stepped back into the chamber, and looked around the plaintive crying bodies there, to see that Lucia was gone and Galileo was lying on the ground, seriously wounded.

Lorenzo rushed across to him and lifted his head. The old man opened his eyes and tried to say something. Lorenzo saw the blood seeping across his tunic and ripped it open. There was a deep stab wound in his stomach. His mentor was dying. "Don't move," he told him and reached into his tunic. He pulled out a small glass cup, bound with brass to protect it.

Galileo lifted his head, trying to tell Lorenzo something, but his breath was coming in short panting bursts. "Lucia," he finally said. "The priest."

But Lorenzo already knew that. He could somehow feel Lucia's fear as the mad priest pushed her along the tunnels ahead of himself. "I will catch him," Lorenzo said, a quiet rage filling him. "But I must tend to you first." Galileo lay his head back once more. "This is going to hurt," he told Galileo, wondering if a dying man needed to be warned about more pain. At least he hadn't told him that he didn't quite know how the device worked, or even if it would have any effect on internal injuries.

He laid the glass cup on Galileo's stomach and looked up at him. The old man looked back with a mix of curiosity and surprise. "It's one of Leonardo's things," Lorenzo said. The old man lifted his head forward again. Clearly he didn't want to miss seeing what it would do.

Lorenzo concentrated, trying to remember what he had quickly read in Leonardo's coded description of the device. He had written his notes backwards, which Lorenzo had quickly recognised and read them in a mirror. There had been so many devices in his workshop, but he only took the ones that he thought might be useful and looked like they were beyond experimental stage. Like this cup.

He placed one hand on top of the glass and with the other he carefully wound a small key in the side of the brass fitting. He then let go and watched the mechanism within move. An arm sprang and struck a flint that ignited some chemical inside the cup and there was a brilliant flash of flame. Lorenzo felt the cup suddenly grow hot and took his hand away quickly. Galileo groaned and Lorenzo felt his body shudder.

The cup was full of cloudy smoke and Lorenzo slowly lifted it away, using cloth from Galileo's tunic to hold it. There was a foul smell of sulphur and burning flesh. Lorenzo waved his hand to clear the smoke and then saw that Galileo's stab wound was now closed, the flesh seared together. He looked up at Galileo who had his teeth gritted in pain.

"I will move you to safety," Lorenzo said. "Away from these men." He placed his arms under Galileo's shoulders to drag him down one of the side tunnels when he realised that none of the wounded men about them were crying out anymore. He stood and walked cautiously across to the closest man. He appeared dead. He reached down and put a hand on his neck. No. He was asleep or unconscious. He stood and looked around carefully, expecting to see the Shadow Master there, but there was nobody. It had to be him. He had done something to these men so that they could not harm Galileo. But why did he not show himself and help Lorenzo?

"Shadow Master?" he called. The words echoed back at him. "Shadow Master," he called again, but the only reply was still his own voice. He was leaving Lorenzo to figure things out on his own again. Or to remind him of what he had to do. So be it. He strode back to Galileo and said, "You will be safe. Friends are watching over you. I must save Lucia." The old man opened his eyes and looked at his apprentice, and then Lorenzo added, "But to do that I must save the city and save civilisation too it seems."

LVII

"Warn the City Council," Sergeant Cristoforo said, looking out over the town walls. He had been summoned by one of the guards who insisted he come at once to look out at the plague people. "There is an army of them," the guard had told him. The Sergeant was reluctant to come. The guardsman was a new recruit. A youngster. And clearly too easily scared. "Yes," Sergeant Cristoforo had said. "There is an army of them there every day."

But the young man was insistent, and so Sergeant Cristoforo had put on his boots and followed him up to the walls. The guardsmen there were all in quite a state and he knew something bad was happening before he even looked out over the surrounding lands. There *was* an army! Not just the growing number of rabble who made their way to the city, but this was a real army. Hundreds or thousands of them. With weapons. Some were riding on donkeys and some were in carts, and some wore the scavenged armour of a dozen different cities and lands, and a few carried tattered and dirty banners, and they were all streaming through the mountain pass towards the city.

He saw the plague people beneath the city walls emerging from their hovels to scurry away. Like peasants the world over, they knew that standing in front of an advancing army was not a place to be. They were gathering their meagre possessions, or precious bags of food, and were hurrying to get clear. Sergeant Cristoforo pondered for a moment whether he should report to the City Council that he had at least succeeded in clearing the walls of the plague people. That at least might get some reaction from them.

"Warn the City Council," he told the young man who had come to fetch him. "Tell them that there is a large army at our gates." The young man was off down the stairs without any more urging and the Sergeant presumed they would pay as much attention to the man as he himself had done. Then he called over two of his more senior and respected guards and said to them, "You must each go to the House of Medici and the House of Lorraine. Tell them that we are under attack and that they must send men to the city walls at once. If they do not we will be overwhelmed and the plague will be free inside the city by nightfall."

LVIII

Dead people were all around them, threatening to trip them at each step. The priest had emerged from the catacombs into a dark corner of the crypt beneath the cathedral. Lucia was having trouble keeping up with him, now, as he bent her head one way and then another, leading them around tombstones and graves underfoot. Twice she tripped and he hauled her to her feet by her hair, causing her to scream in pain. He was close to his goal now though, and there was nothing she could do to slow him down.

The crypt was empty and he hurried along the narrow paths between the graves, mumbling to himself in words Lucia could not understand and could not tell if they were prayers or curses. She had hoped that they would emerge into the cathedral and find it full of people who would recognise her and come to her aid, but when he pushed her up the stone stairs into the back corner of the large building, it was empty.

The priest looked around, as if also expecting to see somebody there, and then hurried down the centre of the cathedral towards the altar. He drove her quickly before him and pushed her past the altar, where she had never dared to step, and into the priest's sanctuary behind it. Lucia was surprised to see the High Priest sitting there. Then who was this man who had her captive? The High Priest had been underlining passages in a book, with a fraught look upon his face, but he stopped and looked up at them and said, "Savonarola! What in God's name have you done now?"

The minor cleric, Savonarola, now that he had been named, said, "No! I am the High Priest!"

"*I* am the High Priest," the other said, standing to his feet. And then Savonarola stepped up close in front of him. "And I am you," he said. Lucia saw the surprise on the High Priest's face, and the then saw him fall to his knees as Savonarola said, "It is the end of days. Judgement Day. Your loyalty is being demanded!"

"What do I need do?" the High Priest asked meekly, his self-importance suddenly gone.

"The artefact of the ancients," said Savonarola.

"It is forbidden," said the High Priest. "It is an object of science."

"So it must be destroyed," said Savonarola.

"It serves to remind us of the folly of the ancients," said the High Priest, but with less conviction.

"It is time to remind us all of that folly," said Savonarola, and the High Priest nodded his head and rose to his feet. He took a small key from around his neck. He used it to unlock a small cabinet behind a red curtain. "Here it is," he said, one madman communing with another.

The High Priest held up a small glass sphere filled with a golden liquid. The cleric lowered the dagger from Lucia's neck and sheathed it, still holding her hair, and then took the object from the High Priest carefully with his free hand and held it up in triumph "The city shall be cleansed of its sins by the hands of the ancients," he said.

"You're mad," said Lucia, struggling to get free. "They'll stop you."

"No one will stop me!" he cried, then he pushed her out into the cathedral.

"I will stop you," she said defiantly, standing her ground.

"You may still have some use as a hostage," he said. "You will submit to me." And he twisted her hair, turning her face to his for the first time. But she was staring into her own face. She did not understand it. Then he bent her head back and Lucia could see the frescos of the ancients staring down at her from the high arched ceiling. How many times had she turned her head up to look at their impassive faces during services, and thought them unseeing of the plight of the people below? But now their eyes seemed to follow her and they looked at her with pity, as if they knew what was to become of her.

"I will defy you," she said and let her body go limp, falling to the floor, knowing he could not drag her and hold the precious glass orb easily.

"So be it," Savonarola said and let go of her. Then he reached into his robes with one hand and pulled out his blooded dagger. He stabbed at her violently and she held up a hand to stop him. "No," she called, and the blade entered her palm with a sharp pain. Savonarola grinned and pulled the knife back to strike again. But it would not come. Lucia felt her fingers melding around it. Felt it becoming a part of her. Savonarola pulled harder but Lucia easily pulled it from his hands and it continued to form and shape into a large talon or claw. Then she stood and lashed out at the cleric's face. Her own face. It caught him by surprise and Lucia felt glass shattering under the blow. It took her some moments to understand that he had been wearing some type of mirror mask on his face. Surely some other product of science, that reflected the visage of the person in front of it back to them.

The shock of the blow nearly caused him to drop the sphere. "No!" he cried, and grasped it in both hands. He fell to his knees and hugged it tightly to his chest, as if it were his own heart, and despite her resolve to see that he killed no one else, Lucia turned and ran. She gathered her skirts in two hands and headed straight for the main doors. There must be people outside on the streets. There must be somebody who could save her.

The madded shout of the cleric boomed around her in the cathedral like it was the very voice of the ancients calling down to her. But the large cathedral doors were closed and bolted. She scrabbled with the large bolts, but the talon inhibited her fingers. She looked back over her shoulder to see that Savonarola was on his feet now and coming towards her. She dragged at one bolt and felt it moving. She smacked at it with her metal hand and then tugged at it again.

It opened a little further. It must open for her. It must. The streets would be filled with her father's men, and if she could just get the door open she would be safe.

She looked at the metal hand and shook it desperately, until she felt the dagger detaching from her fingers and it fell to the floor with a clatter. Then she was tugging at the bolt with both hands as she heard the mad cleric's footsteps close behind her. She almost screamed in frustration to the ancients above her as she knew she would never get it open in time. She would have to turn and defend herself. She spun and looked around on the floor for the dagger. She should have kept the talon. She should have cut his throat with it. She should have done something other than this, because he was upon her now and as he reached out for her she dodged to the side and ran again. Across the stone floor of the cathedral towards a corner door.

She ran through it and started up the spiral staircase, holding her skirts high as her tired legs tried to go faster. She could hear the curses of the cleric behind her, more intent on vengeance now than having her as a hostage, she suspected. She ran up and up and finally reached the door at the top that led out onto the walkway around the cathedral cupola. She had only been up on it once herself, when she was a younger girl. Her father, the Duke, had taken her up to see the city they way the High Priest saw it.

That day had been sunny and calm and she had felt each step was taking her somehow closer to the heavens, up on the level of the murals of the ancients. Today the staircase was just a promise of escape. But when she finally reached the top of the stairs, the small wooden door there out onto the walkway was locked. She banged on it with the flats of her hands and shouted at it. She had to find a way through it. She turned and looked back down the stairs. She could run back down them into the mad cleric's arms, hoping to bowl him over. But he would have the dagger again, she knew. He would hear her coming.

She turned back and grasped the door handle again and tugged on it. Pressed her hand against the lock. Then felt her fingers melding with it, moving into it. She tried to calm herself and concentrate on her fingers, probing and moving them around, feeling the parts of the lock that were becoming a part of her. It only took a moment to turn the mechanism and then she slowly detached her fingers from the metal again. She looked at her hand now and saw that where the dagger had entered her hand the skin was grey and unfeeling and her fingers had also lost colour. She would consider that later, she decided, and threw open the door.

It was an overcast morning outside, but, after the darkness of the catacombs and the empty cathedral, it stung her eyes like bright daylight. She shielded her eyes and looked around. The streets far below were empty. She muttered one of the curses her father used when he was most angry, that even made his guardsmen look to the floor. She had hoped that she would see someone to call for help to. She hurried around the walkway, to look further around the streets below her, but it was empty too. Then she thought of the door behind her. She hadn't locked it. She hurried back and had just put one hand on the door handle when it pushed open, almost knocking her over. Savonarola emerged onto the walkway, red-faced and puffing. His madness had turned to something other, she could see. Some dark fury that was intent on playing itself out only in her death.

She stepped back and thought to turn and run. Thought to look for something to hurl at the cleric. Thought to wrestle the dagger from him. But she did not think an angel would suddenly appear between them. The winged being landed heavily in front of her, and both she and Savonarola threw up their hands to protect themselves. It took her a moment to understand what she was seeing. A man with marble-pale skin and huge white wings was standing there before her. He was reaching out for her and then had her in his grasp. The wings were flapping and she was being lifted from the cathedral roof.

This half man, half bird was lifting her to safety. It was beyond belief. She looked down at the cleric and heard him shout, "Return her to me," he called up, "I am your master."

"You are no longer my master," the bird-man called down. "You should kneel down before me." The cleric called up something she could not understand, that sounded like he said he possessed the power of the ancients, but the man-bird said, "No. I *am* the power of the ancients."

Lucia tried to turn her head and look at his handsome face and she said, "Thank you. You have saved me." The words came out in a stammer.

He looked back to her and he said, "I have saved you to be my bride. I have watched you from afar many times, Lucia Lorraine, and imagined it. Leonardo will make you wings too and together we shall rule over this world." She closed her eyes. Where was it written that she had to be incessantly kidnapped by crazed men? And she recalled the saying about beautiful women having to bear a greater burden in the madness of men than any burden that men ever bore in bearing the whims of a beautiful woman. She would write such aphorisms about men's madness if only she survived this day, she resolved.

LIX

Lorenzo wondered if he could beat the Shadow Master in a fight. He was certain that if he tried to rescue Lucia first he would appear and try to stop him. Frantically, he searched through the scientific devices he still had in the leather bag with him, looking for one that could be useful to him. Perhaps the night glasses would help him see better than the Shadow Master and evade him? He had to find the puce priest. If he had tried to murder Galileo he could just as easily harm Lucia.

He looked at the mole harness, but it was too badly burned to be of use again. Galileo might have been able to advise him, if he were not lying on the ground by him, near insensible. It would undoubtedly have been something wise about using logic and observation to conquer his emotions and find the best path forward. But his emotions refused to be stilled. He had to rescue Lucia first! He stood and looked at the multiple passages that led out of the chamber. One of them would take him to Lucia and the others would not.

He ground his teeth. The Shadow Master would know which way to go, but would not show him. He closed his eyes and tried to think. There must be a logical way out of this. It was like one the puzzles that Galileo sometimes set him. There must be a way to determine which tunnels not to take in order to find the right one.

His feet and his urgency dictated his decision though and he set off quickly down the nearest tunnel, hoping against hope it would prove the right one. Yet he had barely turned the first corner when a dark shape rose up blocking his path. Lorenzo took up a fighting stance, prepared to fight his way past, but a sword appeared under his chin before he even saw it coming. Only one man could move that fast.

"Shadow Master," Lorenzo said, not dropping his offensive position.

"Shhh," said the Shadow Master. "Remember. I don't exist."

"You have to move out of my way," said Lorenzo. "That mad priest has Lucia. I must save her before he harms her."

"He will not harm her," the Shadow Master said firmly.

"Which path will lead me to them?" Lorenzo asked.

"Not the path you must now take," the Shadow Master said.

Lorenzo shook his head. "No. I must go after her. I must save her."

"You will," said the Shadow Master, "But you must save civilisation first. Remember."

Lorenzo felt himself growing angry. "I must save her first. Civilisation can be saved afterwards."

"That is not your choice to make," the Shadow Master replied, pressing his sword tip into Lorenzo's throat. Lorenzo took a step backwards, but the sword tip followed him. "Well, strictly speaking it is your choice to make," the Shadow Master added, "But it would be the wrong choice."

Lorenzo took another step back and came up against the tunnel wall. He had the Shadow Master"s other sword in his hand and looked down at the blade now at his throat. It was longer, heavier and looked quite a bit more dangerous than the sword he held. The Shadow Master looked at him and he glared back at him. "I know what you're thinking," he told Lorenzo. "But you can't save Lucia this way."

"How do you know what I'm thinking?" Lorenzo asked.

"You forget, I know you very, very well."

"How can I believe that?"

"I just told you. You've forgotten."

Lorenzo gritted his teeth and shifted his grip on the sword hilt a little. "I wouldn't do that if I were you," said the Shadow Master.

"How do you know what I'm going to do?" Lorenzo asked.

"Let's not go through this all again," he said. "Look. It's simple. You save the city and save civilisation, and I'll save Lucia. That's just how it has to be."

Lorenzo looked at him carefully and felt the sword point at his throat not waver at all. Then he nodded his head. Very slowly. "What do we do?" he asked.

"You need to go back down to the chamber of the ancients," said the Shadow Master.

Lorenzo frowned a little, as if not understanding, but then said, incredulously, "You want me to wield the power of the ancients?"

"*Bravissimo*!" said the Shadow Master.

"But... but... how?" asked Lorenzo. "Surely only the ancients had that power."

"What if I told you you're older than you look?"

Lorenzo wanted him to stop his stupid word games. "And that will save Lucia?" he asked.

"Without a doubt," said the Shadow Master. "Well, without much doubt. Certainly more than you running around lost in the tunnels down here would." But still Lorenzo hesitated. "Don't worry, it always turns out well in the end," the Shadow Master said. "Trust me."

"Alright," said Lorenzo reluctantly. "I'll do it." He turned and started walking back the way he had come.

"Uh, one more thing," called the Shadow Master.

"Yes?" asked Lorenzo.

"It would please me greatly if you took the right tunnels." And he threw Lorenzo a small device. Lorenzo caught it and looked down at it and saw it was a small glass-covered disc that had a glowing arrow on it. "Just follow the arrow," the Shadow Master said. "It"s an intelligent compass. Probably more intelligent than many people you'd ask directions of."

Lorenzo turned it around in his hand and the arrow stayed pointing in the one direction.

"And just one more thing," he called to Lorenzo.

"What?"

The Shadow Master moved his fingers up and down in front of his face like an imbecile might and said, "Remember, you haven't seen anything." Then he stepped back into the shadows. Lorenzo shook his head. It seriously worried him that the man sometimes seemed more crazed than any of the crazed men they were fighting.

LX

"It is the time of reckoning," the mad cleric Savonarola muttered, as he made his way through the streets of the Walled City, looking around to see what other obstacles might be placed in his path to test him. But the streets seemed deserted. The citizens of the city were either asleep in their beds, or hiding indoors, too wary of the enmity of the two Houses to wish being caught up in it. He looked up into the sky every now and then to see if he could see any sign of his former devotee, Damon. Another traitor. "His time will come too," he muttered.

He kept to the back streets and alleyways, walking quickly and holding the glass sphere close to his body. It was best that he no longer had the girl with him, he decided. It would be too dangerous trying to carry both her and the artefact of the ancients. If she had caused him to drop it before he'd reached his destination, it would be disastrous.

The sphere had been passed down from one High Priest to the next over generations, entrusting the secret to no one else. It was the last treasure of the ancients. A reminder of how they had destroyed their own great civilisation. It was a secret that he had discovered, so it was fitting that it now be used by him to presage the end of days.

He came out onto a square and saw a small group of men on the far side. They were militiamen from one of the Houses. They seemed in a stir about something, sending men running away in different directions. That was good. It would keep them too distracted to observe him. He made his way quickly across the far side of the square and saw one of the men glance quickly in his direction and then look back to his comrades. Nothing strange about a clergyman walking across the square, after all, thought Savonarola.

He was only a block or two away now. He turned another corner and saw the wall of the city ahead of him. There were guards atop the walls calling and shouting to each other. Now, men with arms ran past, but no one challenged him. He saw Medici men and also Lorraine men climbing the walls together. He heard them shouting to each other about a plague army. The foretold army of the night had come and were at this moment at the gates, demanding to be let into the city!

Savonarola made his way down the last street before the wall. At the far end he would emerge by the main gates to the city. Those gates had not been opened fully for many years, but today they would open wide for him and the city would pay the price for its sins. Would be filled with a terrible fear. Would share the horrors and sorrows of his childhood. Would understand what had shaped him. He walked on quickly now and reached the end of the street. He saw a large mob of defenders on the walls, but none of them were at this side of the gates. They did not stop to think that disease spreads from the inside.

He walked closer to the gates and held out the sphere. The yellow liquid inside glowed like a small sun. It was a wonder that it was not hot. He looked about and saw a guardsman call to him. Challenging him. But it was too late. He cast the orb at the gate. It hit the large wooden doors and shattered and flames leapt forth as if a large demon had been freed from its prison. There was an horrendous shrieking noise and Savonarola was knocked off his feet by the blast. He lay there dazed and saw men had fallen off the walls and lay about the gates. Others were on fire, running around, vainly trying to put out the flames. And the gates were off their hinges, burning.

He struggled to his feet and held his hands aloft. He had been tested over and over and had not proved wanting. His followers would now emerge onto the streets and cast all their vanities into the flames. They would hunt out and find all objects of science in the city and would build a giant pyre whose flames would lick at the feet of that traitor Damon and he would fall from the skies, and the plague army would run riot through the city, all as he had foretold. And the few who survived would be just like him.

He would no longer be alone.

Then he saw the flames on his garments. One sleeve was alight. He flapped it to try to extinguish the flame, but the more he flapped the more it grew. It crawled along his arm and took hold his robes. He felt the heat rising up to his face. Felt the flame spreading around his whole body. It was embracing him tighter, eating at his flesh. He felt the pain like a hundred daggers cutting into him.

"No," he shouted, knowing that the flames of the ancients could not be extinguished by earth or water or smothering. They would burn until there was nothing left to consume. He threw his arms into the air and ran about madly, his time of reckoning illuminated by his staggering, flaming body. His own trial by fire.

LXI

Lorenzo felt unequal to the enormity of the task before him. He walked around the huge chamber of the ancients trying to concentrate on what he had to do, and not be distracted by the awe of it all. That they had built all this under the city was so wondrous that he could easily give in to his yearnings to climb amongst it all and examine it from all sides, learning how it was all put together and how it worked. If only he had time in this chamber, what mysteries he would uncover and what learnings he would possess. Then he would bring Galileo down here and the master would become the apprentice.

He looked up at the vast machinery over his head and wondered what power could possibly drive it. There were huge cylinders and cogs of stone and metal that would take over a hundred oxen just to move them a fraction. He walked over to the large metal wheel that the Shadow Master had shown him on their first visit. He had told him that this was the key to operating everything. He looked at it carefully. The huge wheel, which was taller than he was, had a five sided star carved into it and was set firmly into a large block of stone.

Around him stood the statues of the ancients, as if watching over him to see what he did, but unwilling to be his instructors. He stared at the wheel and examined the stars and celestial objects that were inlaid on it, and then ran his hands around the outer rim. It was clearly designed to be turned. But how to turn something that did not even have handholds on it? And something so huge. He tried to grasp the outer edge and pushed at it. It did not move. He looked back at the statues around him and frowned.

Then he tried to move it the other way. Still nothing happened. It made him feel small and insignificant. And not a little angry. He had not come all this way to be defeated by an inability to solve the puzzle before him. The Shadow Master knew how this worked, but would not tell him. Why did he have to discover it himself? And why was he the only one who could do it?

He stared again at the large wheel and then, on a whim, stood firmly against it. Pressed his palms to the metal and felt a warmth there. Then he suddenly knew what he had to do. He turned around and stood with his back to the wheel. Spread his arms and legs out so that each was a point of the star and his head made the fifth. He felt it in his chest first, like his breathing was being constricted. Then his hands started melding with the metal. But nothing else. He slowly detached himself and considered this a moment. Then he placed one hand on the metal wheel and waited to feel the warmth. Then he placed his forearm against it. Nothing. He rolled up his sleeve and tried it again. He felt the warmth all along his arm.

He sighed deeply and then started taking off his clothes, glad this was a secret that was going to stay a secret. He stood back up against the metal and felt his whole body warming and melding with it, like he was sinking back into the metal. This was a bigger metamorphosis than becoming the mole. He was becoming a part of the wheel and a part of the cogs of the vast giant machinery that the ancients had built. He was becoming one of the ancients himself.

He felt the whole machine about him now. He understood how it all fitted together, and its power. He was a part of it. This was knowledge that he had never dreamed of. And all he had to do was turn the wheel to operate it all. He started turning slowly, feeling his body, now a part of the metal wheel, fighting against the resistance of centuries. Stones and dust fell from the edge of the wheel as it turned and he felt the grinding of stone upon stone and metal upon metal as the long disused machine began to awaken.

He felt his valves opening and then could feel the tremor of movement filling the chambers of the large pistons. It was water. He could feel it. An underground river of it. More dust and sand fell as the large pistons creaked and groaned. Then he felt the first piston move slightly. Those massive ancient cogs were moving. Then he understood it fully. The force of the maelstrom was going to drive the machinery. The ancients had harnessed the power of nature to drive this gigantic wonder. He could feel water running through pipes and tunnels all about him. Those tunnels were a part of this machinery.

Stone now creaked loudly upon stone as the pistons started to move a little faster. Small rocks rained down in the chamber as the world of the ancients came slowly back to life. He tried to detach himself from the metal wheel, wanting to see this with his own eyes. Wanting to witness the transformation. But his body had trouble stepping free, as if the wheel and the whole machine did not want to let him go. He broke one foot free, and then another and slowly pulled his body out of the metal. He tried to take a step away from the machine, but his feet would hardly move. And his arms felt like they were made of lead or stone. He felt his breath laboured in his chest and he looked up at the statues of the ancients standing around him and he suddenly understood what the true cost of using the magic of science was on the body that Galileo had tried to warn him of. Finally he understood that the ancients had never died out at all, for they had been standing around them in the city the whole time.

LXII

Lucia was torn between wonder and fear. She was flying. Above the Walled City in the arms of this angel-like being, looking down at the many red-tiled rooftops and grey-stoned streets below them. The feeling was simply incredible. She could feel nothing under her feet but air, and each breath she took in she imagined was filling her with lightness. This was how the ancients had surely seen it, she thought, to paint the city they way they did in many of the frescos they had left behind, as if seen from the air. She could see the streets that she had walked as a child, and could see the tower where her own bedchamber was, and she could see the Council building and the cathedral and the shops and chapels and every nook and cranny of the city. It was wondrous, and she could feel the first faint touches of being as powerful as the ancients, if not as powerful as the gods.

The angel-being turned his flapping wings a little to bring them to a halt in the sky and said to Lucia, "Look upon the world, for you will never see it the same again."

That sounded ominously as much a curse as a promise, and she looked about to see what he might be referring to. "Behold," said the birdman, turning her around so that she could see, "The armies of the darkness have arrived." She drew in a deep breath that no longer felt light. Hundreds of men were at the city gates, with more coming across the plain from the mountain pass. The city was under attack. They would never be able to hold so many back. "So a new era begins," the being said to her. "They will take over the city and we shall rule over them."

Then, before she could even protest that, she saw a flash of fire and heard the distant shriek as the main gates exploded in flames. She saw men on fire running to and fro in the streets and saw the plague army gather around the gates, waiting for the flames to die down a little. Then they would push through and be into the city. She saw men running along the streets by the walls to defend the gates, but could also see they would be hopelessly outnumbered. The city was going to fall to this army of the darkness, whoever they were, and she would witness it from above.

A few of the plague army approached too close to the gates and she saw flames reach out and touch them and turn them into stumbling and running fire-men. One even ran through the open gates to be cut down by swords and axes. She tried to turn her head away, but the angel-being kept turning in the air so that it was before her.

"You must behold," he said. "This is how the ancients watched their own world come to an end."

"I refuse," she said, and closed her eyes. She did not want to see this, perched up in the sky, unable to do anything to save her city. Unable to warn her father or mother. Unable to save a single person from the attacking army and the end of their world. Then she suddenly felt the weightless feeling desert her as the angel-being dropped a little in the sky. She shrieked and opened her eyes. She immediately went from wonder to horror. If he dropped her she would fall and fall and fall until she struck the hard streets below and splattered like a melon dropped from a high window. "No," she called, but she could see the look of confusion on his face. His wings were flapping harder now but were awkward, as if he had been wounded or something. They dropped further. She felt her weight suddenly grown in his arms as he struggled to hold her.

"What is happening?" he asked her, as if she could somehow tell him. Then he answered his own question. "It must be because I did not put the harness on fully to complete the transformation. I must become a giant eagle." She saw him struggle with something around his arms that she now saw was a harness that had previously seemed to be a part of his body. But the more he struggled with it the greater trouble he had remaining aloft.

"No! I am a god," he called, and she felt his arms trying to open and release her. "You are too heavy," he said, no longer wishing that they should be married and rule over the new world. She could feel him trying to drop her, but his limbs would not move how he wanted them to. She clung to him tightly

and screamed at him. Cursed him and told him to fly
down to the ground, but he was losing the control to
even steer them in how they dropped. They would
both plummet to the streets below, she knew. They
would be crushed together. Lorenzo would find her
dead in his arms. She would rather die alone than
that, she resolved, and tried to slip herself free, but
could not wriggle out of his unyielding arms.

She looked down and screamed again as the ground
started rushing up at them, and then, with a sudden
awkward turn of his wings, they tumbled about and
she felt them strike something solid, although they
were still high in the air. The wind was knocked from
her and she took some time to understand what had
happened. They had landed on the peak of the domed
cupola of the cathedral, as improbable as it might be.
He had taken the full force of the collision, and was
lying beside her, back broken, like a statue dropped
from the heavens.

His eyes were moving slowly as if he was searching
for something, possibly an understanding of what had
happened to him and his dreams, but they passed right
over her. She reached out one hand and tentatively
touched him. He felt like stone, but there was a slight
movement in his limbs still. She pulled her hand back.
He had turned to stone while he held her, but a part
of him was still human with blood spilling out. How
was that possible?

Then she looked at the wings and the harness.
Another marvel of science. Or an abomination,
depending on how you looked at it. His eyes looked
around him once more and his mouth opened

just a little. Deep red blood showed inside the pale mouth. It made her shiver. She wanted to get as far away from him as possible but looked around her in despair. There was no easy way down from the dome. It was built of intricately shaped tiles that interlocked together and she knew if she started trying to climb down she would simply slide off the dome as the angle steepened. Workmen undoubtedly had some tools they used to scale the dome, but she had no idea what they might be.

She looked down and found the curve of the roof pulling both her eyes and body towards it, making her feel more vulnerable to be perched on the dome's top than she had felt to be high in the sky over the city. She looked back and saw the man – for he was just a man after all – trying to reach a hand out towards her. She was tempted for a moment to roll him off the roof and let him crash to the streets below, but felt it would somehow be tempting her own fate and she would follow him if she did. She had to get off the roof somehow though. She looked again at the harness wings. It would be dangerous, but what hadn't been today?

It took her some time to get the harness free from under the man's body and then fit it to herself as he had worn it. As soon as she had it strapped tightly to her body she felt the transformation happening. This was something monumental. She stood up and felt the wings move at her commands as she flexed muscles she had never previously possessed. She looked down at the man at her feet and lifted slowly into the air.

It took a moment to gain control of her flying, but only a moment. She had intended to descend quickly to the ground and free herself from the harness, but the feeling of power and freedom that filled her compelled her to fly higher. She would circle over the city and find Lorenzo emerging from the catacombs and fly down to him. She might even take him up in her arms and fly the two of them away from the city to freedom. She turned now to look down at the city gates, to see that many of the plague army were now rushing through the gates as the fires had died down. This was the start of the end, she knew.

But then something entirely unexpected happened. The city started moving. She thought at first it was an illusion caused by her perspective. But the city was definitely moving. She saw one of the taller towers start descending into the ground. Not like it was collapsing, for it was sinking straight into the ground. And she saw another tower nearby rising up higher.

She watched streets disappear and buildings reshape before her eyes. Staircases wound their way up into the air and buildings grew around them. She saw the cathedral descend into the ground, taking the half-statue half-man with it, and then another larger cathedral rose up nearby, with a huge ornate domed roof like nothing she had ever seen.

It was like watching one of those little cogged toys that changed shape after you'd wound the key, she thought, as parts of the city rose up or fell away. Towers that had been erected over years disappeared in an instant and others that had never existed rose up in their place. New streets appeared where none had previously been and then she saw the city walls grow taller, at least twice their previous height and then new branches of the walls started growing, snaking around the invading army of darkness, enclosing them, trapping them.

Then she felt her wings falter a little. She gave a small shriek and tried to concentrate on flapping more furiously, but she could feel them separating from her. "What is happening?" she asked, just as the man had asked when he felt he was no longer an angel, and his wings were becoming nothing but a mechanical set of feathers bound to canvass and wood on a harness on his back. As he fell from the sky.

LXIII

Lorenzo re-emerged into a city in chaos and wonderment. The streets were filled with people walking around looking about themselves in confusion. Some people's houses were gone and new buildings were in their places. Some had run outside and seen towers rise up about them and others had stayed where they were and had new walls and floors rise about them. One woman found herself standing atop a high tower that rose up from the street beneath her, and she shrieked for help, her voice joining with the cacophony of shouts and calls now filling the city. Others had found themselves in cellars or rooms of unfamiliar buildings that they had to search their way out of. Some awoke to the din to find themselves sharing a bedroom with another astounded couple.

Some unfortunates were crushed under the moving parts of the city and others were wandering about, bloodied and dazed. Lorenzo had barely made it to the chamber that carried him to the surface of the city, where once the Council Chambers had been, and staggered out onto the streets, his limbs still awkward and hard to move. But as the city kept moving and changing about him he found feeling returning to his body.

He stared around him in awe. Grand new paved streets spread out before him. Long rows of pillars ran down one side of a building. Large staircases led up into some buildings and small doors hid others. He looked up at the thin windows and the distressed or amazed people staring out of them. He watched people knocking their fists against new walls to test whether they were real. He saw many in their night clothes wandering the streets like sleepwalkers. Others were gathering in one of the new city squares with their belongings, fearful of any more changes that might occur about them. Only the statues of the ancients seemed to remain the same, watching down on the city that had created itself anew. And it was a new city. The imposing palaces of the two Houses were gone. The old order was gone. It was not the end of days, but rather the beginning of them. And he had done this!

Lorenzo pushed his way through the lost crowds; nobody really knew where they were going, nor which streets might take them there. He did not fully know where he was going either, but he had a purpose. He had to find Lucia. And, amongst this chaos, that probably meant finding the Shadow Master – though that meant waiting for the Shadow Master to find him, he knew. He could be watching him now, laughing to himself at Lorenzo's plight. Or he could be battling that mad cleric. He was more a mystery than any of the secrets of the ancients.

Lorenzo was then stopped by two bewildered-looking city guardsmen who asked him if he knew where the City Council Chambers might be now found. They looked about themselves like men awakening from a drunken dream and told him how the very streets had bent and moved and the towers of the city had sunk around them while others rose up, and then, almost as an afterthought, told him that the army of plague people were on the far side of tall walls that had risen around them. They were saved, they told him, though they did not understand how.

Lorenzo told them he was unable to help them and continued along the street, like the two guardsmen, not sure where he should be looking. Then he remembered the compass that he had been given and took it out. The compass needle pointed north, like any compass should. He walked in that direction, waiting for the needle to move and show him which streets to follow, but it did not waver. It was not working any more. He cursed and put it back into one of his pockets. He was, in actuality, as much undressed as he was dressed, having just gathering up a few of his clothes from the floor before he stumbled into that tiny chamber that had carried him to safety. But all about him people were similarly in states of half-dress, having rushed out of their houses or beds in alarm.

He had to think. Where would the Shadow Master be but in the shadows somewhere? But in fact he found him down by the new harbour of the city, standing there as if he had been waiting for Lorenzo for some time. And he held Lucia in his arms.

Lorenzo ran to them, pushing a path through the people in his way.

"Lucia," he cried. But she did not lift her head. Then he saw she was soaking wet. Her long hair hanging damply down to the ground like her limbs. He grasped her hand in his and felt no life in it. "What has happened?" he asked the Shadow Master, more confounded by this than by the changing of the city. Had she been caught by the water in one of the tunnels? He put a hand to her cheek, still not believing what he saw. It was cold. He let go of her hand and it fell back down. Lifeless.

"Um… This wasn't meant to happen," said the Shadow Master. "She fell from the sky and landed in the harbour. Very lucky actually. A moment before, it had been land, but changed just before she struck."

Lorenzo looked at him but the words didn't make any sense. "From the sky?" he asked.

The Shadow Master tilted his head back and looked up. "Yes. From up there. I saw her fall. I'm sorry."

It took Lorenzo some moments to be able to form the words in his mouth. "Do you mean… Do you mean… she's dead?" he asked, shaking his head.

"Let's not think of it as dead," said the Shadow Master. "That's such a negative word, don't you agree. Let's think of it as just not alive."

Lorenzo blinked. "But you said I was going to save her," he said finally.

"And so you shall," said the Shadow Master, laying Lucia gently down upon the ground. "Pucker up your lips."

"What?" asked Lorenzo.

"You need to kiss her to bring her back to life," said the Shadow Master. "Like in a fairy tale."

"But isn't there some scientific device you can use that will bring her back to life? There must be!"

"Ah, yes," said the Shadow Master. "That's something I need to tell you about. When you changed the city you didn't just change its physical form. You changed the world, in a way. The type of science that you are used to thinking of as science won't work anymore. That's why she fell from the sky."

"What do you mean it won't work?"

"That's the greatest secret of the ancients. They discovered how to change the very fabric of nature. But they couldn't leave well enough alone and gambled repeatedly on achieving something better – but in the end lost everything."

Lorenzo knelt down beside Lucia and took her hand. "Show me what to do," he said.

"Well, what any young lover wants to do," said the Shadow Master. "Place your hand on her breast."

"What?" asked Lorenzo, taken aback.

"Her left breast. Just below it." Lorenzo nodded followed his instructions.

"Now, press down on it. Put all your weight on it. And do that five times." Lorenzo did so. "Then you must kiss her," the Shadow Master said. "And not just a gentle chaste kiss, you need to cover her mouth with yours and pinch her nose and breathe your own life into her. Gently mind you."

Lorenzo looked at her slightly parted lips and hesitated. "Do you want me to show you?" asked the Shadow Master. "She looks very kissable."

"No," said Lorenzo. "If anyone is going to do this it will be me."

"Alright then. Go to it lover boy. Five times, then back to her breasts. This is a good technique to keep in mind for later in your life together too."

Lorenzo pressed his lips against hers gently, waiting to feel what he had felt last time. The warmth of her entering him and something of him entering her. The beat of the butterfly wings in his chest joining with hers. But he only felt the coldness of her lifeless lips. He breathed into her, willing the life from him to enter her. Willing to feel the death enter himself in exchange for his life. He did this five times and then looked up to the Shadow Master imploring him for some sign that this was working, as there was no sign from Lucia"s limp body.

"Again," said the Shadow Master. So Lorenzo pressed again on her breast. Kissed her again. Pressed again on her breast. Kissed her again. Breathing his life into her. "How long do I do this for?" he asked.

"Until we have a good audience," said the Shadow Master and Lorenzo looked up to see a small crowd had gathered around them, watching in either amazement or disgust at what he was doing. "Ignore them," said the Shadow Master. "Back to work." Then he grabbed a young apothecary that was in the crowd and pulled him close. "Watch carefully and learn," he said to him. "You will be able to do this yourself one day."

Lorenzo kept kissing and pressing above her heart until he heard a stern voice above him. "What is the meaning of this?" He looked up. It was a Lorraine guardsman, sporting a huge moustache. He had clearly recognised Lucia, but did not know what the half-dressed Lorenzo was doing to her. Lorenzo heard the slither of a sword being dragged from its sheath and saw the guardsmen arming himself. Until a long sharp sword suddenly appeared at the guardsman's throat. "He is performing a miracle and is bringing her back to life," said the Shadow Master coldly. "Now stand back and let him do his work."

"She is dead?" asked the guardsman.

"Not at all," said the Shadow Master. "She just lacks for life and this young man is providing that to her now."

The guardsman scowled at him but made no further move to interrupt them. Not until another voice rang from the other side of the crowd formed about them. "What depravity is this?" Lorenzo paused and looked up and saw the bearded Medici guardsman there.

The Shadow Master sighed heavily and tossed back the sleeve on his free hand, revealing a small cross bow mounted on his forearm. "Such unimaginative questions," he said. Then, "You are witnessing a kiss that will change the whole world." And at that moment, as Lorenzo breathed into her body again, Lucia suddenly coughed and spluttered and vomited up water. Her arms rose up a little as her chest heaved forward. She raised her arms, several times, not unlike the flapping of a butterfly's wings it appeared to those watching, and then she wrapped them around Lorenzo, drawing him in tightly to her. As if they were one.

"What marvels is this?" the Lorraine guardsman asked.

"You will call it science," said the Shadow Master. "Like discovering that the plague is carried by the fleas that breed on rats." He looked to the young apothecary to make sure he had understood that. Then lowered his sword and crossbow and made a deep bow to the audience around them. "That is quite enough miracles for one day," he said. "The Lorraine and Medici men will be dispensing gold compensation to those who have lost their houses."

"What?" the guardsmen asked as the crowd immediately surrounded them, calling out their plight and needs. Lorenzo felt the Shadow Master's strong arms lift him and Lucia to their feet. "Follow me," was all he said.

LXIV

Lorenzo stood with the Shadow Master and Lucia deep in a dark alley. Even though it was new, it smelled of piss and rotting scraps. He remembered everything again and wanted to sit down and rest. It always flooded back into his head too fast. He knew the Shadow Master and knew his and Lucia's role in everything. Again. He looked to the Shadow Master, who gave him a wide smile. "Welcome back," he said.

Lorenzo shook his head. "You're a bastard," he said.

"I think, literally speaking, you were the bastard this time around."

Lorenzo didn't smile. He looked across to Lucia who took his hand. "You did well," she said. She always seemed to manage the recovery better than he did.

"So, what now?" she asked the Shadow Master. "Do we leave the city in chaos?"

"No. Not this time," he said. Lucia shot a quick look to Lorenzo. "What do you mean?" she asked.

"Well," he said. "I was thinking that if you were to whisper a few words to Leonardo and Galileo to whisper in turn to the Head Councillor, Signor Pacciani, he could believe they were his own ideas and in turn suggest them to the Houses of Medici and Lorraine."

"Is Galileo alright?" Lorenzo asked, remembering that he had left him down in one of the chambers under the city.

The Shadow Master waved his hand dismissively. "He is fine. His chamber rose to the surface of the city. As did that of those poor wretches the apothecaries were experimenting on, by the way, and they are wandering around the city somewhere right now, probably scaring people witless. Anyway, if you were to suggest that the army of the darkness be offered either banishment or the offer to stay and join the plague people at the walls, you would sort the wheat from the chaff quickly. And the plague people at the walls be offered work in the fields around the city in exchange for citizenship and food, the two Houses would agree to it as a splendid idea and a gesture of unity."

"Why would they agree to that?" asked Lorenzo.

"Because they would be united in your plans to wed each other."

This time Lorenzo shot Lucia a look.

"This is how it will go," the Shadow Master said. "The Duke and Cosimo will be attacked from behind and within by their wife and mother who will tell them that they wish to hear the sound of children's feet in their households, which would be worth more than any of the wealth they have accumulated over the decades. The Duke will be the first to concede, but he will state that he will only agree to it if Cosimo agrees to adopt Lorenzo into his family so that Lucia is marrying a nobleman."

Lorenzo pulled Lucia close to him and nodded his head a little. "Yes?" he asked. "And what will he say?"

"Well, Cosimo will call you to see him, and he will be sitting there in that chamber beneath the portrait of his father, and will ask, 'Do you know what the riddle before me is?'"

"And what do I say?" asked Lorenzo.

"You will answer, 'Whether any man can see the future and know what it will bring.' And Cosimo will nod, conceding that you are shrewd indeed. But he will say, 'A decision like this could bring more trouble than benefit.' And you will say, 'As could making no decision, my Lord.' And again he will concede that you are wise enough and will say, 'No matter what I decide it will have some unforseen impact.' You will tell him that is true of every decision. And he will then ask, 'But will you respect my decision, whatever it is, and retain your love and loyalty to me?'"

"I will tell him that he always has my loyalty, but that my love belongs to another," said Lorenzo.

The Shadow Master clapped his hands. "A splendid reply. And Cosimo Medici will feel himself in great danger of smiling, and so will set his mouth into a grim line and say, 'We have been at war with the Lorraine household for decades, but if we form an alliance with them, who would we have to fight?' And you won't hesitate to answer him."

Lorenzo knew the line. "The greatest fight is that against those who oppose enlightenment," he said.

"And then Cosimo will say, 'Come back in the morning and I shall tell you my verdict.'" Lucia and

Lorenzo held each other more tightly and Lucia asked, almost breathlessly. "What will he say? He will say yes, won't he?"

The Shadow Master smiled widely and Lorenzo was the first to understand. "You are a bastard!" he said again.

Lucia's shoulders sagged. "Couldn't we stay here this time?" she asked. "We could really do some good. They are going to need so much help here."

The Shadow Master said nothing.

"It's not fair," said Lucia. "There will be more violence and more wars. But we could broker a peace agreement. We could get the plague people working the vacant farms around the city and we could have those poor victims of experimentation settled into a home for them. We could do so much good here." But the Shadow Master just shook his head a little. "This new world is going to need some steering," she said. "We could do it. We could bring peace between the two Houses if we stayed here."

"Yes," said Lorenzo. "If we were betrothed that would bring a peace accord between the two Houses."

"We could make a life here," said Lucia imploringly.

"I'm sure you could," the Shadow Master said. "But they have to work out their own future for themselves. You know that."

"But you intervene when it suits your purposes," she said angrily.

"Our purposes," he said. "You know that the present is held together by the future and the past."

"As is their present," she said.

"Which could have been our past. Which was a

dead branch of historical evolution. A dead branch that needed to be trimmed."

Lorenzo shook his head and let go of Lucia's hand. "Maybe next time, light of my heart," he said.

She smiled at him. "Yes. Light of my life. Maybe next time."

And then the Shadow Master said, "Come. It's time to go. So much more to do, and so little time."

It's *Supernatural* meets *Men in Black*
in a darkly humorous urban fantasy
from the author of *Nekropolis*.

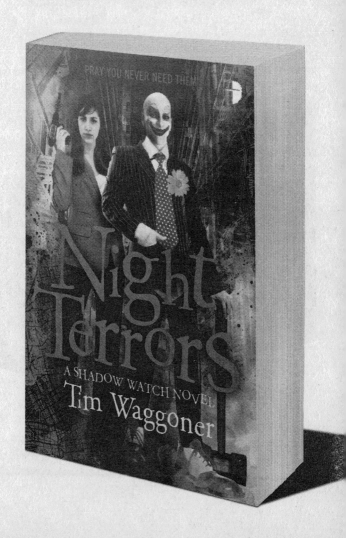

PRAY YOU NEVER NEED THEM

Night
Terrors

A SHADOW WATCH NOVEL
Tim Waggoner

The ultimate divine comedy.

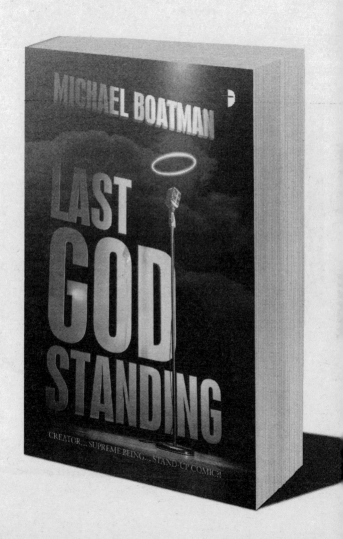

The quest for the Arbor has begun...

Gods and monsters roam the streets in this superior urban fantasy from the author of *Empire State*.

When duty and honour collide...

THE MAJAT CODE, BOOK 1

BLADES OF THE OLD EMPIRE

ANNA KASHINA